Extraordinary Jobs in

GOVERNMENT

Also in the Extraordinary Jobs series:

Extraordinary Jobs for Adventurers
Extraordinary Jobs in Agriculture and Nature
Extraordinary Jobs with Animals
Extraordinary Jobs for Creative People
Extraordinary Jobs in Entertainment
Extraordinary Jobs in the Food Industry
Extraordinary Jobs in Health and Science
Extraordinary Jobs in Leisure
Extraordinary Jobs in Media
Extraordinary Jobs in the Service Sector
Extraordinary Jobs in Sports

Extraordinary Jobs in

GOVERNMENT

ALECIA T. DEVANTIER & CAROL A. TURKINGTON

Ferguson
An imprint of Infobase Publishing

Extraordinary Jobs in Government

Copyright © 2006 by Alecia T. Devantier and Carol A. Turkington

Ferguson
An imprint of Infobase Publishing
132 West 31st Street
New York NY 10001

Library of Congress Cataloging-in-Publication Data
Devantier, Alecia T.
  Extraordinary jobs in government / Alecia T. Devantier and Carol A. Turkington.
    p.   cm.
  Includes index.
  ISBN 0-8160-5857-1 (hc : alk. paper)
  1. Civil service positions—United States. I. Turkington, Carol. T. II. Title.
  JK716.D47 2006
352.6'302373—dc22   2005036749

Ferguson books are available at special discounts when purchased in bulk quantities for businesses, associations, institutions, or sales promotions. Please call our Special Sales Department in New York at (212) 967-8800 or (800) 322-8755.

You can find Ferguson on the World Wide Web at http://www.fergpubco.com

Text design by Mary Susan Ryan-Flynn
Cover design by Salvatore Luongo

Printed in the United States of America

VB KT 10 9 8 7 6 5 4 3 2 1

This book is printed on acid-free paper.

CONTENTS

ACKNOWLEDGMENTS

Thanks to Jon Rand for excellent work, our editors Sarah Fogarty and James Chambers, to Vanessa Nittoli for staying on top of everything, and to our agents Gene Brissie of James Peter Associates and Ed Claflin of Ed Claflin Literary Associates.

ARE YOU CUT OUT FOR A CAREER IN GOVERNMENT?

How does this sound: good pay, room for advancement, and the best retirement and benefit plans on the planet? The U.S. government is the largest employer in the world, but finding and getting government jobs isn't quite like trotting down to your local convenience store and filling out a job application. Every stop along the "find-apply-interview" path has its own little tricks.

Some people are drawn to a particular career early on. If you crave responsibility, stability, job security, terrific benefits, and the chance to work for your country, there's probably no better choice than working for Uncle Sam. Each year the federal government hires tens of thousands of new workers.

Take some time to think about the kind of person you are, and the sorts of experiences you dream of having. Have you inherited a lot of "shoulds" in thinking about the kind of career you'd like to have? These "shoulds" inside your head can be a major stumbling block in finding and enjoying an unusual career in government. Maybe all relatives in your family have entered the family business, or studied to become lawyers, teachers, or ministers.

But if you've always yearned for the excitement of working on Capitol Hill or actually running for office, you owe it to yourself to go after it, no matter how unusual or just plain batty it may seem to others. Don't cheat yourself. If you don't do what you were born to do—well, you're going to get older anyway. You might as well get older doing what you love to do. What you *need* to do.

Getting any job can take perseverance, hard work, and some luck, but getting a government job can be even more challenging. It also doesn't hurt to know someone, so if your cousin's friend's Uncle Joe knows somebody in Washington, use that connection. In government, your political connections can make a really big difference in whether you get the job or a polite rejection. Jumping through all the hoops to land a government job can be tedious, but in the long run, it's worth it. If you allow yourself to explore the options that are out there in government, you'll find an enjoyable, solid career. Push past your doubts and let your journey begin!

Carol A. Turkington
Alecia T. Devantier

HOW TO USE THIS BOOK

Students face a lot of pressure to decide what they want to be when they grow up. For some students, the decision is easy, but for others, it can be somewhat more difficult. If you're not interested in a traditional 9-to-5 job—if you're really looking for a way to contribute to your community, where can you go to find out answers to questions you might have about these exciting, creative, non-traditional jobs?

Where can you go to find out how to become an IRS agent or a staff assistant to the first lady? What does it take to become a government test pilot, helping to make planes safe? Where do you learn how to be an international elections observer? Is it really possible to make a living as a court reporter? What's the job outlook for a press secretary?

Look no further! This book will take you inside the world of a number of government jobs, answering questions you might have, letting you know what to expect if you pursue that career, introducing you to someone making a living that way, and providing resources if you want to do further research.

THE JOB PROFILES

All job profiles in this book have been broken down into the following fact-filled sections: At a Glance, Overview, and Interview. Each offers a distinct perspective on the job, and taken together give you a full view of the job in question.

At a Glance

Each profile starts out with an At a Glance box, offering a snapshot of important basic information to give you a quick glimpse of that particular job, including salary, education/experience, personal attributes, requirements, and outlook.

- ✅ *Salary range.* What can you expect to make? Salary ranges for the jobs in this book are as accurate as possible; many are based on data from the U.S. Bureau of Labor Statistics' *Occupational Outlook Handbook*. Information also comes from individuals, actual job ads, employers, and experts in the field. It's important to remember that salaries for any particular job vary greatly depending on experience, geographic location, and level of education. For example, smaller airports in towns and villages start their air traffic controllers at far lower salaries than they would make at much larger urban airports, which require a much higher degree of experience and skill.

- ✅ *Education/Experience.* What kind of education and experience does the job require? This section will give you some information about the types of education or experience requirements the job might have.

- ✅ *Personal attributes.* Do you have what it takes to do this job? How do you think of yourself? How would someone else describe you? This section will give you an idea of some of the personality traits that might be useful in this career. These attributes were collected from articles written about the job, as well as recommendations from employers and people actually doing the jobs, working in the field.

✅ *Requirements.* Are you qualified? Some jobs, particularly those with the government, have strict age or education requirements. You might as well make sure you meet any health, medical, or screening requirements before going any further with your job pursuit.

✅ *Outlook.* What are your chances of finding a job? This section is based in part on the *Occupational Outlook Handbook*, as well as interviews with employers and experts doing the jobs. This information is typically a "best guess" based on the information that is available right now, including changes in the economy, situations in the country and around the world, job trends and retirement levels, as well as many other factors that can influence changes in the availability of these and other jobs.

Overview

This section will give you an idea of what to expect from the job. For most of these jobs, there really is no such thing as an average day. Each new day, new job, or new assignment is a whole new adventure, bringing with it a unique set of challenges and rewards. But in general, this section provides a general overview of what a person holding this position might expect on a day-to-day basis.

The overview also gives more details about how to get into the profession. It takes a more detailed look at the required training or education, if needed, giving an in-depth look at what to expect during that training or educational period. If there are no training or education requirements for the job, this section will provide some suggestions for getting the experience you'll need to be successful.

Pitfalls takes a look at some of the obvious and not-so-obvious pitfalls of the job. In many cases, the number of pitfalls far outweighs the number of perks. Don't let the pitfalls discourage you from pursuing the career; they are just things to be aware of while making your decision.

For many people, loving their job so much that they look forward to going to work every day is enough of a perk. **Perks** looks at some of the other perks of the job you may not have considered.

So what can you do now to start working toward the career of your dreams? **Get a Jump on the Job** will give you some ideas and suggestions for things that you can do now, even before graduating from high school, to start preparing for this job. Opportunities include training programs, groups and organizations to join, as well as practical skills to learn.

Interview

In addition to taking a general look at the job, each entry features a discussion with someone who is lucky enough to do this job for a living. In addition to giving you an inside look at the job, the experts offer advice for people wanting to follow in their footsteps, pursuing a career in the same field.

APPENDIXES

Appendix A (Associations, Organizations, and Web Sites) lists places to look for additional information about each specific job, including professional associations, societies, unions, government organizations, Web sites, and periodicals. Associations and other groups are a great source of information, and there's an association for just about every job you can imagine. Many groups and associations have a student membership level, which you can join by paying a small fee. There are many advantages to joining an association, including the chance to make important contacts, receive helpful newsletters, and attend workshops or conferences. Some associations also offer scholarships that will make it easier to further your education. Other sources listed in this section include information about accredited training programs, forums, official government links, and more.

In **Appendix B (Online Career Resources)** we've gathered some of the best general Web sites about unusual jobs in government. Use these as a springboard to your own Internet research. All of this information was current when this book was written, but Web site addresses do change. If you can't find what you're looking for at a given address, do a simple Web search—the page may have been moved to a different location.

Appendix C (Getting a Job in the Federal Government) contains information about the special ins and outs you need to know if you're going to get a job in the government.

Appendix D (Graduate School Programs) is a state-by-state list of schools that offer graduate programs in public affairs, public policy, or public administration. If you need more information, try visiting the Web site of the National Association of Schools of Public Affairs and Administration (http://www.naspaa.org).

READ MORE ABOUT IT

In this back-of-the-book listing, we've gathered some helpful books that can give you more detailed information about each job we discuss in this book. Find these at the library or bookstore if you want to learn even more about government jobs.

AEROSPACE ENGINEER

OVERVIEW

Aerospace engineers create machines that once existed only in our imaginations, designing airplanes that weigh more than half a million pounds and spacecraft that travel more than 17,000 miles per hour. They design, develop, test, and help manufacture aircraft, spacecraft, and missiles. Aerospace engineers who work with aircraft are called *aeronautical* engineers; those who work with spacecraft are *astronautical* engineers.

Most aerospace engineers help develop and build aerospace products and parts. About 10 percent of aerospace engineers work for federal agencies, mainly the Department of Defense and the National Aeronautics and Space Administration (NASA).

As an aerospace engineer, you'll find ways to improve aviation, defense systems, and space exploration. You might choose to be an expert in structural design, guidance, navigation and control, instruments, or communication. An aerospace engineer may work on many different products or become an expert on just one—such as commercial planes, fighter jets, helicopters, spacecraft, missiles, or rockets. Aerospace engineers may work with computer-aided design software and other space-age computer software.

But you needn't be limited to working just on planes. Aerospace engineers are also in great demand in other fields. They use their knowledge to improve gas mileage on cars, and work on automated mass transportation, bioengineering, medical systems, environmental engineering, and communications.

Aerospace engineering may sound complicated, but don't let that scare you away. A lot of aerospace engineers once

AT A GLANCE

Salary Range
$50,000 to $105,000.

Education/Experience
Most aerospace engineers are hired right out of college. You'll need at least an undergraduate degree. The aerospace engineering major includes two years of basic physical and engineering sciences and mathematics and two years of aerospace engineering.

Personal Attributes
You need a lot of curiosity and problem-solving skills. You also need to get along with people because engineers often work together on a project team. If you head up a team, you'll need strong leadership skills.

Requirements
Although it's not required, it will help if you pass an engineer-in-training (EIT) test after you get your degree. You'll need strong written and oral communication skills and computer skills.

Outlook
Although the number of total jobs is expected to drop, there should be some opportunities over the next few years, especially in private industry. That's because the number of degrees granted in aerospace engineering has dropped because students don't think they'll be able to find jobs. Foreign competition and weak business for U.S. airlines will limit the new jobs for those who help design and produce passenger planes.

Laurie Marshall Grindle, aerospace engineer

When Laurie Marshall Grindle was a Los Angeles sixth grader, she was assigned to observe the moon. That got her thinking about becoming an astronaut, which got her interested in NASA. Today, she's an aerospace engineer at NASA's Dryden Flight Research Center at Edwards, California.

Although she's worked in space exploration in the past, Grindle now works mainly with aircraft. She was still in high school when she earned a pilot's license. "My father got his pilot's license the year that I was born, so I was always around small planes and loved flying," Grindle says. "My father read in one of his flying magazines about a program at the University of North Dakota for teenagers between their junior and senior years. So in the summer of 1987, I went there to get my pilot's license. It was a great program with concentrated flying time. The following summer, I got my instrument rating from an American Flyers School in Santa Monica, California."

Grindle's flying experience helped her study aeronautical and mechanical engineering at the University of California at Davis. She graduated in 1993. "Having my pilot's license helped me a lot in college because I already knew how an airplane flew," she says. "Lots of times when solving problems, I'd just picture myself doing it and figure out the answer that way. The firsthand experience helped me to understand some of the things that the professors were trying to explain as well. Firsthand experience is the best. Unfortunately, I've never flown any of the aircraft that I've worked on. But I've walked and stood on the bigger ones. I'd love to fly in them, but I don't have the jet engine experience that some would require."

Grindle received a NASA internship at Dryden's aerodynamics branch in 1992 and has been with the agency ever since. She earned an engineer-in-training license in 1994 and a graduate degree in mechanical engineering from California State University at Fresno in 1998. Grindle was lead engineer and chief engineer while working on the X-43A, a 12-foot aircraft with an "air-breathing" engine called a scramjet. She was chief engineer for the X-43A's third flight, in November 2004. Grindle also was an aerospace researcher on the F-16XL Supersonic Laminar Flow Project. This involved improving airflow on the wings of aircraft flying faster than the speed of sound. She also has helped analyze Space Shuttle maneuvers.

"As a lead researcher, although I worked with others to get it integrated on to the aircraft and have it flown, I was responsible for all work associated with the research, including installation, flight test, and analysis," Grindle says. "This is the kind of work I did on the F-16XL. As a lead engineer, I was in charge of a team of people. Prior to the first flight of the X-43A, I was the lead aerodynamics engineer for the project at NASA Dryden. There were five other people from the branch that made up the Dryden aerodynamics team. My job included aspects of a principal investigator and lead engineer, but also included management-type tasks in coordinating the work of the team.

"The chief engineer is a broader scope version of the lead engineer. I act as the lead engineer for the entire project. The scope of the job is always large, but can be a huge responsibility if the project is technically challenging or has several engineers involved. As the chief engineer for X-43A, I was responsible for all engineering decisions, or decisions that affected engineering, in addition to the engineers themselves. It definitely falls into the category of engineering management, but requires a skilled technical background. Most projects, and the X-43A was no exception, have different engineering disciplines involved—aerodynamics, instrumentation, propulsion, flight systems, structures, guidance, navigation, and control. So, odds are that your specialty will only be in one discipline. But you need to be knowledgeable in all. The primary responsibility is monitoring all engineering aspects on the vehicle.

"One of the biggest things about the job is to ensure that engineers are making the right decisions and have thought about the implications and the necessities. The chief engineer has to be able to ask the right questions—even if the technical field is different from your own—to get them thinking and help them to make the right decisions. Since you have to work with several people, it's also important to have good people skills. Figure out how to get along with others and what will motivate people."

Grindle's family background suggested she'd be more likely to wind up in a courtroom than a flight research center. Both her parents, Consuelo and George, and an older brother, Michael, earned law degrees. Grindle's parents were married while attending Howard University Law School. Her mother became chief U.S. District Judge of the Central District of California. Her father was an entertainment lawyer and now practices arbitration. Her brother handles business and legal affairs in the entertainment field. "The day he graduated from law school, I made a sign for my bedroom door that says 'Lawyers,' with a big red circle and cross mark on it," Grindle recalled. "My mother tells me that it's not too late, that I can still go into patent law. Over the years, I have thought about it, but I really enjoy engineering."

Grindle received the 2005 Golden Torch Award as Outstanding Woman in Technology from the National Society of Black Engineers. Though Grindle doesn't want special notice, a black female aerospace engineer obviously breaks a lot of stereotypes.

"Yes, it does come up, and frequently of late," she says. "However, my personal experience—having my mother as a role model—didn't make my choices seem unusual. Also, at work it doesn't seem to be a factor. You're judged by the work you do and the person that you are and the rest doesn't seem to matter.

"I know that seeing someone 'like you' doing something you perceive as difficult or unattainable is very inspiring and makes things seem more doable. So when I address schools, I try to discuss the importance of education and how math and science can and will be used in daily life. I think this also helps to keep them in school. Nothing is beyond reach! Even if the job seems intimidating, just like math and science problems, you can break any job down into manageable parts. If the job seems interesting, pursue it."

thought the work sounded too complicated. But they took tough math and science courses in school and were willing to see the hardest problems through to the end. Once they got hired, they made the most of their on-the-job training. Then they found there were more fascinating jobs for aerospace engineers than they could have imagined.

A flight test engineer uses theories, concepts, and equations to analyze the results of a test flight and may run the entire test program. Analytical engineers use mathematical theory and basic engineering to analyze research. Stress analysts, often with the help of computers, figure out how much weight a product can safely carry. Design engineers meet with a project's other engineers and come up with a design that satisfies everybody. Materials engineers test and evaluate materials used in aerospace products to make sure those materials are right for the conditions in which they'll be used. Manufacturing engineers figure out how to build a product and develop the tools to build it, too.

Pitfalls

It's not all fun and games in this profession. You may see an exciting project that you've really worked hard on killed for lack of money.

Perks

The pay is great, and there's a lot of personal satisfaction in working in a job that can make a difference for the country's future and a better quality of life for everyone. If you enjoy solving problems, it's hard to imagine that you'll ever get bored.

Get a Jump on the Job

Work on school science projects, and enter science fairs. If you're thinking about this type of job, start planning right away—while you're still in high school, if possible. You're probably a whiz in math and science—be sure to take as many courses in this area during high school as possible. Discuss your goals with engineers and scientists. Consider applying for a high school or college summer internship in a business or organization related to aerospace engineering. If you think you might one day work on jets, planes, or spacecraft, consider getting your pilot's license while you're in high school or college. You aren't required to have a pilot's license, but it will help you understand the concepts of air and space flight.

AIR TRAFFIC CONTROLLER

OVERVIEW

If you've ever gazed out at the landing strips of a busy big-city airport and wondered who's keeping all those planes straight, that would be the air traffic controller. Most people probably have a general idea of the controllers up there in the tower—but there are lots of other controllers behind the scenes involved in keeping planes safe. In addition to the tower controllers, there are enroute controllers, radar associate controllers, and flight service specialists. Tower and enroute controllers usually control several planes at a time, which means they often have to make quick decisions about completely different activities. For example, a controller might direct a plane on its landing approach and at the same time provide pilots entering the airport's airspace with information about conditions at the airport. While instructing these pilots, the controller would also observe other planes in the vicinity, such as those in a holding pattern waiting for permission to land, to ensure that they remain well separated.

All the different types of controllers work either in the towers, enroute centers, or in-flight service stations, handling various responsibilities related to safe air traffic. You're probably most familiar with the air traffic controllers up in the control tower—*tower controllers*—who watch over all planes traveling through the airport's airspace. Their main responsibility is to organize the flow of aircraft in and out of

AT A GLANCE (continued)

Outlook

The National Air Traffic Controllers Association estimates half of the nation's controllers will retire by 2010. Still, competition to get into the FAA training programs will be keen, with many more applicants than there are openings.

the airport. Relying on radar and their own eyes as they peer through the tower windows, they closely monitor the airspace to make sure each plane keeps a safe distance away from each other, and guide pilots between the hangar or ramp and the end of the airport's airspace. In addition, these controllers warn pilots about changes in weather conditions, such as *wind shear*—a sudden dangerous shift in the velocity or direction of the wind that can cause a pilot to lose control of the aircraft.

During arrival or departure, several controllers direct each plane. As a plane approaches an airport, the pilot radios the terminal that they're coming in. A controller in the radar room (just beneath the control tower) has a copy of the plane's flight plan, and has pinpointed the plane on radar. If its path is clear, this controller directs the pilot to a runway; if the airport is busy, the controller directs the plane to circle the airport along with other aircraft waiting to land.

As the plane nears the runway, the pilot is asked to contact the control tower, where another controller—who's also watching the plane on radar—monitors the aircraft for the last mile or so to the runway, making sure to stop any departures that would interfere with the plane's landing. Once on the ground, a third controller

in the tower, called a ground controller, directs it along the taxiway to its assigned gate. The ground controller usually works entirely by sight, but may use radar if visibility is very poor.

The procedure is reversed for departures. The ground controller directs the plane to the runway, and the second controller then informs the pilot about conditions at the airport, such as weather, speed and direction of wind, and visibility. This controller also issues runway clearance for the pilot to take off. Once in the air, the plane is guided out of the airport's airspace by the departure controller.

It may sound pretty simple, but it's not. The air traffic control system is a vast network of people and equipment designed to keep all the airplanes safe, but the stress and the responsibility can be harrowing at a large international airport. Although the controllers' main concern is safety, they also must direct planes efficiently to keep delays to a minimum. Some controllers focus on regulating airport traffic; others concentrate on keeping track of flights between airports.

After each plane departs, airport tower controllers notify the *enroute controllers* who now take charge at any of the 21 air route traffic control centers located around the country. Each of these traffic control centers have 300 to 700 controllers, with more than 150 working at the same time during peak hours at the busier facilities. Airplanes usually fly along designated routes; each center is assigned a certain airspace containing many different routes. Enroute controllers work in teams of up to three members, depending on how heavy traffic is; each team is responsible for a section of the center's airspace. For example, a team might be responsible for all planes that are between 30 and 100 miles north of an airport and flying at an altitude between 6,000 and 18,000 feet.

To prepare for planes about to enter the team's airspace, the *radar associate controller* organizes flight plans coming off a printer. If two planes are scheduled to enter the team's airspace at nearly the same time, location, and altitude, this controller may arrange with the preceding control unit for one plane to change its flight path. The previous unit may have been another team at the same or an adjacent center, or a departure controller at a neighboring terminal. As a plane approaches a team's airspace, the radar controller accepts responsibility for the plane from the previous controlling unit. The controller also delegates responsibility for the plane to the next controlling unit when the plane leaves the team's airspace.

The radar controller, the senior team member, observes the planes in the team's airspace on radar and communicates with the pilots when necessary. Radar controllers warn pilots about nearby planes, bad weather conditions, and other potential hazards. Two planes on a collision course will be directed around each other. If a pilot wants to change altitude in search of better flying conditions, the controller will check to determine that no other planes will be along the proposed path. As the flight progresses, the team responsible for the aircraft notifies the next team in charge of the airspace ahead, so that the plane arrives safely at its destination.

In addition to airport towers and enroute centers, air traffic controllers also work in flight service stations operated at more than 100 locations. These *flight ser-*

Ted Johnson, air traffic controller

"This job can be exciting at times," admits Ted Johnson, air traffic control manager at the municipal Reading Airport in Reading, Pennsylvania. Although this airport is fairly small, it serves a population base of 300,000, with a significant number of industries. While not a hub for national airlines, there are many private planes that use the site.

"It's a good job, with steady work, although sometimes it can be boring," Johnson says—boring because, unlike big-city airports, he's not responsible for directing hundreds of planes a day in takeoffs and landings. The airport, which was built on farmland in 1935, opened with a 3,600 foot long runway, a small terminal adjacent to the "City Hangar," a snack bar and a rotating beacon relocated from downtown Reading. In the early days of aviation, there was little need for control towers, but as more aircraft were fitted for radio communication, radio-equipped airport traffic control towers began to replace the flagmen responsible for guiding planes to land. By 1932, almost all airline aircraft were equipped for radio-telephone communication, and about 20 radio control towers were operating by 1935.

Nevertheless, at times, the responsibility of getting planes in safely can be quite stressful, he says. "But it's a lot less stressful," he says, "since the installation of improved radar." The airport is serviced by several air charter companies, as well as Airlink Express, a small regional intrastate airline.

He got his training in air traffic control in the military, as do about 25 percent of the rest of the controllers in the country. A controller for the past 29 years, Johnson chose to direct planes, not fly them, although about a third of controllers do have their pilot's license.

vice specialists provide pilots with information on the station's particular area, including terrain, preflight and in-flight weather information, suggested routes, and other information important to the safety of a flight. Flight service station specialists help pilots in emergency situations and initiate and coordinate searches for missing or overdue aircraft. However, they don't get involved in actively managing air traffic.

Some air traffic controllers work at the Federal Aviation Administration's (FAA) Air Traffic Control Systems Command Center in Herndon, Virginia, where they oversee the entire system. They're always checking for situations that will create bottlenecks or other problems in the system, then respond with a management plan for traffic into and out of the troubled sector. They try to keep traffic levels in the trouble spots manageable for the controllers working at enroute centers. Currently, the FAA is implementing a new automated air traffic control system, called the National Airspace System (NAS) Architecture. The NAS Architecture is a long-term strategic plan that will allow controllers to more efficiently deal with the demands of increased air traffic.

There are still other jobs for air traffic controllers besides the towers, flight service stations, and enroute traffic control centers. Some professional controllers conduct research at the FAA's national experimental center near Atlantic City, New Jersey; others teach at the FAA Academy in Oklahoma City, Oklahoma. Although most work for the FAA, a small number of civilian controllers work for the U.S. Department of Defense, while others work for private air traffic control companies providing service to non-FAA towers.

Civilian air traffic control specialists work for the FAA in airports and control centers around the country.

Learning how to be an air traffic controller can be a daunting experience. It begins with seven months of intensive training at the FAA academy, learning the fundamentals of the airway system, regulations, controller equipment, aircraft performance characteristics, and lots of specialized tasks. To receive a job offer, you've got to successfully complete the training and pass a series of examinations, including a controller skills test that measures speed and accuracy in recognizing and correctly solving air traffic control problems. The test requires judgments on spatial relationships and requires application of the rules and procedures contained in the Air Traffic Control Handbook. The pre-employment test is currently offered only to students in the FAA Air Traffic Collegiate Training Initiative (AT-CTI) Program or the Minneapolis Community & Technical College, Air Traffic Control Training Program.

In addition, you must either have been working full time for three years or completed four years of college. In combining education and experience, one year of undergraduate study (30 semester or 45 quarter hours) is equivalent to nine months of work experience.

Once you're selected, you're still not ready to go to work. Now you must spend 12 weeks at the FAA Academy in Oklahoma to learn the fundamentals of the airway system, FAA regulations, controller equipment, and aircraft performance characteristics, as well as more specialized tasks.

After graduation, you'll spend several years of progressively more responsible work experience, interspersed with considerable classroom instruction and independent study, to become a fully qualified controller. Controllers who fail to complete either the academy or the on-the-job portion of the training are usually dismissed.

Controllers must pass a physical examination each year and a job performance examination twice each year, as well as taking continual drug screening tests.

When you first start, you begin by supplying pilots with basic flight data and airport information. If you can handle this, you advance to the position of ground controller, then local controller, departure controller—and finally, arrival controller. At an air route traffic control center, your first job would be to deliver printed flight plans to teams, gradually advancing to radar associate controller and then radar controller.

Controllers can transfer to jobs at different locations or advance to supervisory positions, including management or staff jobs in air traffic control and top administrative jobs in the FAA. However, there are only limited opportunities for a controller to switch from a position in an enroute center to a tower.

Pitfalls

It's tough getting into the job, and once you get there the stress can be considerable. Because most control towers and centers operate 24 hours a day, 7 days a week, controllers rotate night and weekend shifts. During busy times, you must maintain total concentration to keep track of several planes at the same time and to make certain that all pilots receive correct instructions. The mental and emotional stress of being responsible for the safety of several aircraft and their passengers can be exhausting; the work environment can be very tense during busy periods.

Perks

Aircraft controllers earn relatively high pay and have good benefits, and they enjoy more job security than do most workers. The demand for air travel and the workloads of air traffic controllers decline during recessions, but controllers are seldom laid off.

Depending on length of service, air traffic controllers receive 13 to 26 days of paid vacation and 13 days of paid sick leave each year, life insurance, and health benefits. In addition, controllers can retire at an earlier age and with fewer years of service than other federal employees. Air traffic controllers are eligible to retire at age 50 with 20 years of service as an active air traffic controller or after 25 years of active service at any age. There is a mandatory retirement age of 56 for controllers who manage air traffic. However, federal law provides for exemptions to the mandatory age of 56, up to age 61, for controllers with exceptional skills and experience.

Get a Jump On the Job

If you've got a yen to sit in that air traffic control tower, you might want to think about learning as much as you can about flying, by getting your pilot's license. The requirements for getting a private pilot license are governed by the Federal Aviation Administration of the U.S. Department of Transportation, but you must be at least 17 years old. It's a good idea to read as much as you can about aviation, and see if you can get a part-time or summer job at your local airport.

ATF SPECIAL AGENT

OVERVIEW

If you're like most people, you're probably not sure what exactly goes on at the Bureau of Alcohol, Tobacco, Firearms and Explosives (ATF). The agency's name and crime-fighting mission have been changing since the earliest days of the United States; in 2003, it moved from the Department of the Treasury to the Department of Justice and was given its current title (but the agency still goes by ATF). It enforces federal gun laws and investigates arson, explosions, and thefts of explosives. The ATF also investigates sales of tobacco and alcohol by people avoiding federal and state taxes on those products. To carry out all these responsibilities, the ATF often works with other federal, state, and local law enforcement. For example, a crime causing massive death and destruction—such as the terrorist attacks on New York City in September 2001—usually involves the ATF as well as a host of other agencies.

As an ATF agent, you could be part of one of four National Response Teams including agents and chemists on 24-hour notice to visit major U.S. explosion and fire scenes. Or you could be part of an International Response Team, which helps the State Department assist other countries that need help investigating major explosions or fires. This team has gone to such far-flung places as Peru, Pakistan, and Korea.

But you'll find there's plenty of work to do right at home. Let's say you find that hundreds of weapons used in crimes can be

traced to one licensed gun dealer. Because it's illegal to sell a gun to a convicted felon, you might go undercover and pretend to be a felon asking to buy a gun from that dealer. You'll select one of various electronic surveillance techniques to record the transaction. But to make an arrest, you'll also have to prove the dealer knowingly sold a gun to an actual convicted felon. A case like this takes a lot of time, energy,

---

AT A GLANCE

Salary Range

$30,000 to $100,000+

Education/Experience

Many agents from the Bureau of Alcohol, Tobacco, Firearms and Explosives (ATF) come from other areas of criminal investigation or law enforcement. If you don't have that experience, you'll need a bachelor's degree; useful majors are criminal justice, accounting, sociology, administration of justice, political science, fire science, or chemistry.

Personal Attributes

You need to be tough, physically and mentally. You'll also need to handle exhausting physical training.

Requirements

You must be a U.S. citizen between ages 21 and 37, have a valid driver's license, and pass the Treasury Enforcement Examination and ATF special agent applicant assessment test. You must also pass a polygraph test, a background check for top-secret clearance, and a medical exam and drug test. The ATF will train you to use firearms.

Outlook

The kind of agent with the credentials and dedication to work for the ATF will always be in demand. The ATF's role in firearms and explosives work has become more important than ever because of worries about terrorism in the United States.

and determination. But if you do it right, your evidence will be overwhelming and a dealer usually will plead guilty.

If you want to specialize in arson, you can become a certified fire investigator. You will be called to the scene of major fires to check if they were set on purpose. You'll examine the damage and try to determine how the fire started. With your training, you'll almost always know whether the fire was accidental.

To join the ATF, you'll need a college degree, three years of law enforcement experience, or a combination of experience and college courses. Once you're in the agency, you may find yourself working

Paul Marquardt, ATF special agent

Right after the Oklahoma City bombing in 1995 that killed 168 people and injured hundreds, Paul Marquardt was sent from his Kansas City office to Junction City, Kansas, to join a massive law enforcement team to piece together the bombing plot. Tim McVeigh and Terry Nichols, who were both arrested soon after the bombing, had planned the explosion in the Junction City area.

"The plot was hatched in the Junction City area and that's where all the leads were," Marquardt explains. An ATF agent since 1975, Marquardt was assigned to teams trying to find where the chemicals for the Oklahoma City explosion were bought and where the bombers stayed and met before the blast. The bomb used two tons of ammonia nitrate, a fertilizer, and the first ton was bought from a farm co-op in McPherson, Kansas. The fertilizer was mixed with racing fuel, which McVeigh, posing as a biker, had bought at a Texas track. The explosives were placed in a rental truck and set off in front of the federal building. The investigation helped complete the picture of the plot and built a strong criminal case. Both men were convicted; McVeigh was executed and Nichols was sentenced to life in prison.

Right after the explosion, even federal agents weren't sure if the two bombers had acted on their own or were part of a large group of extremists that might attack investigators. "It was somewhat stressful because you didn't know if it was a broad conspiracy," Marquardt recalled. "It was scary going to these farms and not knowing who you'd run into. We'd run background checks on the people but that wasn't real reassuring because if they were involved in the plot, they'd probably be using aliases. You weren't sure what was going on. One night I got back to my hotel and there was a Ryder truck parked next to my room. It was creepy."

Marquardt was paired with FBI agent Julia Jensen. They'd go to local hotels and acquire the registration cards, then look through them and try to find McVeigh's name or one of his aliases. One night, Marquardt was working late at the barracks, going through hotel registration cards, and he heard CNN updating the latest developments in the bombing investigation. "It's a weird sensation to have the whole country talking about a case and you're watching TV while you're working on that case," he says. "It was a bizarre, surreal situation. All around the barracks they had concertina wire and soldiers with M16s. It was like a James Bond movie. In the initial time frame, nobody knew what was going on, so that was a safe environment for people working the case. It turned out it was unnecessary, but nobody knew that then."

(continues)

with state and local law enforcement in any of several programs.

The National Integrated Ballistic Information Network provides ballistics technology that shows if evidence from more than one crime scene may be linked. Comprehensive Crime Gun Tracing helps trace the movement of guns used in crimes. The Bomb and Arson Tracking System allows agencies to share information about bomb and arson cases. The agency also has bomb-sniffing dog teams around the United States. ATF has three national crime laboratories. It works with other agencies on Project Safe Neighborhoods, a nationwide program to prosecute felons found with firearms. Violent Crime Impact Teams pursue the most violent offenders in more than a dozen cities.

Still confused by how the ATF got its name? The agency that later became ATF was created by Congress in 1862 to

(continued)

Each day, investigators checked out one lead, returned to the barracks, wrote their report, and went out again. Jensen had a laptop computer, however, and wrote her reports on the drive back from interviews. "Ten years ago, that was unusual in law enforcement," Marquardt recalled. "We'd get back, print out the report, and go right out and do another lead. We were like a machine."

Marquardt spent two months in Junction City, and then soon after worked on one of ATF's many undercover operations—cases like Patrick Bark, who was a licensed dealer selling guns out of his Kansas City home and later out of his van. During a three-month period, 30 guns used in crimes were traced to Bark. Marquardt was the "case agent" who directed an investigation that resulted in Bark's arrest in March 1996 and his guilty plea to federal firearms violations. He was sentenced to 71 months in prison and three years of supervised release.

"One of the greatest reasons for the ATF's success is that you're pretty much allowed a great amount of freedom," Marquardt says. "It's very much a self-initiated job. As the case agent, you run your own case. You get a lot of help, but it's your case and it stays your case." Marquardt also thrives on the job's variety. When it was still under the Treasury Department, the ATF helped the Secret Service to protect current and former presidents. "I've guarded every president from [Richard] Nixon on," Marquardt says, pointing to autographed photos of Ronald Reagan and George H.W. Bush.

The Oklahoma City bombing was the most destructive terrorist act ever in the United States until the 2001 attacks, which killed about 3,000. In early 2002, Marquardt was assigned to a Joint Terrorism Task Force, one of many nationwide to bring together experts to combat terrorism. "They decided to put all the agencies in one room," he says. "We had the federal, city, and state working together. When something comes up, you have all the tools in the box." Marquardt stayed with the task force until May 2004, and then moved back to the ATF office as the public information officer.

"After 30 years, I've been exposed to a lot," he says. "One day, you're in some vacant lot in a blighted part of town and the next day you're guarding the president. You see just about every extreme in American life, and that's what's so fascinating about this job."

make sure people who produced liquor paid their federal taxes. The most famous era for the ATF was Prohibition (a period of time beginning in 1919 when it was illegal to manufacture, sell, or transport liquor). ATF agents were then called revenue agents and nicknamed "revenooers." Although Prohibition ended in 1933, illegal production of liquor remained an ATF target for several more decades.

The ATF takes its current name and mission from the Gun Control Act of 1968, passed because of public outrage over the triple assassinations of President John F. Kennedy, his brother Robert, and civil rights leader Martin Luther King, Jr. In 1972, the ATF became a separate division of the Treasury Department and was given responsibility for explosives as well. The ATF also became responsible for investigating arson when it became a federal crime in 1982.

Pitfalls

ATF agents run the same risks to life and limb as do most law enforcement officers. You'll work odd hours, travel a lot, and spend a lot of time away from your family. Special agents also may be transferred anywhere in the United States.

Perks

It might be dangerous work, but as an ATF agent your work will include a wide variety of challenges and experiences. The ATF gives agents a lot of freedom to develop cases from start to finish, and morale has been high over the years, according to government employee surveys.

Get a Jump on the Job

Check the ATF Web site at http://www.atf.gov, under the sections for "Jobs" and "Kids," each of which are helpful to readers of all ages. Note in newspapers and on TV how federal agents are involved in tough, important cases.

BANK EXAMINER

OVERVIEW

Because banks are entrusted with savings and investments of individuals and businesses across America, their honesty and efficiency are an important part of America's economy. The bank failures of the Great Depression were a national nightmare, and effective regulation helps reduce the chance that it will happen again. One way to do that is by having bank examiners check up on the condition and performance of banks, the quality of their operations, and how well the bank's managers follow federal laws.

Banks are regulated by state and federal agencies, including the Federal Deposit Insurance Corporation, the Office of the Comptroller of the Currency (OCC), and the Federal Reserve. Bank examination has become a lot more complicated as banks have evolved from just handling deposits, withdrawals, mortgages, and loans. Today, they're involved in virtually all areas of lending and investment. That means it's gotten a lot harder to find mistakes and problems, too.

The people in charge of finding those mistakes and problems are the bank examiners—experts who perform a wide-ranging evaluation of the practices and financial soundness of an institution (and especially the performance of management). It may only take a couple of examiners a week or two to check out a community bank, while a large bank examination may need a much bigger team. For the very biggest banks, examiners may provide daily supervision

AT A GLANCE

Salary Range

$30,000 to $125,000+

Education/Experience

A bachelor's degree is required, preferably with course work in accounting or business. You'll also need experience at a financial institution in such areas as loan applications, accounting, auditing, and investments.

Personal Attributes

First and foremost, bank examiners should be naturally curious. They must be able to identify clues to problems at banks and have the curiosity and enthusiasm to probe more deeply. Examiners also need good communication skills that allow them to listen to bank officials and, when possible, prevent confrontational situations. Because examiners often work in teams, teamwork and leadership skills are also important.

Requirements

Familiarity with personal computers and word processing and spreadsheet programs; ability to analyze financial and business information; good written and oral communications skills; willingness to travel 30 to 50 percent of the time; and a valid driver's license.

Outlook

Opportunities will continue to grow as bank activities continue to become more sophisticated and examiners continue to need increasingly sophisticated skills.

from their own office right in the bank! If you decide to become a bank examiner, you can be a "generalist"—or you can specialize in one area, such as asset management, bank information technology, capital markets, consumer compliance, or credit and enforcement. Specialists spend their time analyzing specific categories of risk to the bank.

Asset management specialists figure out how well a bank manages the risks of its loans and investments. They check out such activities as personal trust services, estate planning and settlement, investment services, securities lending, and investment advisory services for mutual funds. Bank information technology specialists examine a bank's ability to manage the risks of modern technology and electronically provided banking services. Capital markets specialists examine the risks of a bank's trading activities.

Consumer compliance specialists make sure banks comply with consumer protection laws and regulations, including fair lending laws. Credit specialists review and analyze the quality of a bank's loans by checking out the bank's credit files and the systems established to measure, monitor, and control credit activities.

Then there are the enforcement examiners, who make sure the banks follow the rules, check up on troubled institutions,

Rodney Jokerst, bank examiner

While Rodney Jokerst attended Southwest Missouri State University in Springfield, he belonged to a business fraternity that received a tour of the Federal Reserve Bank of Kansas City in 1991. Little did Jokerst know then that he would wind up as a senior examiner at that very bank. He's one of three examiners in that Federal Reserve Bank's Supervision and Risk Management Enforcement Unit. He's also responsible for the bank's overall supervisory approach for three of the largest institutions in his district.

"I liked the prestige of the Federal Reserve," Jokerst says, referring to the network of 12 banks that are under federal supervision but control their own operations. "I also wanted to be where the money is at."

Federal Reserve Banks are operating arms of the nation's central banking system. They are the bankers' bank, providing services to banks and the government similar to services provided by commercial and savings banks to individuals and business customers. The Fed supervises and examines commercial banks for safety, soundness, and compliance with banking laws.

"You have to have an inquisitive nature," Jokerst says. "You have to have an idea of what's going on in a particular institution or situation. You're in the enforcement world and it's an ongoing learning experience. You learn something new every day."

After earning a degree in finance banking and investment in 1993, Jokerst worked at First National City Bank in Springfield before getting a job offer from the Federal Reserve Bank of Kansas City. He began as a consumer compliance examiner and entered the Fed's exhaustive three-to-five-year training program to be commissioned as a bank examiner. Commissioned bank examiners are responsible for determining a bank's condition and giving their results to the bank's management in a formal Report of Examination.

Jokerst now has the authority to do much more than sign reports. If he finds illegal bank activity, he can turn the case over to the FBI or a U.S. assistant attorney. The Fed also has the authority to ban an individual from the banking business.

(continues)

(continued)

"There are only a few institutions where you have to go in with these tools," Jokerst says. "Usually, we're able to use moral persuasion to get the job done. That makes it less difficult for everybody."

Despite his enforcement role, Jokerst says that most banks don't dread his arrival. Well-managed banks like to know they're doing an effective job.

"If you have a strong bank, you don't mind us coming in," he says. "If you have weak management and weak internal controls, you're not real happy to see us. The stronger banks, I think, are happy to see us on a periodic basis."

Bank examiners rate banks from 1 to 5, with 1 the top grade. The ratings also help gauge progress or deterioration. A bank rated 3 or worse is considered troubled.

"If an institution falls from a 2 to a 3, we place a lot more scrutiny," Jokerst says. "We devote significantly more resources and ongoing supervision. We'll keep close tabs if they're in pretty poor shape and we'll require quarterly reports or even more frequently if it's a dire situation."

Because the Fed of Kansas City covers all or parts of seven states, Jokerst logs plenty of time on the road. It's an occupational hazard.

"We go out to remote places in Oklahoma, Nebraska, and Kansas, and it's very common to drive 30 miles from the bank to where you're staying," he says. "You can stay anywhere from a great hotel in a large city to somewhere where the only place to eat is at the filling station. We go to a lot of farming communities, so you get the fresh smell of manure in the mornings."

If nothing else smells bad, it's been a highly successful examination for both Jokerst and the bank.

---

and take action against insiders who have acted inappropriately or embezzled bank funds.

Pitfalls

If you don't like to live out of a suitcase, you might not enjoy this type of work. Travel for bank examiners can be taxing, especially if they have to travel outside major cities. In fact, it's common for examiners to perform 60 or 70 percent of their work on the road. Some examiners travel internationally, while others focus on metropolitan or rural areas.

Travel may sound like fun, but it isn't always glamorous. A lot of small banks are located in small towns and rural areas, and can require lots of driving time.

Perks

Bank examiners are well paid. Salaries can reach six figures, especially for specialists working with large banks. Plus, you can feel good about knowing you're keeping everybody's money safe and protecting the integrity of the nation's banking. If detective work and learning all the time sounds like fun, bank examining could be for you.

Get a Jump on the Job

If you have an interest in bank examining, you might start out working as a bank teller while attending college. This can help you get a feel for some of the areas in which a bank examiner will become involved.

BORDER PATROL SEARCH AND RESCUE AGENT

OVERVIEW

It can be a tough and dangerous trek in the illegal flight from Mexico into the United States. Although many immigrants do illegally cross the U.S. border, there also are many who don't get very far. While crossing mountains or deserts, they can get lost, dehydrated, sick, and injured. If they need emergency medical treatment, they may be hours away from a doctor or hospital. Although people illegally crossing into the United States usually hope to avoid Border Patrol agents, the ones who get stuck and need medical care are happy to see them.

Border Patrol Search, Trauma, and Rescue (BORSTAR) teams primarily help illegal aliens, but they also aid U.S. citizens—other Border Patrol agents, hikers lost or stranded in the mountains, and motorists in serious accidents. The Border Patrol, despite having no formal program, had been rescuing people since the mid-1980s. But in 1998 officials in the Border Patrol's San Diego Sector asked permission to start an official rescue team because it was hard to treat agents or civilians who needed help in remote border areas. In July 1998, the first San Diego BORSTAR team started up.

That October, an academy open in San Diego, and 29 agents went into training. That encouraged the Tucson Sector to start its own unit; in April 1999, a BORSTAR academy began in Tucson and graduated

30 agents. Today there are nearly 150 BORSTAR agents in California, Arizona, and Texas—aided by search and rescue dogs who were added in 2001.

Becoming a BORSTAR agent is no day at the beach, however. The academies require intense training that usually eliminates half of the applicant pool before the session concludes. Graduates are required to pick a rescue specialty that requires advanced training to be completed within a year. Although a college degree isn't required, you'll stand a better chance of advancing in the Border Patrol if you've graduated with a degree in criminal justice or another major related to law enforcement.

BORSTAR agents start their workday as enforcement agents, on the lookout for illegal aliens, terrorists, and smugglers of immigrants and drugs. But when people need medical help, BORSTAR agents switch into search and rescue mode. In April 2005, the Tucson team rescued 77 illegal aliens lost on a desert Indian reservation. Many in the group were sick, vomiting, and unable to continue. Their guide was preparing to abandon them, so the ailing aliens grabbed his cell phone and called 911. The caller was connected to the BORSTAR team.

Agents first had to find the lost group. After asking the caller to describe any

Ron Bellavia, BORSTAR commander

Many illegal aliens pay smugglers to lead them out of Mexico, but then discover their trip isn't what the smugglers told them to expect. "They're told that it's just an eight-hour walk and they'll need only a gallon of water," says Ron Bellavia, commander of the BORSTAR team in Tucson. "By the time they're on their fourth day, they're out of water and the smugglers have abandoned them in the desert. We're a friendly face. Now they just hope to get out of the desert alive."

The smuggling crews are a multimillion-dollar business. "They know the terrain very well, they know where they're going, and they're in it for the money," Bellavia says. "We've had numerous people we've saved and apprehended in our daily enforcement activities who tell us the smugglers abandoned them because they heard the Border Patrol was in the area or because they got lost. They run away from the group in the middle of the desert and leave them without any water."

Once the smuggler abandons the immigrants, they're in big trouble. Typically, they have no idea where they're going. "Once the smuggler leaves, all they're doing is going north or in the direction of a light they see in the distance," Bellavia says. "Once the smugglers leave them, their chances of survival are considerably less."

Arizona is the most popular state for those who illegally cross the U.S. border from Mexico, but it's not all environmentally friendly terrain. Temperatures of 115 and higher are common in the Arizona desert. "It's often very treacherous," Bellavia says. "We're hours from any backup or building."

The team operates from the lowlands in the desert areas to high mountain areas, performing rope rescues when people fall into the canyons. "That's why it's very challenging," Bellavia says. "It's a hard environment and we need people who are in top physical condition. We're putting those agents' lives in danger to rescue people already in peril."

Many illegal aliens assume it's warm enough in early spring to cross the southeastern Arizona mountain ranges—but they're mistaken. In some years, more than 300 immigrants have been rescued from wintry weather in just one week. The trails are steep and exhausting, and hypothermia (a dangerous loss of body heat) is common when temperatures dip below freezing at night. That's why Bellavia's team carries blankets and heat packs. Shortly before Christmas in landmarks, they were able to use mapping software to determine the search area. The group was on the Tohoho O'odham reservation, close to a silver mine. The caller phoned back to say he could hear the BORSTAR helicopter, and the group was found near the base of the Silver Bell Mountains. By the time an agent jumped off the helicopter to see who most needed medical attention, two people had stopped breathing. The agent managed to revive them, and they were airlifted to Tucson hospitals. Although illegal aliens found by BORSTAR are arrested, if they're in danger of losing their lives, getting arrested always beats the alternative.

Pitfalls

You'll have to deal with the stress of working irregular hours on treacherous

2004, Bellavia took reporters into the Huachuca Mountains to show them the hazards faced by illegal aliens. When reporters quickly got tired and thirsty, Bellavia explained, "These people aren't any more prepared than you."

Bellavia joined the Border Patrol in 1995 after earning a degree in criminal justice from Valparaiso University in Indiana. He and some friends made an Internet search for law enforcement jobs and he narrowed his choices to the Chicago Police Department in his hometown, and the Border Patrol.

"I decided it was time to get out of Chicago, so I took a job in the Wild West," Bellavia says. He became a patrol agent after graduating from an 18-week academy, where he learned Spanish, immigration law, arrest procedures, firearms use, and all-terrain driving. After seven years as an agent, Bellavia's friends convinced him to join them on the BORSTAR team. He was accepted into the five-week academy and graduated.

"Not only are we going out every day to enforce the laws of the U.S., but we're going out and saving lives," Bellavia says. The team uses Humvees outfitted with medical gear, IV solutions, backboards for transport, and baskets for carrying people out. First, the team transports the immigrants out of the heat, giving them EMT care and summoning an ambulance if necessary.

"You have to have a lot of inner strength to see a mission through," Bellavia says. "But you also have to have the compassion to treat people who on one hand are breaking the law, but on the other hand have to be rescued and cared for.

"We've rescued plenty of U.S. citizens, too," he added. "We see people going on hiking expeditions in mountains where they don't take enough supplies and get in over their heads. We also respond to motor vehicle accidents. Those sometimes are the hardest things to respond to because of the vast amount of trauma."

Bellavia's team rescued 561 people during one 12-month stretch. He also led the April 2005 rescue of 77 people. "That was particularly satisfying because there were some young people in that group," he says. "The youngest boy was 12. Once you draw parallels from that to your own family and next of kin, that makes it all the more gratifying."

terrain in life-or-death situations. When you're not doing search and rescue work, you're routinely putting your life at risk.

Perks

You'll get the challenge and satisfaction of being part of an elite team and saving lives; it's especially rewarding to be able to rescue children. BORSTAR members also enjoy the variety and freedom that comes with rescue work.

Get a Jump on the Job

When you pick a foreign language to study, Spanish is the obvious choice if you're interested in someday becoming a Border Patrol agent. Study immigration issues, including the problem of illegal aliens.

CENSUS BUREAU STATISTICIAN

OVERVIEW

You've probably grown up hearing the statistics about this country: how many one-parent families there are and how that's changed since the 1950s; how many different racial or ethnic groups make up this country's population. Yet behind each and every statistic that helps define this nation stands an individual employee at the U.S. Census Bureau—a demographic or mathematical statistician whose job it is to look at the vast amounts of material that the bureau assembles and make sense of it for the rest of us.

The U.S. Census Bureau has been around in some form for just about as long as there have been log cabins and settlers to count. After the American Revolution, then-Secretary of State Thomas Jefferson ordered a census to be taken to survey the population of the fledgling nation. As people began to spread across the country, the census kept adding up information to help plan for growth during the 1800s, asking questions about taxation, churches, manufacturing, product value, and crime, earning the nickname "America's Fact Finder." Congress made the Census Bureau a permanent institution in 1902.

Today, Census Bureau employees figure out the nation's makeup using statistics—the scientific application of mathematical principles to help manage details to make data clearer. Statisticians also apply their mathematical and

AT A GLANCE

Salary Range
$30,380 to $91,680+

Education/Experience
A master's degree in statistics, mathematics, or demographics is the minimum educational requirement for most jobs with this title. The training required for employment as an entry-level statistician at the bureau is a bachelor's degree, with at least 15 semester hours of statistics or a combination of 15 hours of mathematics and statistics, if at least six semester hours are in statistics. Qualifying as a mathematical statistician at the Bureau requires 24 semester hours of mathematics and statistics, with a minimum of six semester hours in statistics and 12 semester hours in an area of advanced mathematics, such as calculus, differential equations, or vector analysis. Many other schools also offer degrees in mathematics, operations research, and other fields that include a sufficient number of courses in statistics to qualify graduates for some beginning positions in the federal government.

Personal Attributes
Good mathematical and communications skills are important for prospective statisticians, who often need to explain technical matters to people without statistical expertise.

Requirements
Because computers are used in so many statistical applications, a strong background in computer science is highly recommended. Courses in sociology and demographics are also highly desirable.

Outlook
Although slower than average growth is expected in employment of statisticians over the 2002–12 period, job opportunities should remain favorable for individuals with degrees in statistics. Competition for entry-level positions at the bureau is expected to be strong for persons just meeting the minimum

(continues)

statistical knowledge to help design better surveys and experiments.

One technique that is especially useful to statisticians is sampling—obtaining information about a population of people or group of things by surveying a small portion of the total. Statisticians decide where and how to gather the data, determine the type and size of the sample group, and develop the survey questionnaire or reporting form. They also prepare instructions for workers who will collect and tabulate the data.

Some government statisticians at the bureau develop surveys that measure population growth or unemployment. Finally, statisticians analyze, interpret, and summarize the data using computer software.

Pitfalls

The job of counting citizens may seem straightforward, but it can get pretty confusing because of disagreements about how to divide the population, or think of population groups. Also, there is enormous pressure to be mathematically perfect, since a small mathematical mistake in the Census Bureau can have enormous effects on the information disseminated to the public about the direction the country is headed. To a considerable degree, just about everyone relies heavily on the Census Bureau to accurately count everything from how many indoor toilets we have to how many single parents are living alone. A minor mathematical slipup can affect government aid, programs for the poor, sociological data, and much more.

Perks

Using statistics to make the country's trends more understandable to everyday Americans brings great satisfaction to those in this profession.

Get a Jump on the Job

You can start preparing for a career in statistics or demographics in high school by taking sociology, psychology, and math classes. In college, you'll want to focus on courses in statistics and demographics. Required subjects for statistics majors include differential and integral calculus, statistical methods, mathematical modeling, and probability theory. Additional courses that undergraduates should take include linear algebra, design and analysis of experiments, applied multivariate analysis, mathematical statistics, and sociology.

In 2002, about 140 universities offered a master's degree program in statistics and 90 offered a doctoral degree program. Many other schools also offered graduate-level courses in applied statistics for students majoring in sociology, education, psychology, and other fields. You don't need an undergraduate degree in statistics to join a graduate statistics program, although good training in mathematics is essential.

Angela Brittingham, demographic statistician

Forget the stereotypical bookish mathematician that you may think of when you hear the word "statistician"—for Angela Brittingham, her interest has always been the human side of the equation, which is why she majored in sociology in college.

Today, she's a bona fide government numbers cruncher—a demographic statistician for the U.S. Census Bureau in Washington, D.C. The job has a big title—but basically, she says, she uses statistics to help people understand demographic trends. "I do a little bit of statistical testing," she says, "but mostly it's based on data that the mathematical statisticians have put together."

Brittingham came to the job by way of Georgetown University, where she earned a bachelor's degree in sociology and a master's degree in applied demography. Demography is really the study of the size, structure, and distribution of populations, and how populations change over time as a result of births, deaths, migration, and aging. Demographic analysis can focus on entire societies, or smaller specific groups defined by different criteria, such as education, nationality, religion or ethnicity. Brittingham works in the ethnicity and ancestry branch of the Population Division of the Census Bureau.

If you're interested in social anthropology, sociology, and demographics, there are a number of universities around the country with demographic programs, she explains, although her program at Georgetown is no more. Most people go on to earn a Ph.D. in demography, she says. Demography studies tend to be centered in sociology departments, although the field is really a hybrid of sociology and statistics.

While the Census Bureau is a big employer of statisticians and demographers, there are lots of other places you can work with a degree in this field, Brittingham explains. Before she came to the Census, Brittingham worked at a nonprofit national opinion social research center affiliated with the University of Chicago. Working for a nonprofit opinion research center means you'll do a lot of social research, surveys, and methodological research on how to take surveys. You might work at the Population Reference Bureau in Washington, D.C., or at the Pew Hispanic Center studying characteristics of Hispanic populations. Professional pollsters, such as the Gallup poll, also hire a lot of statisticians and demographers.

"Any kind of social research organization or survey research companies will hire demographers," she says, or you can veer off and bring your knowledge of statistics to the field of marketing.

After six years at the bureau, she still likes her work. "What I like is that I do things at the Census that's an important tool that everybody can use to get information on how our society is changing," she says. "I guess I grew up looking at those snapshots [of interesting facts] in *USA Today*, and I was fascinated by them." What she doesn't like is the fact that much of the work in ethnicity and ancestry is very vague. "A lot of different people think of it differently, so what seems right to one person might seem wrong to another person." Constantly having to deal with

(continues)

(continued)

different people's opinions about how to present data on ethnicity can be frustrating. "Still, it's important for someone to do," she says.

If you're interested in statistics or demography, you should take all the classes you can that relate to human populations. Brittingham recommends you take a human geography course, and then beef up your statistics background, along with classes on survey design or survey methodology. "Everything we use is based on a survey, asking people questions, so it's important to get a good background in learning how to effectively design surveys."

CITY PLANNER

OVERVIEW

Have you ever flown over wide-open spaces and imagined the kind of town you would build if you could? Have you driven down a street clogged with ugly storefronts and wished you could replace them with modern businesses? Have you ever looked at blighted downtown buildings and wished you could build a gorgeous new sports arena in their place? If you have that kind of vision and passion for changing a community, city planning might be right up your alley. We all have ideas on how we'd like to change our town or city, but planners are trained to know which ideas can actually work. They know which plans meet zoning, environmental, and other laws.

Planners get most of their training on the job. But they'll have an easier time if they have a degree in urban or regional planning. They'll also get a boost from studies in architecture, landscape architecture, urban design, civil engineering, law, earth sciences, geography, demography, economics, finance, health administration, and management.

Planners figure out the best way to use land and the money a city can afford to spend for housing, business, recreation, and public transportation. They show city officials how to promote growth, preferably without more traffic jams, air pollution, and other problems that may come with new projects. Officials who run a city (such as a mayor, city manager, or city council member) are always being asked

AT A GLANCE

Salary Range
$47,000 to $100,000 and up.

Education/Experience
You'll have an edge with a master's degree in urban or regional planning or a related field. Job experience in architecture, engineering, environmental work, or public administration will come in very handy for a city planner.

Personal Attributes
You need to get along and communicate with developers, public officials, and citizens. It helps to have a thick skin when elected officials reject your ideas or citizens complain that your planning decisions are ruining their community.

Requirements
You'll have to be able to think in terms of spatial relationships and visualize how your plans and designs will turn out. You'll need to be able to communicate well both orally and in writing every day on the job.

Outlook
Most jobs for urban and regional planners will open up in well-to-do suburbs. In these places, demands for new houses, schools, shopping malls, arenas, and office parks are exploding. All local governments need planners, although not all can afford to hire them. More architectural firms are hiring their own planners so they can get a head start on projects when they sit down to discuss them with government planners.

to consider new building proposals and designs. Maybe a developer wants to build a new shopping mall or office building, or a neighborhood group wants a new school. Or maybe a professional sports team wants a new arena or stadium. Almost everybody can agree that progress is important, but public officials want that progress to be orderly, legal, and affordable. Before officials agree to start new projects, they want to know what their planners have to say.

City planners will explain how a new project fits in with the surrounding area and if it meets zoning, building, and environmental laws. Planners will outline the needs for improvements in streets, highways, and water and sewer lines around the project. They'll suggest the layout for new buildings and other facilities. They'll write detailed reports to show how new projects can be built and what they will cost. A developer who asks public officials to look over a project usually will be sent to a planner. The planner may suggest changes that will avoid problems down the road. As a planner, you'll often be asked to defend or explain your opinions at public meetings and you should expect to be criticized. Citizens often disagree

Bob Lindeblad, city planner

Most people come home from their vacations with photos of beaches, mountains, and friends and relatives in tourist poses. Bob Lindeblad comes home with photos of shopping centers, office buildings, and parking lots. He's manager of current planning for Overland Park, Kansas, and likes to compare his city with others. "If you see designs and buildings you like, a picture's worth a thousand words," Lindeblad says. "Sometimes, a developer comes in and says, 'We can't do that here,' and I say, 'You did that there.' I'm pretty well known for my camera. My friends say, 'That's it, we're not going to another shopping center!' "

Lindeblad's city is a perfect place for a city planner. Overland Park is a fast-growing, forward-looking suburb of 165,000 people in one of America's wealthiest counties. A new arena and a huge open-air shopping mall were on the drawing board when Lindeblad was interviewed. "It's hard for me to go to a church or a meeting without somebody saying, 'What's going on here? Why did you do that?' " Lindeblad says.

But he and the planners who work under him can't do anything by themselves. They report to the city planning commission, which holds public hearings to discuss the pros and cons of new projects. If the planning commission likes a project, it gets sent to the city council for consideration. "You're making a difference in the fabric of the community and you've got to love it or else you can't stand the heat," Lindeblad says. "You have to have the passion to really make a difference."

Lindeblad had a passion for planning early in life. While he attended grade school in Hutchinson, Kansas, he was assigned to plan his own city. His plan included a wide main street, a park, a college, a river, and an expressway. That plan now hangs in a frame on a wall of Lindeblad's office. "My mom gave it to me one Christmas," he recalled. "She says, 'You were meant to be a city planner.' "

Lindeblad's walls also included a design for the Overland Park Events Center and Entertainment District, including a sports arena, bars, restaurants, and retail stores. Lindeblad with planners. Public officials don't always agree with their planners, either, but at least they listen carefully.

Many cities and suburbs have so many projects that their planners must be specialists. They may be experts in housing, transportation, environmental issues, economic development, or historic preservation. If you want to become a planner in a smaller community, you may be asked to become a jack-of-all-trades. If you see a city that's clean, well designed, and a good place to live, chances are it's had good planners.

Pitfalls

You can work long hours when a full day's work is followed by a city council meeting that night. Moreover, city planners can expect to get criticized by citizens and officials. It can become very frustrating when a well-thought-out plan gets rejected.

also had drawings for a mall that would cover one million square feet. "These open-air centers—we call them lifestyle centers—are the new design in shopping centers," he says. "This is what everybody's doing around the country. Our city budget is based highly on a retail sales tax and we can't let our outdated shopping centers fall apart."

Indoor malls were the rage for decades, but many shoppers suddenly got tired of them. There's also a trend for suburbs to move shopping centers closer to homes. "That's what we're getting back to—a new urbanism," Lindeblad says. "We're encouraging mixed-use development. If you still want to live on a cul-de-sac, in low density, you can still do that. But we want to offer options."

Lindeblad graduated from Kansas State University in 1975 with a bachelor's degree in landscape architecture. That qualified him to evaluate how a piece of land can be developed. "It's how to lay it out and how to create people spaces," he says. "You have to know about the soils, the grading, and the environment impacts. It's the big picture. If you have 300 acres to develop, these are the people you should give it to."

Lindeblad and developers don't always agree on how to develop land. But he's always willing to suggest different approaches that will suit both. "We're in partnership with the private sector to develop these projects," Lindeblad says. "You don't just say, 'No.' You give them options—move this building here, put the parking lot there. They'll thank you because you're giving them other alternatives."

Overland Park's city planners don't forget that they're really employed by their residents. Every weekday one of eight planners takes a turn at being "planner of the day." That planner sits at a desk in City Hall and takes phone calls and visits that may come from a major developer or a local resident with a question or gripe. "It's not rocket science," Lindeblad says. "Personality, work ethic, and creating relationships, to me, are most important. If you can't relate to people, you're history. You're toast."

Perks

It will make you feel good to know that you've made a community a better place to live, work, or go to school. And it's nice to have a job in which your opinion is important. Because new projects are usually in the works, the job never gets boring.

Get a Jump on the Job

You can attend a public hearing or meeting at which new projects are being considered and a city planner is making a presentation. These events often are televised on public access channels. You could also make an appointment with a planner and ask for career advice.

CONGRESSIONAL PRESS SECRETARY

OVERVIEW

If you love to talk, express yourself clearly in writing, and think politics is just about the most fascinating career around, you might have what it takes to become a press secretary for a state or U.S. congressional leader. Many press secretaries begin their careers on Capitol Hill, where the offices of the nation's 100 senators and 435 representatives have long been the training ground for some of history's most influential power brokers. Capitol Hill offers a virtual immersion program into all aspects of government and politics, and press secretaries are often in the eye of the storm.

As a press secretary, you'll serve as the mouthpiece for the politician, building and maintaining positive relationships with the public. As politicians recognize the growing importance of good public relations to the success of their tenure in office, they increasingly rely on their press secretaries for advice on strategy and policy. After all, a politician's reputation and success—even a successful re-election campaign—can depend on the degree to which the constituents support the politician's goals and policies.

Press secretaries are responsible for analyzing public opinion by constantly monitoring the press and by keeping up with the latest polls. Press secretaries also need to organize media campaigns by using press conferences, media interviews,

AT A GLANCE

Salary Range
$25,000 to $100,000+

Education/Experience
College graduates with a degree in journalism, public relations, advertising, political science, English, or another communications-related field with related work experience.

Personal Attributes
To be an effective press secretary, you'll need excellent research, communication, and writing skills so that you can persuade people that their politician understands the issues and is doing something about it. Creativity, initiative, good judgment, and the ability to express thoughts clearly and simply are essential. Decision-making, problem-solving, and research skills also are important. You'll also need an outgoing personality, self-confidence, an understanding of human psychology, and enthusiasm. You should be competitive yet able to function as part of a team and be open to new ideas. You'll need good organizational skills and an understanding of how government works. It's also vital that you are able to be trustworthy and keep important information confidential. Finally, you need to be tough, look good, and speak well.

Requirements
A college degree in journalism or communications, plus experience in some type of newsgathering organization, newspaper, radio, or TV.

Outlook
Although employment is projected to increase faster than average, keen competition is expected for entry-level jobs in this field. Many people are attracted to this profession due to the high-profile nature of the work. Opportunities should be best for college graduates who combine a degree in public relations, journalism, or another communications-related field with a public relations internship or other related work experience.

and public events, as well as writing press releases, speeches, and other related material. As a press secretary, you'll spend time answering media queries for your politician and arranging official responses, while at the same time managing issues with the potential to generate negative media coverage. Most press secretaries also advise politicians on appropriate responses to questions, especially on key projects or policy. Press secretaries (also called information officers, public affairs specialists, or communication specialists) keep the public informed about the activities of government agencies and officials. For example, a press secretary for a member of Congress keeps constituents aware of the representative's accomplishments.

The day starts very early for a press secretary, as you read all the major newspapers from the district and scan the national media outlets, including the *Washington Post*, *New York Times*, *Wall Street Journal*, *CNN*, *Washington Times*, National Journal's *Congress Daily*, and so on. You'll gather a set of media clips from major newspapers for your boss to check out, and perhaps brief the boss over the phone about what's in the papers, including local coverage of Congress and breaking national stories.

Next, you might spend some time writing a press release on the bill your boss has written that's just made it out of committee, or some new funding obtained for the local library back home. This kind of funding coup shows your boss's commitment to helping the people back home, so it's pretty important—especially to a hometown paper. As you work, you might get calls from reporters checking out stories or looking for a quote; it's your job to check out the facts and see if you can obtain the information before the reporter's deadline.

Next, you might work on a summary of important "talking points" for your boss's upcoming interview with a Washington paper—and then it's time to meet with the legislative director to get a handle on legislation coming to the floor over the next couple of weeks. At any point in the day, you may need to interrupt your work in the wake of breaking news—perhaps the president has just closed a number of military bases around the country, and one of them happens to be in your boss's home territory. If something like this occurs, you'll have to draft a quick response to the announcement, and then track down your boss and read the statement over the phone. Once it's approved, you'll release it to the media. As a press secretary, however, your boss isn't the only one you've got to please—you may be called on to attend a meeting of all the press secretaries for members in your political party to hear the best way to discuss the party's education agenda.

You can expect to put in long hours, and unpaid overtime is common. Occasionally, you must be at the job or on call around the clock, especially if there's an emergency. On the job, the office can be hectic; work schedules can be irregular and the press secretary is often interrupted. Schedules often have to be rearranged so that your boss can meet deadlines, deliver speeches, attend meetings and community activities, or travel.

There are no definite minimum standards for becoming a press secretary, and you can't major in "press secretary." But a college degree in political science, journalism, English, or communications, combined with experience as a journalist or in public relations, is typically required. A public relations internship is one way to get this experience. In fact, internships are becoming vital to obtaining employment. Some congressmen seek college graduates who've worked in electronic or print journalism, whereas others consider whether the applicant has demonstrated communication skills and training or experience in a field related to politics. And of course, on Capitol Hill, who you know can count for a lot.

Many colleges and universities offer bachelor's and postsecondary degrees in journalism or communications. A typical communications program includes courses in writing, emphasizing news releases, proposals, annual reports, scripts, speeches, and related items; visual communications, including desktop publishing and computer graphics; and research, emphasizing social science research and survey design and implementation. Courses in advertising, journalism, business administration, finance, political science, psychology, sociology, and creative writing are helpful.

People rarely make a permanent career out of being a press secretary, however.

Alison Power, former congressional press secretary

Being on the inside of what was happening on Capitol Hill made the job of press secretary something special for Alison Power, who worked as press secretary for Republican Congressman David O'Brien Martin of northern New York. Her four-year stint on the Hill gave her a fascinating peek at the inner workings of the federal government. "It was just interesting to be on the inside, interesting to see how things worked," she recalls. "I saw how bills were written, laws were made, how things were negotiated, how representatives worked with their constituents. I saw how Washington worked."

A graduate of Smith College, Power had begun her career as a general assignment reporter and then managing editor for the *Ogdensburg Journal* and the *Sunday Advance-News*, the small newspapers close to her hometown. From there she moved on to work in the public relations office at St. Lawrence University in Canton, New York, when Martin tapped her for the press secretary job.

"It wasn't that hard, being a press secretary," she says. "You're constantly reading newspapers, always watching the news. The TV was on all the time." Having spent so long as a journalist, intent on covering politicians, finding herself on the opposite side was a bit disconcerting. But she realized that her experience in journalism made her more empathetic to reporters and what they need.

Her advice for students thinking of a press secretary career? "Learn to spell," she cracks, and then turns serious. "If you can, do a [congressional] internship—even an unpaid internship. Learn how to write, and remember that no task is too small. Always ask if you can help."

After four years working on the Hill, Power moved to New York City to work in public relations for the Central Park Zoo. Today she is director of communications at the main headquarters of the Wildlife Conservation Society at the Bronx Zoo, the flagship of the largest network of metropolitan zoos in the country.

Press secretaries lose their job when their member leaves office, and even if they don't get laid off, few can stand the pace for long. That's why press secretaries typically see these positions as stepping-stones to other careers in politics, federal agencies, or business.

Pitfalls

This is an exciting career, but one fraught with incredible stress as you juggle the needs of your congressperson with the desires of constituents, the public, and the press. You're looking at long hours, lots of travel, and little overtime pay. You also have to contend with job security issues, depending on how likely it is that your boss will be re-elected every four to six years. If your boss loses an election, you're out of a job.

Perks

For electrifying excitement and a sense of being right in the thick of the action, it's hard to beat the job of press secretary. The income can be quite satisfying and the contacts you make will greatly strengthen your chances of moving up the job ladder. This can be a once-in-a-lifetime opportunity to meet the leaders of our country and know that you're playing an important role in government. This job also carries a lot of prestige and some power, depending on who you're working for.

Get a Jump on the Job

Most press secretaries have at some time been a working member of the press, so think about first getting a job in journalism. You can start in high school, working for your school paper and taking journalism classes. In college, you can major in journalism and work on your college paper. Try for a summer internship at a news organization, or TV or radio station, and practice writing every chance you get.

During high school and college, you might also want to volunteer for local, state, or national political campaigns. Offer to stuff envelopes, ring doorbells, or help drive voters to the poll—anything to get involved in politics and see whether a future in government work might interest you.

If you think you might like working in national, state, or local government as a press secretary, your best bet is to try to land a congressional internship during or after college. Many colleges and journalism schools can help you obtain a part-time internship that provides valuable experience and training either in state government or on Capitol Hill in Washington, D.C. Membership in local chapters of the Public Relations Student Society of America (affiliated with the Public Relations Society of America) or the International Association of Business Communicators provides an opportunity for students to exchange views with public relations specialists and to make professional contacts that may help them find a job in the field. A portfolio of published articles, television or radio programs, slide presentations, and other work is an asset in finding a job. Writing for a school publication or a TV or radio station provides valuable experience and material for your portfolio.

CORONER

OVERVIEW

No matter what time of day or night, whenever or wherever an unexplained or unexpected death takes place, someone has to investigate. In the United States, death investigations are handled differently in each state. In some states, deaths are investigated by a state, district, or county medical examiner. In other states, a state medical examiner oversees the investigations done by county or district medical examiners or coroners.

The types of deaths investigated also vary from state to state. In almost all states, violent, criminal, suspicious, or unexplained deaths are always investigated. Coroners are also usually called when a body is found dead. Depending on the state, coroners might investigate the reasons for other deaths as well. They might look into the sudden death of a person who was in good health, or they might investigate if the death appears to be a suicide. Some states ask that accidental deaths be investigated, including drowning and motor vehicle accidents. If a child dies, coroners may be called on to find the cause.

To figure out the cause of death, the coroner will collect evidence at the scene of the death, interview anyone who might have witnessed the death, and review the dead person's medical history and records. Coroners sometimes have assistants who help them with the investigation. The coroner will also read through the autopsy report as part of the investigation.

After analyzing all the evidence, the coroner makes a decision about how the person died; that cause of death will

then be listed on the death certificate. The coroner may need to write a report explaining the cause of death, and how it was determined. If the person died as the result of a crime, the coroner may have to testify at a hearing or trial.

Not surprisingly, the requirements to become a coroner vary from state to state. In some states, the requirements are left up to the district or county. Coroners are usually appointed or elected. In some places, qualifications only specify that the person be 18 years old and a resident of the county or district he or she serves. In other places, the coroner must be a medical doctor to be appointed or elected.

If you're interested in being a coroner someday, there may be few or no requirements for you to run for election or to be appointed to a coroner position—but in reality you really need a very strong background in many different areas. Knowledge of law enforcement or criminal justice will help you collect and analyze the evidence. A medical background or coursework will help you read and analyze medical records and autopsy reports. College classes in criminal justice, forensics, anatomy, biology, pharmacology, fire science, nursing, management, and business administration will help give you good background. Some colleges and universities even offer a degree in death investigation.

After you're appointed or elected, you might be required to complete a training class, and you'll probably be required to go to training each year to learn new information and techniques while keeping your skills up to date.

Pitfalls

Coroners are on call 24 hours a day, seven days a week. They are called to death scenes on holidays, weekends, and in the middle of the night. In many areas, coroners make less than other elected officials (such as managers and treasurers) who put in 40 hours a week, Monday through Friday.

Perks

You'll be able to give a family answers about how their loved one died. That can be important for a family in a time of grief.

P. Michael Murphy, coroner

With almost 13,000 deaths in Clark County, Nevada, each year, it's hard to imagine that the coroner's office would ever have an average day. But occasionally, "there is that average day when everything is running according to schedule and appropriately, while rare," says P. Michael Murphy, Clark County coroner.

Clark's background is in law enforcement, and he received his training during his 30 years on the job and from some advanced education. He notes that experience and training comes into play on almost every case. "Some of the forensic challenges that are placed on us require some unique skills and forward thinking," he says, "not accepting the status quo and understanding the need to think outside the box."

For Murphy, one of the things he likes most about his job is the ability to interact and help families at their time of crisis. He takes seriously the responsibility of speaking for the people who died, and telling the truth about their situation. "But the actual time that it requires to do the job and do it effectively and appropriately," he adds, "has always put a strain on personal life and the ability to balance both."

A medical background or at least a background in anatomy would be helpful, Murphy believes, and the investigative experience he got while working as a police officer was important. "For this particular job," he says, "you'd need an administrative background to run the office itself. Gain as much experience as possible, get the education early on, and associate yourself with an office either in a volunteer status or in some type of intern status so that you can gain the insight and knowledge that you need to make sure that this is the type of career that you want. Then begin the process of working your way through the system."

Get a Jump on the Job

Find out what the requirements are for death investigators in your area, or in the area in which you'd like to work, and work toward meeting those requirements. If there are no requirements, take college courses in criminal justice and pre-medicine, along with a variety of other classes to give you a broad background. Some coroner's offices have volunteer opportunities. Sometimes these volunteers get to help the coroner with death investigations.

COURT INTERPRETER

OVERVIEW

Have you ever felt helpless in a foreign country because you couldn't understand the language? Then just think how helpless you'd feel if you had to appear in court in a nation in which you couldn't understand the judge, prosecutor, or witnesses. Imagine if your freedom or financial well-being was being decided in a courtroom in which you felt lost. Because the U.S. judicial system guarantees everybody a fair trial, special measures are needed when a defendant or other individual involved in court proceedings doesn't speak English or doesn't speak well enough to feel comfortable in court.

That's why local, state, and federal courts hire interpreters. Those who can translate Spanish into English are in highest demand. An interpreter must not only be fluent in a foreign language and English, but must understand slang as well as correct grammar in both languages. Interpreters must also understand legal terms, court proceedings, and court documents. If the defendant speaks only Spanish, the interpreter will repeat his or her words to the court in English. The interpreter will also tell the defendant in Spanish everything that's being said in English.

Although court interpreters are full-time employees in some larger jurisdictions, most are freelancers and paid by the hour. Interpreters may be required to pass written and oral examinations and get certified by federal,

AT A GLANCE

Salary Range

$5,000 to $60,000 a year.

Education/Experience

You'll need to be fluent in English and the language you'll be interpreting. Most court interpreters have college degrees, though they may not have majored in a language.

Personal Attributes

You'll need to inspire confidence in people who need your service, especially defendants. They'll count on you to help them express themselves and present their case. You'll need to be a people person and relate to officers of the court as well as defendants and others who come from many different walks of life.

Requirements

Most states require certification earned by passing oral and written exams. But some states allow both certified and non-certified interpreters, although those who are certified receive higher pay. You'll need to be thoroughly familiar with the U.S. court system.

Outlook

The need for court interpreters, especially those specializing in Spanish, is expected to grow. As Spanish-speaking immigrants keep coming to the United States in large numbers, more interpreters will be needed for those who require legal help.

state, or municipal courts. The National Association of Judiciary Interpreters and Translators also trains and certifies court interpreters. You can also get training from such organizations as the National Center for Interpretation, Testing, Research and Policy at the University of Arizona. Many jurisdictions don't require their interpreters to be certified. Many interpreters were

Ivonne Hournou, court interpreter

When Ivonne Hournou retired as a Spanish teacher from the Kansas City School District in 2000, she began looking for other ways to stay busy. Her son, Luis Belaustegui, who teaches Spanish at a local university, saw a flier that advertised training for court interpreters. He realized immediately that this job was right up his mother's alley. Not only does she speak both Spanish and English fluently, but she had attended law school in her native Argentina.

Hournou went to Jefferson City for training and became certified by the state of Missouri as a court interpreter. However, she noticed that few applicants could pass the oral and written tests. Most were handicapped by their lack of a legal background and behaved inappropriately. "I saw a lot of goodhearted people but who wanted to do everything they're not supposed to do, like give advice," Hournou says. "My drawback was that I didn't have the legal training in English."

She was a fast learner, however, and today she often freelances in the Jackson County Circuit Court in downtown Kansas City and several small-town courts within easy driving distance. "I love small towns," she says. "The courthouses have the strength and status of the law and everybody is quiet as mice and does what they're supposed to do. And because the dockets are not so crowded, the judges are more personable."

It didn't take Hournou long to realize the importance of her services. She interpreted for a woman who was trying to regain custody of an infant she initially had agreed to give up for adoption. The woman claimed she'd called the adoption agency to change her mind, as was permitted within 30 days. But the agency ignored her request and later argued that she had failed to make a written request. "Her lawyer called me," Hournou says, "and the court ruled that nowhere did it say the request had to be written." Another time, she remembered feeling startled to see a harmless-looking teenage boy facing a forgery charge. "He was caught with a forged I.D.," Hournou recalled. "He wanted an I.D. that said he was 17 so he could go to work. The judge was very understanding once he had all the facts." Hournou also interprets for motorists who buy cheap cars and fail to consider the need for a title, registration, driver's license, license plates, insurance, or inspection.

If she's interpreting for a defendant, she'll try to make the person feel comfortable. "I always introduce myself," Hournou says. "I say, 'I will be your interpreter. You can tell me whatever you want and I will tell your lawyer what you want to say.' You do get satisfaction when people say 'Thank you,' and the lawyers say: 'I'm glad you were here.' I want these people to get the best of the system, not get screwed up by the system."

Though Hournou interprets for people from various Spanish-speaking countries, she has little trouble understanding different dialects. "We come across some dialects that we don't know, but generally any Spanish speaker can understand another," she says. "But you have to know all the bad words and slang, then be able to go up to the sophisticated language. Whether we're in common usage or formalized language, we have to know it."

Judges seem to appreciate her contributions and several federal judges in Kansas City, Kansas asked Hournou to give them Spanish lessons. The judges were seeing so many Spanish speakers before the bench that they at least wanted to be able to pronounce their names correctly. Hournou gave the judges one-hour lessons twice a week for eight months. "They wanted to be able to say something to these people," she says. "So I think this was a very good idea."

born overseas and learned to speak fluent English while living in the United States. But as more and more Americans become fluent in foreign languages, often through intensive grade school programs, the number of U.S. natives working as court interpreters will only increase. Many foreign-born interpreters hold college degrees in both their native lands and the United States.

When anyone involved in a court proceeding doesn't speak English, a court officer who's working for the judge will contact an interpreter who can provide either simultaneous or consecutive interpretation. A simultaneous interpreter will repeat the speaker's words almost immediately. In consecutive interpretation, the interpreter waits until the speaker has finished a thought or sentence. While simultaneous interpretation is common at international proceedings (such as those at the United Nations), many judges find it distracting and prefer consecutive interpretation.

Court interpreters don't do all their work in court, however. They're also hired for depositions and attorney-client meetings, which are sometimes held in jail. And they don't work only for defendants. They may be requested by a prosecutor, judge, or anybody else who needs their help in a legal proceeding. They're also required to interpret letters or legal documents; this is known as "sight translation" and can be very difficult when a document includes complicated legal or financial information.

If you're a court interpreter, you'll be expected to maintain an impartial tone and act as an innocent bystander: No changes may be made to what has been said. As a trained interpreter, you'll help a defendant and lawyer present the strongest case possible and perhaps prevent a little misunderstanding from becoming a big one.

Pitfalls

A freelance interpreter may find that work is often irregular. Most freelancers experience feast-and-famine cycles, and the dry spells can be stressful. If you're working outside major metropolitan areas, you may have to do a lot of driving.

Perks

Many court interpreters find this a rewarding career. Interpreters get a great deal of satisfaction from helping somebody whose legal problems may be related to their inability to speak fluent English. Freelance interpreters can earn extra income while also working full-time jobs. Many interpreters find court cases interesting and stimulating. They're also made to feel like important parts of the legal system.

Get a Jump on the Job

You'll want to learn as much about a foreign language and the U.S. court system as possible. Start studying a foreign language as early as you can. Some schools offer immersion programs in which students receive instruction exclusively in a foreign language and become fluent while they're still in grade school. Try to visit a country where the language you're studying is spoken. Take a seat in a local courtroom and observe how a trial or other proceeding is conducted. Contact the court's public information officer or a judge's clerk and ask if a court interpreter will talk to you about his or her occupation.

COURT REPORTER

OVERVIEW

You couldn't hold an important trial without a court reporter. There'd be no transcript of testimony for a judge or lawyers to review, and no official record to prove the trial was properly conducted.

Court reporting is an important job in the judicial system—and it may be the best-kept secret in government work! Expanding opportunities, good pay, flexible hours, and the ability to work at home make this a terrific job, especially if you don't have a college degree.

Court reporters are employed outside the courtroom as well. In fact, court reporters work in so many other places that there may be a shortage of them in the courtroom. You'll find court reporters taking depositions and providing transcripts of news conferences, conventions, corporate shareholder meetings, or government agency hearings. Needs of people with hearing problems also have created jobs for court reporters known as steno-captioners, who provide closed captioning on TV. Court reporters also are hired to take class notes for college students with hearing problems.

Court reporters use their keyboard and computer skills to make exact records of speeches, conversations, legal proceedings, meetings, or any other event that requires an official record. In the courtroom, a court reporter has more responsibilities than you could possibly imagine. Jerry Kelley, a federal court reporter from Sherman, Texas, wanted to show his bosses he and other

AT A GLANCE

Salary Range

$20,000 to $75,000; weekly salary includes transcript fees at about $2.50 per page (a transcript can pay between $2,000 and $5,000).

Education/Experience

You can get training at one of about 160 postsecondary vocational schools and colleges. Although secretarial or administrative work can teach some of the skills needed for court reporters, you'll have to take specific courses.

Personal Attributes

You'll need to be able to relate to a wide variety of people. In court, you'll interact with lawyers, judges, witnesses, plaintiffs, and defendants from many kinds of backgrounds. You must be a careful listener and able to concentrate.

Requirements

Some states require court reporters to pass a certification test. You should be able to capture at least 225 words per minute when you finish training.

Outlook

Jobs will grow as quickly as in most occupations, and court reporters keep branching out into more areas.

court reporters do much more than report and transcribe testimony. His list of his tasks (totaling 156) included: get business cards from lawyers and witnesses, make seating charts, help swear in witnesses, approach the bench as necessary, seal notes and transcripts as ordered, answer mail from prisoners, prepare docket sheets and pretrial orders for the next day's cases, put trash out for the cleaning crew, go home and read professional law magazines.

Court reporters, who are hired by their judges, are usually stenotypers or voice writers. Stenotypers use a stenotype machine that lets them press several keys at once to create a phonetic stream of syllables that produce words or phrases. Most machines are hooked up to a computer and as the reporter keys in the symbols, they instantly appear as words on the screen, a process known as communications access real-time translation (CART). The computer also has a digital voice recorder that the reporter can play back when editing the final transcript. The stenograph machine has 24 keys, including just 17 for the 26-letter alphabet. Computer software provides a dictionary that can include symbols for more than 100,000 words or phrases. Court reporters are constantly adding to their dictionaries.

The other method of court reporting is voice writing. A voice writer repeats testimony while speaking into a stenomask—a hand-held mask with a microphone and a voice silencer. They can produce an almost immediate transcript as they speak, thanks to the development of computer speech recognition technology. It usually takes less than a year to become a voice writer but can take almost three years to become a stenotypist.

Just because court is adjourned for the day doesn't mean that court reporters are finished. They must edit their transcripts

Nancy Fox, court reporter

When Nancy Fox was playing the clarinet and oboe in fifth grade, it never dawned on her that she might be training herself to be a court reporter. "The best court reporters are the ones who've played musical instruments," says Fox, official court reporter at Division 10 in the Jackson County Circuit Court in Kansas City, Missouri. "I spoke with other people who'd played musical instruments and they say the same thing. It started coming really easily to me while other people were struggling. Playing the piano requires about the same manual dexterity as court reporting. I never played the piano, but the oboe and clarinet employ the same multiple finger movements."

Fox is certified as a court reporter by the Missouri Supreme Court. She's also a registered "merit reporter," which means she can capture at least 260 words per minute, and a certified "real-time reporter," which requires 96 percent accuracy in a five-minute test. She's a huge booster for her occupation because it's given her a career that she loves, even though she was the only one of six brothers and sisters not to attend college.

"My father was a lawyer and he was not disappointed, but he was surprised when I said I wanted to be a court reporter," Fox recalled. "I remember when I was in third grade, I thought I'd try to write down every word my teacher ever said. Of course, I couldn't." To acquire that knack, Fox attended business school. She picked up a flier for a court reporting training course, then quickly became convinced that she'd found the right job.

Fox spent four years as a full-time court reporter after getting certified, then switched to freelancing after having her first child in 1983. "You go to attorneys' offices, doctors' offices, prisons, office buildings, wherever anyone needs a deposition taken," she says. "I also did a few conventions, but those required a lot of traveling." Fox worked about three days a week, which she says was ideal for a new mom who needed to work. "But I didn't want to be away for accuracy, grammar, and spelling of proper names. Some attorneys ask for drafts each day during a trial. They'll need the official final transcript to show they may have grounds for an appeal.

Courts don't use audio or videotapes to replace court reporters, although some states have tried. So far, these devices haven't been able to match the almost-perfect accuracy of court reporters. That's because reporters sit right next to the witness stand and can watch a witness's lips. They can ask a mumbling or soft-spoken witness to speak up or repeat testimony. A good court reporter will make sure that testimony isn't missed when a fire engine, with its siren blaring, passes outside the courtroom.

Pitfalls

Court reporters have to watch out for carpal tunnel syndrome and other repetitive motion injuries. Court reporters also can suffer wrist, back, neck, or eye strain.

Perks

Court reporters often get involved in important or interesting cases and can feel good about playing an important role in the judicial system. Opportunities for freelancing and part-time work have never been better.

from home 40 hours a week. My husband worked the second shift at General Motors, so we really cut baby-sitting costs that way."

Fox was ready to return to full-time work in 1995 and was appointed to the Jackson County Circuit Court, where she often works on major criminal cases. "I was fascinated by the criminal side and it's just a challenge every day to do something different," Fox says. "One day, you can be on a car wreck case, the next one you're hearing DNA evidence, and then a civil case with a $6 million judgment." It's not all fun and games, however. "It can be very disturbing," she says. "I get very upset hearing about child abuse."

Fox sits just to the left of Judge Charles Atwell's bench and works behind a computer that's hooked up to her stenograph machine. Once she starts working her magic, testimony streams across her screen almost as quickly as it's uttered. Fox's software dictionary includes symbols for 109,000 words or phrases. "It's like a foreign language, with a code that translates to your dictionary," she says. "My transcribing rate is over 99 percent. You're like in a Zen subconscious zone when you start to get a rhythm." Sooner or later, though, even Fox gets weary from physical and mental strain. "My judge knows I can go an hour and a half in my little prison," she says, laughing.

Fox takes enormous pride in the history of her occupation and court. She keeps in her desk a file of newspaper stories about major cases on which she's reported. She also likes to show visitors a 1911 machine once used by court reporters. That machine is a good reminder that, despite space-age technology, a human is still required to meet a court's standard of accuracy. "Ever since I started, people have said the tape recorders would take over," Fox says, smiling. "To this day, they haven't."

Get a Jump on the Job

Take any classes you can that emphasize keyboard, stenotype, and computer skills, and keep playing musical instruments. These activities will help build your eye-hand coordination, which is vital for court reporters. Try watching Court TV to get an idea of whether you'd enjoy becoming an important part of the judicial system. And if you want to see a trial in person, courtrooms usually are open to the public. Just pop in for a visit and watch the court reporter at work.

DISASTER ASSISTANCE EMPLOYEE

OVERVIEW

Do you ever wish you could zoom to the site of a hurricane or flood and pitch in to help people who've lost their loved ones, homes, and businesses? You might consider joining the thousands who sign up to help with Federal Emergency Management Agency (FEMA) assistance efforts. As a disaster assistance employee, you may be assigned to check on people's safety and tell them how to get help. You might answer phones on a toll-free line for disaster victims, or work in a relief center.

Disaster relief in the United States is headed by FEMA, which is part of the U.S. Department of Homeland Security. Any time you see a natural disaster on the news, you'll probably see FEMA reservists there, too. They were there after the Oklahoma City bombing in 1995, the World Trade Center attacks in 2001, the loss of the Space Shuttle Columbia in 2003, and the devastation following hurricanes Katrina and Rita in 2005.

State and local governments are the first line of defense against natural disasters. Officials in Florida, for instance, will warn citizens to board up their houses or evacuate when a hurricane threatens. But if the hurricane strikes and destroys thousands of homes, state and local help won't be enough, as the country discovered only too clearly during the 2005 hurricane season. Effective federal assistance is also needed.

AT A GLANCE

Salary Range

$10.15 to $37.81 per hour; $21,190 to $79,920 based on 52 weeks.

Education/Experience

Disaster assistance employees, also called Stafford Act employees or reservists, are temporary workers hired by the Federal Emergency Management Agency (FEMA). They range in age from students to retirees and come from all kinds of jobs and walks of life. There are no educational requirements.

Personal Attributes

You must enjoy helping people, have a sense of adventure, and be willing to give up creature comforts. You'll head into a disaster area on a moment's notice and work long days without getting much sleep.

Requirements

A willingness to help disaster victims. It helps if you have experience in jobs like fire fighting or emergency medical care.

Outlook

Natural disasters aren't going away and neither will the need for disaster assistance employees. At the same time, FEMA has taken on a bigger role in homeland security, so jobs should only increase.

The 1988 Robert T. Stafford Disaster Relief and Emergency Assistance Act allows the governor of any U.S. state or territory to ask the president for federal disaster aid. Once the president declares a major disaster or emergency, the call goes out for assistance through a FEMA regional office. That assistance won't pay for all losses, but it helps disaster victims get back on their feet in a dozen different ways. Its "individuals and households" program gets money and help to those whose property damage isn't insured. Then there's housing assistance, so that people can try to find a safe place to live. Disaster victims may get money to find an apartment or temporary housing built by FEMA. The agency also may pay for medical, dental, funeral, personal property, transportation, storage, and other expenses.

To find these jobs, you can click on "Employment Opportunities," at the FEMA Web site (http://www.fema.gov). Once a federal emergency is declared, jobs are advertised in newspapers throughout the disaster area.

If you're a disaster assistance employee, you'll work under a full-time FEMA employee and join a team to help deal with

Candy Newman, response and recovery expert

Candy Newman became a disaster assistance employee when she was a single mom who needed part-time income. She enjoyed the job so much that she kept it for 11 years. In fact, she was so good at her job that in 2002 she was hired as a full-time employee in the Response and Recovery Division at FEMA's Region 7 headquarters in Kansas City, Missouri. "I thrive well in chaos," she says. "It's always a challenge. It gets your adrenaline going; it keeps you moving and on your toes. It keeps you young—till you get to the end [of a disaster relief effort] and then you're exhausted."

Despite her promotion to full time, Newman remains a reservist at heart. "Reservists are the backbone of FEMA," she explained. "We couldn't function the way we do without this bundle of resources. I miss being a reservist. I like being out there 10 months a year. I like the 16-hour days, I like getting dirty."

Newman hasn't exactly taken a cozy desk job. She still works long hours and spends most of the year on the road, often going straight from one disaster to the next. "I love working with disaster victims," she says. "I can't imagine a more emotionally rewarding profession. It's absolutely the best job in the world."

She's officially the human services branch director in field operations, although during disasters she'll be given other jobs, too. She traveled to Florida during 2004 to help victims of hurricanes Charley, Frances, Ivan, and Jeanne. All struck in a six-week period starting in mid-August, the first time since 1886 that four hurricanes hit one state in the same season. The devastating winds and rains killed 96 people and damaged one of every five homes in Florida.

Property damage losses were estimated at more than $40 billion, but Newman worries most about a disaster's human cost. "My part is the people," she says. "You see people initially at their worst. A lot of people we see have lost everything. It's really amazing to see the strength of the people out there, particularly the elderly. I don't know if it's because of the lives they've led and what their hardships were growing up."

After Hurricane Charley, Newman pulled together community relations teams of reservists and full-time employees to operate disaster centers. Newman was barely finished with Hurricane Charley when Hurricane Frances loomed on the horizon. She was evacuated to Atlanta, home of the FEMA office responsible for Florida. FEMA began hiring reservists for community emergency the disaster. Many sign up again and again. Many first-timers sign up because they live in the disaster area, and get the extra satisfaction of helping friends and neighbors.

Pitfalls

Disaster areas are nasty places. Flooding can contaminate water and bring out poisonous snakes, disease-carrying mosqui-toes, and bacterial infections. Working in a disaster area also can be psychologically upsetting.

Perks

There's tremendous satisfaction in helping disaster victims get back on their feet. The pay won't make you rich, but it comes in handy if you don't have a full-time job

response teams: Thousands of firefighters, emergency medical workers, contractors, retail employees, and others temporarily left their jobs to join teams in Florida. Although Newman wasn't officially assigned to hiring, she helped, anyway. "I did some interviews and sat on the floor making file folders," she says. "Versatility and being adaptable is a big part of this job."

Once Hurricane Frances left, Newman went back to Florida and led a team of housing inspectors in Brevard County on Florida's east coast. Retired people in one mobile home community had nowhere safe to live. "We worked out of the trunks of our cars, made referrals, and started bringing in travel trailers," Newman says. "You do a lot of really quick team building. It requires people from across the U.S. and you pull together these people with different backgrounds as quickly as possible. You assemble a team and move it to a goal."

After Hurricane Ivan slammed the western Florida panhandle, Newman was sent to Pensacola to take care of massive housing needs and to coordinate volunteers. Then came Hurricane Jeanne, which traveled the same path as Frances but packed an even bigger wallop. Newman went back to Florida's east coast and led another team to sign up people for assistance, inspect property damage, arrange to remove debris, move people into travel trailers, and run a recovery center. "It's managed chaos," Newman says. "You have to be able to think on your feet."

Newman can't tell you exactly where disasters will strike, but she knows what time of year to expect them. Atlantic Coast hurricanes hit from June through November; when spring rolls around, it's time for tornadoes and floods back in her own four-state region.

When one tornado destroyed about a third of Hoisington, Kansas, in 2001, it cut a path nearly three quarters of a mile wide and caused one death, 28 injuries, and $43 million in damage. "We counted the destroyed homes, saw how many businesses were damaged, and talked to community leaders," she says. "There are a number of skills you need in a situation like that, so my varied background really helped a lot."

Newman was still a reservist in Texas when she was assigned to Midwest flooding in 1993—one of the worst U.S. natural disasters, causing 50 deaths and $15 billion in damage while destroying 10,000 homes. She stayed so long in the Midwest that she never left. "I spent two and a half years working on a series of disasters," she says. "That's not unusual."

or you're retired. Plus, there's a lot of overtime pay. Skills and experience gained as a Stafford Act employee can lead to a full-time job at FEMA.

Get a Jump on the Job

While in school, you can read about hurricanes and other tropical storms and the damage they cause. Check out the FEMA Web site (http://www.fema.gov) for news about its disaster relief efforts and to familiarize yourself with the agency and its relief programs.

GSA ASSOCIATE

OVERVIEW

The U.S. General Services Administration (GSA) is like a gigantic department store and real estate agent for other government agencies (especially the Department of Defense). It buys goods and services from federal or private businesses at the best price possible, and then sells them to government agencies. The GSA is the most unusual federal agency there is, because it's expected to make a profit. While other agencies may have to stay within their budget from Congress, GSA gets very little money from Congress. It's expected to pay for itself, just like any other business. And thanks to its managers and associates, the GSA has been able to do that. The GSA, in fact, makes enough of a profit to pay for 99 percent of its operation.

So if you're unsure if you'd rather have a career in government or business, you can do both as a GSA associate. You will buy and sell properties, goods, and services just as you would working for a huge business. Depending on your specialty, you'll be leasing the office space, products, technology, and anything else it takes to set up a government agency. Or you can provide furniture, computers, and telephone service. You might sell surplus federal property, including real estate and cars, to the public.

There are about 14,000 GSA employees around the country helping more than a million federal workers in 8,300 buildings. The jobs at the GSA vary widely, but most require a college degree or at least 24 hours

AT A GLANCE

Salary Range
$20,000 to $100,000+

Education/Experience
To work in the U.S. General Services Administration (GSA), you'll need a college degree or some business education. You can be hired right out of college, though business experience definitely is a plus.

Personal Attributes
To be a GSA associate, which is what most agency employees are called, you'll need the qualities you'd need in any business. You'll have to be smart, hardworking, and thorough. When dealing with customers, you'll have to be friendly and trustworthy.

Requirements
You must be a U.S. citizen or a national (a resident of some U.S. territories). You must show your ability during a one-year probationary period.

Outlook
Because 50 percent of its employees are eligible to retire during the next five years, there should be plenty of openings for GSA associates.

of business courses. If the GSA sounds like something you might want to do for a living, you should considering majoring or taking courses in accounting, business, finance, law contracts, purchasing, economics, industrial management, marketing, or management.

As a GSA associate, you can find just about any job you'd want in any business. That's why one recruiting slogan was, "You Can Do That Here!" With all the goods, services, and properties bought by the GSA, you'll be kept busy if you're involved with contracts for what you buy

Brad Scott, GSA administrator

Working as a GSA administrator seems like an odd job for Brad Scott. Before taking over as administrator of the Heartland Region of GSA, he spent years managing various political campaigns and working behind the scenes in politics.

And then came the call to join the GSA as an appointee of President George W. Bush. Most of his workers at the GSA are career government employees, so Scott had to have the know-how to direct more than 1,000 people at the huge GSA regional headquarters in Kansas City, Missouri.

"It was always known as probably the most prestigious appointed position in the region, because the GSA can get so much done," Scott says. He was recommended to the President by his old boss, Republican Senator Kit Bond of Missouri. Scott has a lot of help. His top assistant, James Ogden, is a long-time GSA employee.

To help his employees understand their strengths and weaknesses, he uses the StrengthsFinder program, which was created by the Gallup Organization. Each worker takes a three-hour test with hundreds of questions, and each must be answered within 20 seconds. The results identify five main strengths for each employee and they are listed on the back of each employee's I.D. badge. Among Scott's strengths is command. "When planning work objectives, always ask this person for his ideas," a GSA guidebook explains. "He isn't likely to sit back and agree with everything."

Understanding your strengths, Scott explained, helps you perform better. "It tells you basically how you view the world and process information," he says. "What does my customer look like? How do I deal with the customer, taking into account what his strengths and my strengths are? We've got people who can evaluate real estate who you wouldn't want to put

and sell. You'll need to make deals to buy at the best prices available so you can sell goods to government agencies at fair prices but still make a profit. Because you'll work for an agency that's such a big buyer, you'll be able to get great deals on services like phone service. You'll buy a lot of products from small businesses, so if you negotiate a good contract, you'll be able to help a small business, save the taxpayers money, and help the GSA make a profit—all at the same time.

Because the GSA owns federal buildings and builds new ones, architects and engineers are always needed for improvements, renovations, and new construction. The GSA leases a great deal of office space,

and it needs a lot of real estate experts, who can tell the value of property and know how to manage property. The GSA does billions of dollars in business and needs all kinds of financial experts, including accountants. Information technology workers are always needed because the GSA buys so many computer products. With a fleet of 170,000 vehicles for government agencies, the GSA also needs all kinds of transportation experts and maintenance employees.

A lot of business-minded college graduates don't think of applying for work in government, so there's room for a GSA associate to move up the ladder much faster than in private business. You with a customer. We've got people you'd want with a customer who you may not want in the back office. In a sense, it's liberating because it says to quit wasting your time on things you don't do well. It's really helped me broaden as a manager and communicator of ideas. I spent 12 years working for congressmen and senators and there was no leadership training. They didn't have time for that stuff. You performed or you were gone."

Scott graduated from the University of Missouri with a master's degree in political science in 1987. He was encouraged by a former classmate to apply for a job researching legislative issues in Bond's office. As a campaign worker, Scott helped Bond win re-election in 1992 and 1998. Next, he served as campaign director for Jim Talent's unsuccessful run for governor in 2000. "It was a heartbreaking election," Scott says. "But it was a blessing for both of us. He wouldn't be in the Senate and I wouldn't be at the GSA. The morning after the election, I watched the sun come up because I'd been up all night. And I wept. And I didn't have a job."

Next, Scott became chief of staff for Congressman Sam Graves in 2001, but he left when Bond asked him to take the GSA post.

Politics is still an important part of Scott's job. When he wanted the GSA to spend $378 million for a new IRS headquarters, Scott was able to use his political contacts to get federal approval. "If it's not for Brad, we'd probably still be talking," notes Ogden, his deputy. "Somebody has to convey the message."

Scott jokes that his big mouth always gets him in trouble. But he knows it's important to get his point across. "What I found was that the best idea without an advocate is just an idea," he says. "The worst idea with an advocate sometimes comes to pass. What I try to do around here is make sure that good ideas have an advocate."

may soon be writing checks to your suppliers for millions of dollars or asking U.S. congressmen to let you build a new federal courthouse.

Pitfalls

Because the GSA is such a huge agency, you may find that your best ideas take longer than you'd like to move up the chain of command. That can be frustrating.

Perks

With 11 regional headquarters in large metropolitan areas, you can live in just about any part of the country you like. According to a survey of federal employees, the GSA is considered one of the best U.S. agencies in which to work.

Get a Jump on the Job

Get involved in any kind of business, whether it's pumping gas, selling Christmas gifts to help support a youth sports team, or working in a retail store. Join a business program like Junior Achievement, and start reading the business pages of your local newspaper.

INTERNATIONAL ELECTION OBSERVER

OVERVIEW

The collapse of Europe's Communist governments—especially the Soviet Union in 1991—left dozens of nations faced with the unfamiliar job of holding democratic elections. One-party elections had been the norm, and any semblance of a democratic race was a sham. The job of boosting democracies around the world fell to the Organization for Security and Cooperation in Europe (OSCE), the world's largest regional security organization. Involved in 55 countries, in 1992 the organization established an Office for Democratic Institutions and Human Rights (ODIHR) to monitor elections and guard against intimidation, fraud, and incompetence.

Election observers are hired to help guarantee fair elections and serve on a long- or short-term basis. The ODIHR fields a team of six to nine long-term observers, who arrive in a country months before the election. The team will include a head of mission, deputy head of mission, and officers in charge of the elections process, media relations, logistics, and security. There's also a political officer, who acts as a go-between for the observers and government that holds the election. Short-term observers are brought in as watchdogs on election day.

ODIHR observers will try to point out problems with fairness long before an election. Political officers may complain to

AT A GLANCE

Salary Range

$300 per day, as well as $100 per diem; extra hardship pay in some countries.

Education/Experience

Election observers come from such fields as politics, journalism, public relations, and law enforcement. Some background in elections is important. It's a good idea to have a college degree in political science, history, or another major to help you understand the importance of elections in a new democracy.

Personal Attributes

You should enjoy travel, be adventurous, and be able to adapt to new cultures and different forms of government.

Requirements

Previous election monitoring or other helpful national or international experience; ability to cope with difficult situations; respect for local attitudes; good communication skills; ability to maintain professional independence and strict impartiality; commitment to democracy and human rights; and fluency in the working language of your team (usually different from the language of the host country).

Outlook

Opportunities for paid election observers will expand as the world increases its appetite for democracy. But this is a tough job to get because you need such a highly specialized background. There are a lot more opportunities for volunteers.

government officials that the local police are bothering peaceful protesters. Media officers may tell a government-controlled TV station that it should provide fairer coverage of an opposition candidate.

All of this may sound like more trouble than it's worth—so why do governments put up with international observers? Simple: They hope that a favorable report about the election may help them become less isolated from the rest of the world. A good report might even help them join the European Union.

Many Americans, including former President Jimmy Carter, have joined observer teams around the country. The best way to get started is to become a volunteer for the National Democratic Institute in Washington, D.C., a group that has organized more than 50 election observer delegations throughout the world. By volunteering, you'll be helping to spread democracy and also will get the experience you'll need if you want to get hired by an organization that pays election observers.

Observers have jumped into some of the world's most controversial elections.

Steve Glorioso, election observer

Steve Glorioso was a new voter in 1968 when he experienced his first crooked election. Voting in an old-fashioned booth, he found that he couldn't pull the lever for a school board candidate. Only after removing some pins from behind the lever did he realize the lever was sabotaged! As a result, the dirty tricks he witnessed were no surprise to Glorioso when he began international elections work in 2000. His overseas work began when a relative, an employee of the World Bank in Europe, recommended him to an organization that promotes freedom of the press in former Communist countries. Glorioso, who once published a political weekly, was invited to Albania for six weeks to train journalists to become part of a free press.

"I went to Ghana after our 2000 presidential election and people asked me, 'What are you doing here?'" Glorioso recalled, laughing. "Florida was going on." Still, he says he's seen elections much worse than Florida's, where many irregularities led to a controversial recount. A long-time political adviser and consultant, Glorioso has observed elections in former Communist republics, including Albania, Serbia, and Ukraine. Ethnic hatreds and undemocratic governments make some Eastern European countries difficult places to work. "That was the first time I came face to face with real evil," Glorioso says. "You do know you're being watched. You know your Internet [communications] are being watched by the state police."

Trying to start democratic elections from scratch can be quite a challenge, he noted. Voters may distrust any kind of paperwork that reminds them of their old governments. "There are no centralized records (for voter registration)," Glorioso says. "If you gave them voter I.D. cards, in former Communist countries people would tear them up and throw them away. To them, it was like the cards that were used to control people."

Glorioso, a resident of New Orleans, was hired by the ODIHR to help monitor the 2004 Ukrainian presidential election. "When I got there, there were all kinds of tales," he says. According to an ODIHR report, votes couldn't be counted in some places where challenger Viktor Yushchenko was known to be popular. Ballots lacked the ink marks needed for the votes to count because the government sent disappearing ink to the polling places. "When it came to the runoff, that's when the stealing was wholesale," Glorioso says. "It was so bad, the whole international community went crazy."

(continues)

Ukraine's 2004 presidential election was a hotly contested race that involving a face-off between incumbent Viktor Yanukovych and former prime minister and opposition leader Viktor Yushchenko. Although the initial election was fair, a runoff wasn't clean at all.

Although Yanukovych was declared the winner and his victory was endorsed by Russian president Vladimir Putin, ODIHR observers insisted the election was rigged.

Yushchenko's supporters staged a series of protests, and ultimately the Ukranian Supreme Court agreed the runoff wasn't fair and called for another. Yushchenko won the second runoff, but he appeared in poor health during his campaign and medical tests revealed that there was poison in his system. Many claimed his opponents were the culprits. Without election observers, that election might never have turned out fairly.

(continued)

Glorioso faced his biggest challenge as an observer when he became the ODIHR political officer for the South Serbia election in July 2002. The Albanian majority hadn't been allowed to vote before it waged a guerilla war against Serbian soldiers. Albanians had been persecuted and driven from their homes in former Yugoslav republics when Serbian president Slobodan Milosevic stirred up old ethnic hatreds. At one point Glorioso was told, " 'You Americans forget your history. Our biggest issue is that we can't forget ours.' "

A cease-fire and peace treaty between Albanians and Serbs made possible the 2002 election in South Serbia. "Just two months earlier, they were killing each other," Glorioso says. "It was incredibly tense. Almost all the offices were held by Serbs because Albanians were not allowed to vote. It was not unlike the American South after the Civil Rights Act. There was lingering animosity from the war, there was real hate. There were guns everywhere. Throughout South Serbia, there were thousands of land mines still around. In small villages, we were very nervous about that."

Yet Glorioso has had heartwarming experiences, too. He was working in Albania as an OSCE press officer in 2001 during the September 11 attack on the World Trade Center. "My office was the only place in the building with a TV and an Albanian named Elvis grabbed my elbow and says, 'Watch CNN now!' " Glorioso recalled. "What was incredible, after the attacks, was that you couldn't go anywhere without Albanians, in broken English, telling you how sorry they were. You couldn't pay for a drink, you couldn't pay for a meal. About 20,000 people marched in sympathy with America."

A few months later, on another assignment in Albania, it was Glorioso's turn to show his sympathy for people who'd experienced tragedy. He and dozens of Albanians watched on TV as Milosevic made his first appearance as a defendant before an international war crimes tribunal in The Hague, Netherlands. "One older woman says three of her family were killed," Glorioso says. "The first day they brought him into the court, everybody in the room was crying. To see the appreciation . . . that this is justice and in a civilized society there is a rule of law . . . I was crying, too."

Pitfalls

The job can be dangerous and observers usually are evacuated if fighting breaks out. Observers are sometimes harassed by people who don't want democratic elections because they see them as a threat to their power or way of life.

Perks

If you love to travel and want to help others, this is an ideal job. Observers travel around the world, meet people from different cultures, and get satisfaction from promoting democracy. Observers are paid well for their work, too.

Get a Jump on the Job

It helps to travel to foreign countries and get a feel for other cultures and forms of government. While you're in high school and college, you might volunteer to stuff envelopes or answer phones for a political campaign to get a feel for how the election process works.

IRS AGENT

OVERVIEW

If you're interested in winning a popularity contest with your customers, this is probably not the job for you. Most taxpayers would rather go through a root canal than meet with an IRS agent. But if you enjoy working with numbers and you're interested in a job that's important to the financial health of America, working as an IRS agent may be just the job for you.

The Internal Revenue Service (IRS) is a branch of the U.S. Department of Treasury. Each year, the IRS processes more than 220 million tax returns and collects about $2 trillion in revenue. The IRS deals directly with more Americans than any other public or private institution. It's an agency with roots stretching all the way back to the Civil War. It was President Abraham Lincoln and the 1862 Congress who created the Commissioner of Internal Revenue, designing an income tax to pay for war expenses. Never popular with the folks back home, the income tax was repealed 10 years later.

Congress dredged up the income tax again in 1894, but it was ruled unconstitutional a year later by the U.S. Supreme Court. Congress finally received authority to enact an income tax when the states ratified the 16th Amendment in 1913. At that point, Congress placed a 1 percent tax on net personal incomes above $3,000, adding an extra 6 percent tax on incomes above $500,000.

The IRS was run by political appointees until the agency was reorganized in the

1950s. Now, only the IRS Commissioner and Chief Council are political appointees, nominated by the President and confirmed by the Senate. In 1998, the agency was reorganized into four major divisions, with each division auditing different types of taxpayers. The Wage and Investment Division is responsible for about 116 million taxpayers who file individual and joint tax returns. The Small Business/Self-Employed Division serves about 45 million small businesses and self-employed taxpayers. The Large and Mid-Size Business Division serves corporations with assets of more than $10 million. The Tax-Exempt and Government Entities Division serves employee benefit plans, tax-exempt organizations, such as charities and religious groups, and tax-paying organizations within the government. Other IRS divisions include Appeals, Communications, and Liaison and Criminal Investigation. The Office of the Chief Counsel is the legal department for the IRS.

One of the main things the IRS does is selectively audit citizens' tax returns. Although the IRS had slightly more than 99,000 employees in 2004, that's not nearly enough to audit all the tax returns sent in every each year; in fact, the IRS audits only one or two percent of all taxpayers and conducts few random audits. The agency focuses on returns with the kinds of deductions that seem to invite the most mistakes or dishonesty. Taxpayers who claim unusually high amounts of deductions in charitable donations, for instance, might be logical candidates for an audit.

Agents who audit individual and joint tax returns are called tax compliance officers—they're the face of the IRS most taxpayers see. The auditors from the Large and Mid-Size Business Division work individually or in teams to examine the tax returns of America's largest corporations. These auditors face complex tax

Bert Snider, IRS administrator

When Bert Snider joined the IRS in 1973, he didn't try to avoid taxpayers who might have been unhappy with him. In fact, he couldn't avoid them. After earning an accounting degree from the University of Sioux Falls, Snider started as an IRS agent in Pierre, South Dakota. That city was small enough for him to be as well known as a teller at a local bank.

"Everybody knows you as an IRS agent and, in a sense, that's a good way to work because people come up to you and give you information," Snider recalled. "On the other side, you don't have a private life."

The IRS, the city of Pierre, and Snider's resume all have grown considerably since 1973. He's become the compliance territory manager for Minnesota and central Iowa. Based in St. Paul, he oversees nine groups of 8 to 12 examiners. He also helps the U.S. Treasury to give foreign governments tips on improving their tax collection. "I've been doing some international consulting work and we have the best tax system there is," Snider says. "For taxpayers in other countries, integrity [in a government's handling of tax money] is a real problem. I don't think people realize that our tax system has the highest level of integrity in the world."

That may not console any U.S. taxpayers who are upset about owing money on April 15, when tax payments are due, or getting audited. And when you also consider all the politicians who try to get elected by telling voters that they shouldn't pay so much in taxes, it's easy to see why IRS agents aren't all that popular. "There's a little bit of isolation and alienation, much like anybody in law enforcement feels," Snider says. "[It's like] 'Oh, you're a policeman . . . a state trooper . . . or an IRS agent.' "

People who apply to become IRS agents are evaluated for their ability to handle confrontation and stress. An agent's most important talent, however, is connecting the dots when he or she is examining a financial picture with a lot of blank spaces. "I personally look

(continues)

issues and need help from a variety of IRS experts. They include economists, international examiners, financial product and transactions examiners, employment tax specialists, and computer audit specialists. These people often are needed to deal with such matters as tax shelters, mergers and acquisitions, and global operations.

A typical taxpayer audit goes like this: The taxpayer is notified by the IRS that the tax return has been selected for review. The taxpayer may choose to have the help of an accountant at the audit. The IRS agent asks for the needed tax records, reviews the return and tells the taxpayer if the return is correct. The agent usually tries to be polite but businesslike. The taxpayer may owe more money or, in some cases, may even get a refund. Individual taxpayers are liable to be audited for any of the three previous tax years.

Pitfalls

IRS agents are the government employees the rest of us love to hate—these agents often face even more suspicion and hostility

(continued)

for natural inquisitiveness [when hiring an IRS agent]," Snider says. "You have to make decisions based on partial data." Accountants typically like rigid rules and lots of details, but taxpayers won't always let you see their records and you have to make decisions based on partial data. "You'd like to see a checkbook and if there are 20 transactions, you might want to look at all of them," he says. "But rarely do we have everything."

Snider also represents the Treasury Department overseas, traveling in Africa and Europe to help governments simplify their tax forms and improve their auditing and collection. "It's not a matter of me going over there and telling them what to do, because our taxation system is much different than the rest of the world's," Snider says. "One of the first things I have to do is learn the tax code and I try to design something around that."

The U.S. model probably would only work in western Europe, he noted. In the developing world, things are much different. "There's virtually no middle class," he says. "They're extremely poor or you have large multinational companies."

Snider spent a year in Greece working to improve their tax collection—but sometimes he's given only a week. "When I went to Uganda, you leave the Twin Cities on Saturday, and on Monday at 7 o'clock, you get up, all jet-lagged, to meet with the people at the embassy. They were promised a report by the close of business on Friday, so you have meetings every day from 7 in the morning until 10 at night. You want to develop a good product and at times it's very hectic."

The overseas work can be grueling. Then again, you could say that everything Snider's been doing for the past three decades has been "taxing." "It's very rewarding and the people are wonderful to work with," Snider says. "The reason I do it is the challenge. You're coming up with a work plan: This is what I can do for you. You're never bored. I've done so many things here and it's been a quick 30 years. You never get in a rut."

than law enforcement officers. It can be a frustrating, lonely business.

Perks

There's lots of variety in this profession; an agent deals with a great variety of taxpayers and laws and there's a wide variety of jobs within the IRS. There's no forced overtime, unlike private accounting firms that may require 70- or 80-hour workweeks. And when IRS agents retire,

they often get good jobs in other areas of the Treasury Department.

Get a Jump on the Job

Work hard on math. If your parents do their own taxes, ask them to show you how they do it. Or you can pretend to file your taxes using inexpensive tax preparation software programs that are available at any office supply store.

LOBBYIST

OVERVIEW

Politicians affect our lives and businesses by the laws they pass, so it's not surprising that people with money and influence try to affect the way politicians vote. They do this by lobbying, and they hire lobbyists to make their case.

Lobbyists try to figure out the best ways to get lawmakers on their side. That usually involves delivering campaign donations, votes, or favors. The most persuasive lobbyists sometimes even write bills. Lobbyists have an easier job if they're visiting lawmakers who already agree with them. For example, a lobbyist for a labor union may find a natural friend in a U.S. congressman from a district in Michigan where autos are manufactured. A lobbyist for the oil industry should have an ally in a congressman from the heart of Texas.

That doesn't mean that lobbying is easy. Nearly every large group of people with special interests—such as labor unions, doctors, lawyers, and senior citizens—hire lobbyists to promote issues important to them. Sometimes they'll hire ex-lawmakers or ex-administration officials who already have a lot of friends and influence. But most lobbyists have to work their way up after getting political experience. Most have college degrees in such majors as political science, law, journalism, public relations, and economics. Those who lobby in the public interest shouldn't expect to get rich. But those who influence major legislation that can bring huge sums of money to clients can earn seven-figure incomes.

A good lobbyist has to be armed with information. Because opposite sides on an

AT A GLANCE

Salary Range

$35,000 to $1 million+

Education/Experience

Lobbyists usually obtain know-how and contacts through experience in other lines of work, like law, public relations, economics, and politics. You'll need a college degree.

Personal Attributes

You have to be outgoing, because a lot of schmoozing will be required. You have to be persuasive to get across your client's viewpoint. And you must be patient and thick-skinned when you don't always get a friendly reception.

Requirements

Lobbyists don't need licenses, but must register with state and federal governments.

Outlook

Because lobbying is such an important part of the lawmaking process, there will be lobbyists as long as there's a democracy.

issue usually put a different spin on facts, a lobbyist needs to make sure a politician isn't listening to just the other side. But many lobbyists offer politicians more than information. They offer campaign donations, often through political action committees. Lobbyists also may offer politicians free meals and drinks, free tickets to concerts and sports events, or free trips. Some lobbyists, as the headlines often tell us, even resort to bribery and illegal gift giving. While lobbyists may promise to help elect a politician who votes the way they want, they also may work to defeat a politician who doesn't.

As a lobbyist, you'll work nonstop to get support. You'll go in person to meet

Ridge Multop, lobbyist

Ridge Multop has had lots of odd jobs in government. He was a congressional economic adviser for most of his career, before he was hired to lobby for the American Association of Retired Persons in 2002. He became a senior legislative representative in federal affairs, lobbying on federal issues important to AARP's 35 million members.

Multop likes lobbying for senior citizens instead of a big corporation or association that relies on making campaign contributions. AARP does not give politicians money, but the organization can deliver a lot of votes from its members. Older people tend to vote regularly, and politicians are well aware of that. And as the baby boom generation ages, the ranks of voting members is ever increasing.

"There are a lot of different kinds of lobbyists," Multop explained. "The typical picture is somebody who's schmoozing and giving out campaign contributions and taking members of Congress and their staff to luncheons and on expensive trips. Or somebody standing around in a thousand-dollar suit and having the country club membership." Tax lobbyists, real estate lobbyists, and defense lobbyists often fall into that category, he says. "But I didn't really see myself as one of those people," he says, "and I don't think I could've gotten hired as one."

Lots of other lobbyists are advocates for positions or policies with nonprofit groups. Multop sees himself as somewhere between the nonprofit lobbyists and the "hired guns."

"A lot of nonprofit groups have small budgets and the pay is very low," he says. "These folks are pretty young people who've been on Capitol Hill in a [congressional] office and then they go to a nonprofit organization. They also end up in places like AARP."

AARP lobbyists have expense accounts, but they don't make campaign contributions, they don't have a political action committee, and they don't receive country club memberships. "On the other hand," Multop says, "and this is the thing that attracted me—you actually have 35 million people backing you up. Walking into a congressional office, that makes a huge amount of difference."

(continues)

with a lawmaker, and you'll have to attend or organize fund-raising dinners and golf tournaments to get the ear of a politician or group that may help your cause. You'll stay in touch with key politicians before legislation that's important to your client comes to a vote. You might need to hire public relations experts to make sure that newspapers, magazines, and radio and TV stations hear your side of an issue.

A lobbyist may be a "hired gun" who'll work for any cause as long as he or she is well paid, but many lobbyists work for causes in which they believe deeply. Lobbying at its best educates our leaders about important issues and helps them to vote intelligently on bills. Lobbying at its worst helps those with the most money and influence get their way, even at the expense of most Americans.

Pitfalls

Lobbyists work long hours, spending long evenings at cocktail parties, awards dinners, or fund-raising events. They also may have to spend a lot of time on the road.

(continued)

One of Multop's most important jobs was to oppose major changes to the social security system proposed by President George W. Bush. The President claimed that social security would go broke unless it was changed to give younger workers the chance to invest some social security taxes in the stock market. AARP insisted that social security would not go broke and says that workers could lose benefits under the President's plan.

Multop received degrees in economics at Allegheny College in Pennsylvania and then at Case Western Reserve University in Cleveland. From 1994 to 2002, he was senior economic adviser to Representative Dick Gephardt, a Democrat from Missouri and the House minority leader. Multop advised Gephardt on taxes, budgets, and social security.

So how does economics lead to lobbying? Most big political issues are based on whether they will bring more or less money to most Americans. But the issues are complicated and if you don't understand economics, you won't understand many big issues.

Multop tries to visit congressmen in their Washington offices, but if they're away or too busy to see him, he'll ask a staff member where the boss stands. "House members basically are in town Tuesday through Thursday," Multop says. "So on Monday, you get ready. Tuesday through Thursday you run around like a chicken with its head cut off and Friday you have meetings to plan what you're going to do the next week."

Don't even think about becoming a lobbyist unless you're willing to work long hours. One morning, Multop left his house before 8 a.m., then spent the next few hours lobbying on Capitol Hill. He spent the afternoon in strategy meetings back at AARP headquarters, attended an awards dinner sponsored by the Hispanic Chamber of Commerce, and got home about 11 p.m. "It was a pleasant enough dinner," Multop says, "but nonetheless I was working. I was able to lobby a state senator from Puerto Rico who's thinking about running for Congress."

Nightlife and travel may sound glamorous at first, but they get old in a hurry.

Perks

Some lobbyists enjoy the money, power, and country club memberships that may come with the job. Lobbyists have the satisfaction of knowing they're on the front lines fighting for an issue they feel passionate about.

Get a Jump on the Job

Get active in campus politics, and if you get a chance, volunteer for election campaigns for local, state, or federal candidates in whom you believe. Working on the staff of a state, local, or national lawmaker is another great way to learn how laws are written and passed. Think about getting a job as a congressional page to really find out how government works on the inside. Or check to see if you qualify for an internship offered by a congressional office, government agency, or lobbying firm.

MAYOR

OVERVIEW

In small-town lingo, the buck stops on the desk of the mayor. Mayors are usually elected officials (although some are chosen by city council) whose job is to steer their city's growth and development—sort of like the president, but on a much smaller scale. However, the job is quite different depending on the size of the city or town, from tiny rural spots with a church and a bank to a bustling metropolis such as New York. Some mayors, like Rudolph Giuliani, attain hero status of near-mythic proportions, while others make a name for themselves as shady, crooked, progressive, arch-conservative, visionary, or party boss.

However large or small the municipality, the mayor's job is to present some sort of vision for what the town can become. This is never easy because there's never enough money and there are always more than enough problems—education, poverty, safe streets, drugs, racism, housing, economics, environment, infrastructure, and crime. Somehow the mayor has to guide his or her town through these political minefields, balancing the needs of a wide variety of different groups.

Almost every day the mayor schedules meetings with a wide variety of special interest groups along with business owners, financiers, political leaders, neighborhood leaders, and others. And every step along the way, the mayor's every move is scrutinized, both by political enemies and by the media. To the extent that a mayor can articulate a strong vision for the town

and then fight for legislation backing up that vision while appeasing voters—he or she will be successful. The true test of a mayor's ability comes in times of hardship, such as the 2001 terrorist attacks in New York City and the massive flooding in New Orleans and Gulfport, Mississippi, in 2005.

In most cities, the work is intense, as the mayor combines the everyday business of the town with more ceremonial duties. Most are on call 24 hours a day.

Most cities also have term limits on a mayor's length of service, and when the term is up and the campaign must begin for reelection, the political challenge can be difficult and expensive, in even the smallest towns.

Thomas M. McMahon, mayor

Few would suspect that the mayor's office would possibly appeal to somebody who's spent his entire life as an engineer, but that's exactly how Thomas McMahon came to the mayor's job in Reading, Pennsylvania. "I guess I'm an unusual case in that I've been an engineer my whole life," he says. Although the engineering profession was his primary interest as a young man (he holds a B.S. in engineering from the Rochester Institute of Technology and a master's in engineering from Penn State), McMahon was also bitten by the political bug and minored in political science.

McMahon started up his engineering business in Reading, and, on occasion, "the idea of being mayor crossed my mind, and people encouraged me." He was too busy then, but once he retired, he began to rethink his plans. "When I finally retired from my business, I saw things that were going on in the city that bothered me." At the time, Reading was a city crippled by political scandal, poverty, and inner-city violence. "Maybe this is what impels people to take that step," he says. "I felt I had the qualifications to be able to do something different and better for the city of Reading. I've been here for 40 years, it's been my adopted home, and it seemed to be going in the wrong direction."

McMahon, a former Peace Corps volunteer, was just the man to step in and try to stem the tide. "Somebody has to," he says. "Democracy can't be a spectator sport. People need to be involved in it. If we step back and nobody gets involved, sometimes the lowest common denominator takes over. People don't only serve for publicity or power."

It makes McMahon sad that young people seem to consider politics a dirty word.

"I tend to look back on the founding fathers," he says. "They all had full-time productive careers, they were educated men who came forward and spent a lot of time worrying about how to get this country off to a good start. These are the people I respected, they did things for the right reasons. Maybe that's why I looked at it as an opportunity."

It's an opportunity that he clearly loves. McMahon thinks one of the strengths of being a mayor lies in making things happen by putting the right experts together. "I like the fact that I can make some connections between people who have needs and people who have resources, or who have like minds," he says. "I like the fact I can reach across the spectrum and I can introduce people to others to get things to happen."

One of his favorite things about being a mayor is being able to interact with students in the city school district. "A mayor theoretically doesn't have responsibility for the school district," he says, "but 17,000 of my citizens are in schools, and I'm concerned about that." He likes to go in and work with kids in the younger and middle school grades, so that he can make an impact on their lives. For example, the fifth graders go through a drug awareness program, and McMahon tries to be at all the graduations from the program, shaking each kid's hand, getting his picture taken with them, and hamming it up. "I'm hoping that my being there might make an impact. Maybe they'll say: 'Hey, the mayor was interested!'"

Sometimes, he says, the job makes him feel a bit like a minister. "I try to inspire people to do a lot better than we have done in the past," he explains. "Why else would we get up every day and go through any kind of struggle if we didn't think we could make it better? Sometimes," he says, "people have been looking at the tips of their shoes instead of the tops of a building. You've got to raise your head and look around."

McMahon says that although he came to the mayor's desk without a lot of specific political experience, he was an engineer for 35 years and was in management for most of that time. "I draw on my managerial skills," he says. "I've got to delegate, manage, assign resources, develop goals and objectives, come up with mission statements, and work with people to select from alternatives."

The only thing he doesn't like about the job? The process of getting elected. "That's a challenge, and you have to be prepared for it," he says. "You have a series of hurdles if you want to get to the other side. The hurdles, going through the electoral process, is very demanding time-wise and you have to raise money to pay for air time, organize a committee, do reporting at the proper times, knock on doors." He loved meeting the citizens, but found the process of the campaign "a little bit tedious at times."

Once he was elected, he stepped into a $53 million business with 1,900 people working in various jobs throughout the city. "Most are doing a very good job, but a lot don't have very good systems in place. I'm trying to find ways to make things more efficient, trying to bring an element of professionalism to the job." He's found that there's an enormous amount of work with a small staff. "It's a challenge," he says. "I have to do as much as I can at any given time. Then when I'm tired, I rest." No matter where he goes, he carries the mantle of mayor with him. "You can't stop," he says. "If you go to the restaurant or the supermarket, it's not long before someone comes up [to you] with a problem—but that's part of the job and I understand that. Even if I think I'm off duty, I'm not."

His advice to young people is to not get into the mindset that government is "somebody else's job." Volunteer, he says, and do what you can in your community. "The time I spent as a volunteer with the Peace Corps has been the most rewarding of the things I've done in my life. If you can make a difference in the community, if you've been given some gifts that you've been able to give back. I'm afraid young people think they don't have a voice, they should hang back and let older, wiser minds prevail—but sometimes those older minds aren't the wisest minds. I can often learn more from young people than from those who've been around a long time."

McMahon appreciates what's been given to him over the years. "Sometimes when I cross a 100-year-old bridge, I think of the teams of horses dragging the timbers, someone designing that bridge, and we're enjoying the fruits of their labor. I think it's only fair that we pass that on to the next generation."

He's most proud of the neighborhood organizations he's worked with to try to reclaim the city. "I firmly believe reestablishing a sense of neighborhood is the only way to survive," he says. "There's not enough tax money to hire cops on every corner, but there are enough neighbors who can observe what's going on in the neighborhood. Right now we have 32 groups who are adopting playgrounds, doing block cleanups, outdoor social picnics, parties, getting to know each other. Especially when people are speaking different languages, you have to have the ability to understand each other."

Pitfalls

Many cities' problems can seem insurmountable, and there is always the risk of being the subject of negative political campaigning.

Perks

For outgoing political hounds and those who simply love their community, few jobs can compare with the "top position" in the city. The mayor has the power to effect changes in his or her town or city and improve citizens' lives.

Get a Jump on the Job

You can volunteer at any age for a political campaign on the grassroots level, so if you think you're interested in politics, this is a great place to start. You can attend community meetings—they're almost always open to the public unless personnel issues are being discussed. Study the news and pay attention during history and civics classes; when you get to college, consider majoring in political science. In the summers, see if you can volunteer at the mayor's office.

MILITARY DENTIST

OVERVIEW

If you're about to graduate from dental school and you're interested in a military career—or the chance to get more dental experience than you'd expect in your early years of private practice—becoming a dentist in the Army, Navy, or Air Force might be just what you're looking for.

New military dentists receive an officer's commission of two to four years and are sent to officer indoctrination school, where they receive a military orientation to help them feel comfortable in a military environment. (Because they're officers, for instance, they must expect to be saluted by lower-ranking personnel.) Dentists also must meet the same physical requirements as other soldiers and are subject to regular fitness tests.

New military dentists usually serve as general practitioners in a clinic, treating soldiers and their spouses and dependents. Like most dentists, they're kept busy examining patients and treating cavities and other problems. They're especially busy if they're assigned to a training center that receives large numbers of new recruits. Dental examinations are an important part of processing those recruits.

Military dentists often have the opportunity to specialize in areas such as periodontal dentistry (the treatment of gum disease) or endodontics (root canal treatments). Larger military clinics encourage dentists to rotate through various specialty areas. Versatility will come in handy for a

AT A GLANCE

Salary Range

Military dentist salaries range from $42,000 to $60,000, along with 30 days' paid vacation plus 11 paid holidays each year.

Education/Experience

You'll need to have or be working toward a dental degree from an accredited U.S. or Canadian dental school. Most incoming military dentists are recent dental school graduates.

Personal Attributes

You'll need the discipline and physical fitness to fit into a military environment. Your patients will appreciate a friendly and sympathetic dentist, though in the military you don't have to worry about your patients going elsewhere.

Requirements

You must be a citizen of the United States. You'll have to submit an extensive application, including letters of recommendation. You'll be interviewed by at least one dental officer.

Outlook

U.S. armed forces can't function effectively without health care professionals, including dentists. Since the military is not expanding significantly, opportunities for military dentists should remain near their current level.

dentist who winds up at a base with just one or two colleagues.

New military dentists learn specialty work from experienced dentists, who'll help them perform surgeries and other advanced procedures. Because of these opportunities, dental school graduates who undergo their residency after military service will find they have a big edge in experience over their fellow residents.

Laura Brown, military dentist

When Laura Brown was sent to the Marine Corps training center at Paris Island, South Carolina, she didn't have to worry about screaming drill instructors and an exhausting training routine.

Mostly, she had to worry about teeth.

While Brown was in dental school, she enlisted in the Navy, was commissioned as a lieutenant and sent to Paris Island from the summer of 1991 to the fall of 1992. That was after she attended a six-week officer indoctrination school in Newport, Rhode Island. "When you go in as a physician or a nurse and don't have military experience, they want you to know enough so that you don't embarrass the uniform," Brown says. Once at Paris Island, she embarrassed neither her uniform nor the dental profession.

Her day started around 5 a.m.; by 6 a.m. she was admitted to the base. When the first company arrived, they'd line up at the door for X rays and oral hygiene instructions. "Then, they'd see us and we'd do exams," she says. "There'd be 60 recruits in a company and you'd have six or seven exams in an hour." After seeing three companies in the morning, she'd go work out in the middle of the day, and do paperwork all afternoon. She'd chart their problems and determine whether they needed further treatment. "It was a good experience," she says. "You learned to diagnose quickly." As young men, most didn't usually have a lot of dental problems. "But a lot of kids from Mississippi, Alabama, and Tennessee had a lot of problems," she recalls. "And there were older recruits, some in their early 30s, and they would have a lot of problems, too."

Brown, who today is a periodontist in Olathe, Kansas, considered military dentistry as a way to help her career and finances. She accumulated about $100,000 in debt on student loans which carried high interest rates, but because of her enlistment the interest was waived and she was able to pay off a good deal of her debt. She also wanted to learn if periodontal dentistry was the right field for her before she took the big step of opening her own practice. After Paris Island, she was assigned to the Naval Training Center at Great Lakes, Illinois.

" It was a very, very good experience," she recalls. "I spent a good year and a half in periodontics. I was at a large clinic and they would try to get the lieutenants to rotate through there. Most people don't enjoy periodontics, so I would just take somebody else's rotation. It made me realize that's what I wanted to do."

Brown was performing surgery before she did her residency. "I remember my first soft tissue graft," she says. "Normally it would take 45 minutes. My first one took me four hours. An experienced periodontist was with me, assisting me.

"I didn't know it was going to be so much fun. At Great Lakes and Paris Island we had about 70 other dentists and they were all fun people. We weren't worried about office overhead, or whether the patients came."

That experience, Brown adds, gave her excellent preparation for her residency, which she started in 1995 after being promoted to lieutenant commander. "A lot of students go right from dental school to residency," she says. "But you don't understand dentistry until you've practiced it for a while. For me, it helped that I practiced before I went back to school. It helped me understand things more fully."

The services offer incentives for dentists to continue military careers, including pay raises, attractive retirement benefits, continuing education, and the chance for specialty training. When military dentists attend professional courses, they receive a leave of absence and expenses for travel, lodging, and tuition.

After four to six years of active duty, dentists may be able to receive intensive training in a specialty. Some dentists choose to remain in the service for the rest of their careers, while others use their military training to start a private practice once their service obligation ends.

While career military dentists may sacrifice a private practice income, they also avoid many of the risks, expenses, and responsibilities. They don't have to worry about taking out a big loan to open an office and buy dental equipment, or bother about hiring a staff. They don't have to worry about bookkeeping, accounting, or losing patients to a competitor. And they generally don't have to worry about complaints or lawsuits.

A military career may not be for everybody, but if you think you'd enjoy working as a dentist while serving your country as an officer, becoming a military dentist might be right up your alley.

Pitfalls

You could be assigned to a combat area and be in danger. If you have a family, you may have to move your spouse and children periodically when you're reassigned, and you won't earn as much as you could in private practice.

Perks

You'll have job security and health, disability, and retirement benefits. You can become eligible for military retirement pay and benefits after serving 20 to 22 years. Your experience will prove valuable as you continue your education or start a private practice.

Get a Jump on the Job

When you see your dentist, pay attention to the instruments and procedures. There's usually time at the start and end of each visit for small talk, so ask your dentist some questions about the job. Ask your dentist if there's any possibility of a summer job or internship in the dental office. Check out books about dental careers.

MILITARY LAWYER

OVERVIEW

If you've watched many movies and TV shows, you already know plenty about the Judge Advocate General Corps. Known as JAG, this is the legal branch of the Army, Navy, and Air Force that provides prosecutors and defense lawyers for all military and many civilian cases. JAG defense lawyers are the military's public defenders. Once almost invisible outside the military, they've suddenly become celebrities because of movies such as *A Few Good Men* and the long-running television series, *JAG*. In real life, JAG lawyers handled many highly publicized and controversial cases that arose from charges of espionage and prisoner abuses involving military personnel during wars in Afghanistan and Iraq.

Many law school graduates seek commissions in the JAG Corps because of the opportunity for a wide variety of legal experience in the United States and abroad. JAG Corps attorneys may practice civil litigation or criminal, administrative, labor, international, operational, medical, or contract law. They also may teach incoming military lawyers and help soldiers, retirees, and their families with personal legal problems.

In criminal law, JAG attorneys serve as prosecutors or defense lawyers in courts-martial. In civil litigation, JAG attorneys represent the United States in cases that include injuries to military personnel and

damage to military property. An administrative lawyer will give legal advice to commanders and staff officers.

Because the military branches employ so many civilians, the services must also be represented in labor cases. High-ranking military personnel overseas need lawyers who can give advice about international agreements and foreign laws. In operational law, JAG Corps lawyers provide

AT A GLANCE

Salary Range

$27,000 to $60,000.

Education/Experience

You'll need to graduate from a law school approved by the American Bar Association. It helps if you've already had civilian experience practicing law, though most military lawyers are recent law school graduates.

Personal Attributes

You need to be mentally and physically fit and be of good moral standing and character. You'll have to have the discipline and personality to fit in a military environment. And you need to be passionate about practicing law.

Requirements

You must have passed an examination that allows you to be a member of a federal, state, or the District of Columbia bar. You must be no older than 34 at the time you're commissioned.

Outlook

Legal services always will be needed in all branches of the military. But because military law is considered such excellent preparation for a civilian law career, there will continue to be more applications than openings.

Jana Torok, Army JAG Corps lawyer

When you're in the JAG Corps, Jana Torok discovered, you can be thrown into the fire quite quickly. She'd been a lawyer at the military prison at Fort Leavenworth in Kansas for about two months when an inmate died and her commander asked: "What do we do?" Torok was flustered at first, but recovered quickly. "You're put in a position where you have a lot of authority very quickly," she says. "You learn to be a lawyer quickly. You learn trial skills. When you go into civilian practice, you have practiced more than any other associate. To have a judge yell at you . . . to talk to a jury . . . I don't think you can underestimate the importance of that."

Torok enrolled in the Army ROTC program at Purdue University to earn financial aid for her education and follow the military tradition in her family. Her father, Ernest, was a career soldier who served in the Gulf War, and her brother, Douglas, served in Vietnam. She attended law school at the University of Kansas, was commissioned as a lieutenant and went through a 14-week JAG Corps officer basic course. It included four weeks of military orientation at Fort Lee, Virginia, and 10 weeks of military law on the grounds of the University of Virginia.

Torok was assigned to Fort Leavenworth in 2001 and immediately found herself very busy. "There were always people suing the prison and I worked with the U.S. Attorney," she recalls. "Inmates were suing for things like no air conditioning, for cruel and unusual punishment, for violations of their First Amendment rights, or because of uniform rules of the cutting of their hair. Some of the suits were pretty serious, others were pretty silly." Torok also prosecuted military cases and civilian cases, too, because of charges involving civilians employed at Fort Leavenworth. "Post 9-11, all vehicles were open to search and drug crimes went through the roof," she says. "All vehicles coming on the base had to have a decal and if there was no decal, they'd be searched. And we started finding drugs."

Torok was next assigned to Tongduchon, a South Korean city about 20 miles from the North Korean border. Because of the post's sensitive location, security was tight and soldiers weren't permitted to have cars. "When you have a bunch of 18- to 20-year-old men and all they have to do is drink, a lot of bad things happen," Torok says. "You had soldiers beating each other up and you had date rape situations. I wound up being the sex crimes expert in the office."

After serving in Korea, she returned to Fort Leavenworth and practiced administrative law. Despite a four-year commitment, she stayed for a fifth year, then accepted a job as an associate with Shook, Hardy & Bacon in Overland Park, Kansas. Although Torok says she never got bored practicing military law, she found that her job had little in common with its movie and TV portrayals.

"It is very not glamorous," she says. "As a lawyer in the army, you just don't have the resources. I painted more in the JAG Corps, sprucing up my office, than I ever did before. I did my own filing. In one movie they talked about 'actions unbecoming a Marine.' There is no such thing.

"But you always feel good about what you're doing. You can take pride in helping people in the green suits, who are trying to do the right thing and defend their country. That's the piece people love about it."

courses in military orientation and military law. Not only do new officers usually lack courtroom experience, but they'll be practicing a code of law different from what's covered in law school. Courts-martial are conducted according to the Uniform Code of Military Justice, in which court procedures and rules of evidence differ from those in U.S. civilian courts. While the military will be represented by a prosecutor at a court-martial, the charges are brought by a commander. The verdict is submitted to that commander, who can reduce a sentence or throw it out entirely.

For JAG Corps attorneys, important assignments come much sooner than they would in civilian law firms. JAG Corps attorneys often serve as prosecutors and defense lawyers and also work in some type of noncriminal law. They are moved into different roles because they may wind up at a small base where just one lawyer could be required to handle almost any type of legal issue. JAG Corps attorneys usually sign up for four years, then can move to private practice or continue a military legal career. Many former JAG Corps attorneys specialize in military law when they enter private practice. Although soldiers are assigned military lawyers, they're allowed to hire civilian lawyers instead. While the job may not be as glamorous as the movies and TV shows suggest, many law school graduates find that serving in the JAG Corps is an ideal way to serve their country while becoming better lawyers.

Pitfalls

It can be difficult to gain the confidence of clients in criminal cases because they might view you as an arm of the military instead of as their lawyer. You won't be paid as well as an associate just starting out with a large private law firm.

Perks

The variety of cases and different types of law will give you much more experience than you'd get starting out in private practice. The pay, on an officer's scale, is decent, and you're encouraged to take time to exercise. You may get the chance to live abroad, and you'll have the satisfaction of helping people who've volunteered to serve their country.

Get a Jump on the Job

Though the movies and TV shows about JAG Corps attorneys aren't exactly true to life, they can give you a rough idea of what the job entails. Watch Court TV and read books, newspapers, magazines, and Web sites to learn as much as you can about legal issues. Each military branch has online information about its JAG Corps.

PARKS DIRECTOR

OVERVIEW

Do you love a stroll in the park or a bike ride, horseback ride, or a jog on a public trail? Do you enjoy seeing lots of green grass and water and birds? Do you enjoy taking your dog for a walk in the park or tossing around a football with a friend? Do you wish you could make sure that beautiful open areas will still be there for your children and their children and many more generations after them?

If so, you might consider becoming a parks director, who's responsible for finding the best uses for public parkland. You will oversee recreation, environmental protection, and historical preservation on land owned by a city, county, state, or the federal government. A parks director develops and manages programs for parkland and park facilities. Directors will be asked to give technical advice to a park commission, city council, county commission, or any other body that oversees a parks department. Because they have so many responsibilities, parks directors often hold master's degrees. The field is so popular that many universities offer majors in parks and recreation administration.

A parks director often is responsible for vast areas, which require constant maintenance and repair. The director usually needs a large staff to cut grass, trim trees, resurface trails and parking lots, build rest rooms, manage wildlife, and make sure that parks rules and ordinances are being obeyed. Parks directors also help decide exactly how land will be used, and those decisions can invite controversy. While almost everybody loves parks, not everybody agrees on what should be put in them.

Some citizens want their parks department to build ball fields and organize youth and adult sports leagues. Others would rather have tennis and basketball courts, without organized leagues, and some would rather have a golf course or swimming pool. Some would rather have open spaces preserved for their natural beauty. Still others might want the parks department to preserve a Civil War battlefield or historic home on public property. And some might argue that parkland be sold to developers for new homes or a shopping mall.

That's why it's important for a parks director to come up with a master plan for the use of parkland. Such a plan can be developed with the help of city and environmental planners, who can show how to make the park plan compatible with the rest of the area's needs and laws. That plan ultimately will be taken to the city government and the public for approval.

Because park plans involve a lot of money, the officials who oversee them want to make sure that taxpayers are getting their money's worth. A good parks director stays in touch with local officials

Ron Ahlbrandt, director of parks

As director of parks for Montgomery County, Pennsylvania, Ron Ahlbrandt oversees 6,500 acres of land, six parks, 60 miles of trails, four historic sites, and 100 full-time and 75 part-time employees. Clearly, there's a lot more to running a county parks department than sending somebody out to mow the grass once in a while!

"A position like mine requires you be able to be an administrator who handles budget and planning," Ahlbrandt says. "You have to have a background in construction development, resource development, and historic sites and keep brushing up to make yourself aware of what's going on." You also have to deal with management issues, he notes, so it helps to hire the proper people and surround yourself with the expertise you need.

Ahlbrandt's projects range from solving an erosion problem to teaming up with the National Audubon Society to preserve the only existing American home of naturalist John James Audubon. The home, Mill Grove estate, was built in 1762 and covers 175 acres owned by Montgomery County. The estate includes a house, barn, miles of winding trails, more than 175 species of birds, and more than 400 species of flowering plants. Preserved by the county as a museum and wildlife sanctuary, the estate's long-term improvements proved too costly for taxpayers to handle alone. "Now, with National Audubon, we can do long-term improvements," Ahlbrandt says. "We have a nice partnership and it satisfies a lot of needs for people in the area."

In one county park, powerboats caused a severe erosion of the shoreline, which the county restored, with help from a federal Environmental Protection Agency grant. The County Planning Commission and Parks Department hired consultants who suggested a plan for stabilizing 1,800 feet of eroded shoreline. By using a combination of tree roots, rocks, and soil, the county began restoring the shoreline in 2003. "We went to an outside consultant because you can't be experts in everything," Ahlbrandt says.

But all park directors need to be experts in knowing how to get things done, which usually involves cooperation. A nine-member parks board comprised of Montgomery County residents and attends public hearings that affect the parks department. The director presents technical information and answers questions from officials and the public. They may be upset that new recreation facilities will be too close to their homes, or that the playground equipment hasn't been upgraded lately.

An area's size, needs, and resources will determine just how many citizens a parks department will serve. In a large metropolitan area, a parks director may be responsible for swimming pools, ice rinks, and other facilities. Parks department workers may be responsible for maintenance, repair, and gardening work in public housing complexes. In a national park, a director may devote a lot of time to fish and wildlife management and safety of campers, boaters and hikers. Public parks just may be among the most democratic places in America. Anybody can use them and they offer something for just about everybody.

Pitfalls

It can be frustrating to try to convince elected officials and the public that your

advises Alhbrandt's staff and the three county commissioners on park operations. But decisions affecting county parks also often need to involve municipalities in which parkland is located. One of Montgomery's jogging and biking trails covers 22 miles and runs through more than a dozen townships. Each of those townships wants to stay informed about what the county parks department is doing in its neighborhoods. "There are 62 townships and boroughs in our county, and one of my responsibilities is to further develop relationships with the professionals there," Ahlbrandt says.

"All these municipalities require us to interact. It's our responsibility to make that connection, especially where parks impact the towns they're in. We have people who want more active recreation and people who like to have preservation of open spaces and have the land not used at all. It's my responsibility to make it all workable. The residents of this county are strong about preserving open space. We don't have an attack of developers wanting to develop that land. More people are concerned with, what are we doing to prevent that? One of our primary responsibilities is to provide open spaces to our residents, not to developers."

Ahlbrandt received a bachelor's degree in economics from King's College in Wilkes-Barre, Pennsylvania, and a master's degree in parks and recreation administration from Penn State. He worked in municipal parks administration for 14 years, spent eight years in private business, and was hired by Montgomery County in 1992. "I really enjoy being able to assist and develop and help make decisions to benefit people in the future," Ahlbrandt says. "These are decisions that have to be reached now or we won't have these parks. It's satisfying to be in that role of involvement. It's also frustrating because a lot of the time you don't get things done because an issue is politically oriented or because the dollars are not available. On the flip side, it is satisfying when you do get it done."

plans for their parks make sense. As is often the case in government, the wheels of progress don't always turn as quickly as you'd like.

Perks

As a parks director, you will maintain and improve land and facilities important to the quality of life of the community. With sound planning, you can make sure that the community's parks will be enjoyed by the public for many generations to come.

Get a Jump on the Job

You can get a summer job as a lifeguard, youth coach, or maintenance worker in your local parks department. This will help you understand the many functions performed by parks directors and their staffs. Any time you use a park, check out the facilities and think how you might improve them if you could.

POLITICAL CONSULTANT

OVERVIEW

When a candidate runs for political office, we see him or her out there alone, giving speeches, shaking hands, debating, or asking for votes in a TV ad. But the candidate isn't alone. In today's complicated and expensive campaigns, a candidate needs to have a small army to win an election. Many of the soldiers are political consultants.

Political consultants are freelancers—hired guns who sign on as consultants, as opposed to a campaign's full-time paid staff. Consultants fill a broad range of jobs, including political strategist, media strategist, pollster, researcher, and fundraising consultant. Some consultants fill more than one role. A political consultant might work as a strategist, determining which issues and groups of voters to target, or as a media strategist, producing campaign ads for radio and TV. Political and media strategists may help shape the campaign's message and prep the candidate for debates. Pollsters conduct polls and help develop a strategy based on those results. Polling in the final stages of a campaign is almost an around-the-clock job.

A public policy researcher studies key issues and briefs the candidate. An opposition researcher studies the opponent's history on issues, especially the person's voting record, speeches, and writing. A diligent opposition researcher can give a candidate plenty of ammunition because some of the opponent's past votes or speeches may prove embarrassing. An opposition researcher may also focus on

AT A GLANCE

Salary Range

If you're a political consultant who works on high-profile campaigns, you'll often earn between $100,000 and $150,000 per year. Top consultants earn in the high six figures and even millions.

Education/Experience

Many consultants start at the lowest ranks of political campaigns, whether as volunteers or paid employees. Others may come from jobs in government, journalism, public relations, marketing, and nonprofit organizations. Political science, journalism, statistics, and communications would be useful majors.

Personal Attributes

You'll need a lot self-confidence to put up with strong personalities; an ability to communicate with just about anybody; and the savvy to understand what makes both your allies and enemies tick.

Requirements

A college degree is preferable, though not necessary. You must be a strategic thinker and problem solver and be able to handle stress. It also helps to have a strong belief in the candidate for whom you'll be working so hard.

Outlook

There are about 7,000 political consultants in the United States, but there's high turnover because of the long hours, constant demands, high stress, and nasty campaigns. That means there's usually room for energetic, well-qualified, and smart people.

his or her own candidate to get an idea what the opposition may find. Fund-raising consultants do just what it sounds like—they worry about the money and plan fund-raising events.

Many of the best consultants at some point manage an entire campaign. They direct the full-time staff and consultants and try to move them all in the same direction to win the election. Most consultants at the national level are committed to one party.

Pitfalls

The fast pace and long hours of campaigns won't let you get much sleep or see a lot of your family. It hurts to lose a race into

---

Marc Farinella, political consultant

Marc Farinella is one of those top-notch consultants who's sometimes hired to manage an entire campaign. In fact, he's the only campaign manager ever to have gotten a deceased candidate elected to the U.S. Senate. It's a distinction Farinella wishes he didn't have. His candidate was Governor Mel Carnahan, a Democrat from Missouri who was killed in a plane crash during his campaign in 2000 against incumbent Senator John Ashcroft. Carnahan, his son, Roger, and adviser Chris Sifford all were killed while flying in a small plane from St. Louis to New Madrid, Missouri, for a campaign rally.

"My sense was, 'All right, it's over, there's nothing to do but pack up and send everyone home,' " Farinella recalls. "But nobody wanted to go home and we quickly decided the right thing to do was continue the battle." Under Missouri law, Carnahan's name had to stay on the ballot, and if he won, the acting governor—Lt. Governor Roger B. Wilson—would appoint someone to fill the vacancy. Wilson let it be known that he'd appoint Carnahan's widow, Jean, and she finally agreed to accept the seat if he won.

"We were prepared to continue whether or not Jean decided to accept an appointment to fill the vacancy," Farinella says. "We knew it was going to be tough to persuade people to vote for a deceased candidate but we also knew that if people approved of the person who would replace him if he won, that would make our campaign much more viable. About 10 days before the election, Jean announced that she would accept the appointment, and we won."

Carnahan's victory climaxed a heated campaign between candidates who differed sharply on many issues, including abortion and gun laws. "It was an extraordinary episode, one of the most unusual elections in history," Farinella recalls. "But the whole two-year campaign was extraordinary. It was the toughest, meanest, nastiest campaign I had ever seen. It was hand-to-hand warfare. The candidates were two political titans who had very different philosophies about public service, and from day one it was a very intense battle."

The Carnahan campaign spent the final weeks fighting and grieving at the same time. It ordered 750,000 buttons that read, "I'm Still With Mel." "It wasn't until his death that we came to understand how much Mel Carnahan had meant to the people of Missouri," Farinella says. "You couldn't go anywhere in Missouri and not see people wearing the button. There were spontaneous gatherings for candlelight services, people gathering in parks to do their own private memorials."

Three days after the crash, more than 8,000 lined up for blocks to view Carnahan's casket, as he lay in state at the governor's mansion in Jefferson City. The next day, a memorial service on the state Capitol grounds attracted a huge crowd, including President Bill Clinton, Vice President Al Gore, Ashcroft, and several U.S. senators. Carnahan's daughter, Robin, gave a which you've poured your heart and soul. You may need clients outside politics in years when you don't have any candidates running for office.

Perks

You'll get a chance to make a difference in who gets elected and what kind of leadership a city, state, or the nation gets.

eulogy on behalf of her family. "We set up chairs for 3,000 people and 15,000 came," Farinella says. "They stood on top of buildings, on window ledges—there was a crowd as far as you could see."

As the Carnahans drove the casket home to Rolla, for the next day's burial, Robin Carnahan phoned Farinella to tell him of the overwhelming response along the motorcade's path. People lined the roads, holding banners and leaving memorials. "She called to say, 'You won't believe what's going on here,' " he says. "The motorcade left three hours late and people were still lining the roads, waiting to catch a glimpse. We knew that something extraordinary was happening as far as how people felt about Mel. We knew at that point we were not going to stop. We owed it to him to go on. Many of the pundits felt this was sure defeat, that people would not elect Mel Carnahan. But they didn't see what we saw. They didn't understand what was happening."

Farinella joined the political media firm of Murphy, Putnam, Shorr and Partners in 2003. Besides other consulting duties, he became interim manager for the U.S. senate campaign of Bob Casey, a Pennsylvania Democrat. "I feel strongly about my Democratic values and philosophy," Farinella says. "I just feel like an old soldier and there's a war going on and it's time to reenlist. At this point in my life, I'd like to find something with less stress and more control over your environment and not get late-night phone calls. I'd like to be doing something in which every decision isn't so high stakes. But the political parties have two very different perspectives on what America ought to be and I feel like I've got to stand up for what I believe."

Despite the most careful plans, a political consultant quickly discovers that you can't have much control over a political race. "It's a freewheeling environment with a lot of strong personalities and many personal and political agendas," Farinella says. "You need a lot of self-confidence and self-esteem to be able to represent your point of view forcefully, be able to accept rejection of your advice without taking it personally, and have the confidence to both stand up for what you believe and be willing to recognize when you are wrong. Campaigns are complicated, very fast-paced, and very difficult to manage. It's like riding a bull. You have to realize you're not going to have control over everything. You just try to point the bull in the right direction and hold on. It's crisis management all day long."

It's a job that can often become unpleasant. "Campaigns have become meaner, nastier, and uglier and have driven a lot of good people out because they just don't want to deal with that environment," Farinella says. "You have to be tough and strong and let it roll off your back. You have to maintain character and integrity and be true to your values."

The pay can be excellent, especially in the most important races.

Get a Jump on the Job

You can volunteer for campaigns while you're still in high school or college, canvassing voters, stuffing envelopes, and working the phones. This can give you a good idea of what it's like to work in the trenches during a campaign.

POLYGRAPH EXAMINER

OVERVIEW

Forget what you've seen in *Meet the Parents*—polygraph tests aren't conducted in dimly-lit rooms with noisy machines that scribble lines on paper. And a polygraph machine isn't actually a lie detector, but a machine that measures physical stress that may suggest when people aren't being truthful.

Experts explain that there's no such thing as a pure lie response. Lying is a mentally challenging thing to do. When you lie, you know what you're doing is wrong, and it often shows up in various physical responses in your body. There are a lot of good liars out there, but they can't fool themselves.

Typically, polygraph exams are conducted in a brightly-lit room, with the subject sitting in a chair next to the examiner. Two rubber tubes filled with air are placed around the subject's chest and abdomen to monitor breathing; a blood pressure cuff is wrapped around the upper arm, and fingerplates are attached to two of the subject's fingers to detect sweat. The subject sits at a desk with a computer hooked up to these tubes and wires connected to the subject. The old-fashioned analog instruments that once scribbled lines across the paper are now displayed on a computer screen, representing the subject's heart rate, blood pressure, breathing, and sweat on the fingertips.

To begin, the examiner asks a few simple questions to which he already knows the answer, so that he can identify how the subject's body reacts to truthful answers. The test, which usually takes at least 90 minutes, starts with a pretest interview. The examiner tries to make sure the subject is emotionally and physically ready for an exam. The examiner explains how the polygraph works and reviews the questions with the subject before the exam. During the test, the examiner asks about the issue being investigated, and then will later analyze the responses.

Lots of people may think they can beat the test by trying to fake their reactions—but it's actually pretty hard to do. Some subjects try to fake the test by taking

AT A GLANCE

Salary Range

$30,000 to $120,000.

Education/Experience

At least a bachelor's degree is required. Police officers learn many of the skills and principles needed to become a polygraph examiner, but you don't have to have a law enforcement background to enter the career.

Personal Attributes

You'll need to have rapport with people from all kinds of backgrounds, and you should be eager to take advanced courses because polygraph technology keeps improving.

Requirements

Excellent speaking and writing skills, integrity, willingness to work with people who may become confrontational, and a valid U.S. driver's license.

Outlook

There are about 3,500 polygraph examiners active in the United States; most work in law enforcement, national security agencies, and private companies.

Jim Sackett, polygraph examiner

Kansas City, Missouri, police detectives usually don't ask for Jim Sackett's help until they've reached a dead end. "The police usually go to polygraph only because they can't solve the case otherwise," says Sackett, a civilian who works at the department. "We're a last resort."

Sometimes that last resort pays off. Sackett recalled a young mentally retarded man who stayed in jail for a year because a witness saw him standing over the body of a man who was beaten to death. Sackett says the police were unable to tell if the suspect was involved in the death because of his developmental disability.

The suspect finally was given a polygraph exam. He told Sackett that he actually was trying to protect the victim from two other men. Sackett concluded that the suspect was being truthful. The men he identified as the killers were arrested and convicted. "I sat down with him for six hours and did an examination in terms he could understand," Sackett says. "He was free the next day."

Sackett at first gives his subject the benefit of the doubt. "I don't know of any examiner who wants the person to fail," he says. "To provide a high-quality test, you need full knowledge of the case facts and a desire to do your best. That way, you work for the truth, not for the outcome."

Sackett is wise to every trick that some people think can fool an examiner. Internet ads sell manuals that claim to show people how to cheat a polygraph exam. "Anybody in this business keeps up with what the bad guys are doing," he says. "You never beat the polygraph, you beat the examiner. That's why you have to continually maintain advanced education."

Examiners aren't always perfect. If an examiner gets truthful answers and interprets them as being deceptive, he'll get a false positive. If an examiner gets deceptive answers but interprets them as truthful, a false negative will result. According to Sackett, the best way to avoid mistakes is to use the most advanced equipment and study current trends in psychology and physiology. "To the public, it seems mystical, subjective, and wishy-washy," he says. "But it requires a sound knowledge of physiology, psychology, biology, and interpersonal and interrogational skills. A lot of this job is simply knowing people—how to read people and how to talk to people."

Sackett spent 22 years in the U.S. Army as a military policeman, criminal investigator, and polygraph examiner. A graduate of the Department of Defense Polygraph Institute, he retired from the military in 2000 and joined the Kansas City Police Department. He also runs a private polygraph company, and conducts exams at the police department for job applicants, internal affairs investigations, and the Office of Citizen Complaints (OCC), which handles complaints against the police.

Angry subjects are the exception for Sackett, a 6-foot-2, 230-pound man with a military bearing. "There's usually enough rapport," he says. "But they might get a little hostile, especially when they know they're lying and get caught. They don't like anybody calling them a liar. Nobody's taken a swing at me yet, but it's been close."

Still, there's a bit of mystique that clings to what he does. People who know what Sackett does for a living often try to avoid catching his eye, because they think he's a human polygraph machine who has some mystical power to size up their honesty. "That's one of the reasons," he says, smiling, "that I don't stare at people."

sedatives, putting antiperspirants on their fingertips, doing mental arithmetic, or changing their breathing patterns. Some people even bite their tongue, lip or cheek, or press on a tack in their shoe to try producing pain, hoping this will hide their normal reactions. Experienced examiners are wise to these tricks.

Results that suggest deception will lead to a post-test interview by the examiner or a detective. Although polygraph results seldom are admissible in criminal cases, any statements—including confessions—are admissible. The courts have ruled that scientific evidence can't be admitted into court until it's been accepted by the scientific community, and the reliability of polygraph results is still controversial among scientists.

Polygraph examiners usually learn their trade by being sent for special training by their police department, the military, or a federal agency such as the CIA or FBI. You also can attend a polygraph school on your own, and then apply for a job in law enforcement or start a private agency.

Pitfalls

Polygraph examiners often encounter hostility or tricks. Some subjects may be uncooperative because they consider the examiner an adversary. Others may attempt deception and become angry when they're caught. Examiners quickly learn that they won't enjoy good rapport with every subject.

Perks

A polygraph examiner can earn up to $100,000 or more a year, with private examiners usually earning the most. In law enforcement, polygraph work also can bring the satisfaction of solving cases and saving detectives many hours of work.

Get a Jump on the Job

Join a law enforcement agency or military service that will give you polygraph training. Or, you can pay for your own tuition at a polygraph school, and then apply to become an examiner in law enforcement or at a private agency.

PRESIDENTIAL SPEECHWRITER

OVERVIEW

Imagine how proud you'd feel to hear the words you wrote coming out of the mouth of the President of the United States. You'd be helping the leader of the free world express opinions and policies that might make America a better place to live. You might even get famous doing it. Once upon a time, presidential speechwriters were unknown—but not anymore. Now they are sometimes better known than some members of the president's cabinet. When they write a famous phrase, they get the credit.

George H.W. Bush brought the 1988 Republican Convention to its feet when he said, "Read my lips: No new taxes!" Speechwriter Peggy Noonan got famous for writing that line, although it came back to haunt Bush when he went ahead and raised taxes anyway, and lost his bid for reelection in 1992. Ronald Reagan made headlines in 1987 when he visited West Germany and told Soviet leader Mikhail Gorbachev to get rid of the infamous Berlin Wall. Uttering the words penned by speechwriter Peter Robinson, Reagan cried: "Mister Gorbachev, tear down this wall!"

Presidential speechwriting has become more sophisticated since the time Abraham Lincoln used the back of an envelope in 1863 to scribble down the Gettysburg Address—the most famous presidential speech ever. In fact, there were no full-time presidential speechwriters until Judson Welliver went to work for Warren Harding, who was elected in 1920. Back then, the

only way to hear the president speak was to jostle for a place in a crowd and listen in person. Today, every president speaks before a worldwide TV or radio audience—and no longer has the time to write or research his own speeches.

Presidents depend upon strong speeches to get elected, make the annual State of the Union address, welcome foreign leaders,

---

AT A GLANCE

Salary Range
$60,000 to $75,000.

Education/Experience
You'll need an undergraduate degree, preferably in journalism, political science, English, history, or another major relevant to politics or writing. But you don't go right from school to the White House. Presidential speechwriters include former journalists, professors, and campaign workers.

Personal Attributes
You should be a serious student of the day's issues. You'll need to be patient and tactful because what you want to put in a speech can get tied up in office politics. And working in the White House involves the ultimate in office politics.

Requirements
You must be able to take complicated issues and express them in forceful yet simple words. You must be able to react quickly to important events and be able to meet a tight deadline.

Outlook
These jobs open up in each new administration, but there aren't many of them and those lucky enough to get hired consider this an important stop along the way, and not a final destination. There are no career presidential speechwriters, and unfortunately, there's no clear path to this job. Most people just fall into it.

and talk to the nation about events that change our lives. After the 9-11 attack, the American public looked for reassurance from President George W. Bush, who rose to the occasion with a ringing speech pro- vided by his speechwriters: "We will not tire. We will not falter. We will not fail."

The most important events usually produce the best speeches. And if you're a speechwriter, it helps to have a president

Gordon Stewart, presidential speechwriter

Gordon Stewart met his future boss when Jimmy Carter was a political nobody. Carter was seeking support in New York City and asked for help from Howard Samuels, a wealthy businessman with a lot of political contacts. One of those contacts was Stewart, who'd been a speechwriter and aide to New York Mayor John Lindsay.

"Back then, Jimmy Carter carried a garment bag and slept in people's apartments," recalls Stewart. "Howard says, 'I need people to come see this guy.' We sat around the breakfast table one morning and I left with a very strong impression of Jimmy Carter. This guy was smart and intense and it hadn't occurred to him that he might lose. He had appealing ideas to Americans who didn't know if they could trust traditional politicians. But there were not a lot of New Yorkers supporting Jimmy Carter."

That changed when Carter accepted the Democratic nomination for president in New York in 1976. Stewart was asked to help write Carter's acceptance speech as well as some of the nominating speeches. Carter completed his rise from nowhere when he defeated President Gerald Ford in November 1976.

Stewart didn't go to Washington right away, however. His many interests include drama, and he was directing the Broadway hit *Elephant Man* at the time. But when Carter's first chief speechwriter resigned, he was replaced by Hendrik Hertzberg, who asked Stewart to become deputy chief speechwriter.

"That's one of the funniest titles in all of government," Stewart says. "I had just finished directing *Elephant Man*, and I was directing a play in a church basement somewhere. I thought: 'Who am I to say no?' You get only so many opportunities to get involved in something you think is important. One of the nice things about this job is you use everything you've learned."

Stewart wrote a 1979 speech for Carter to greet Pope John Paul II, the first pope ever to visit the White House. The pope opposed Soviet control of his native Poland and later would support a democratic movement led by union leader Lech Walesa. That movement helped end Soviet control over Poland. Carter's national security advisor, Zbigniew Brzezinski, was born in Poland, too. "Zbig comes up to me," Stewart recalls, "and says, 'Can we insert a line in that speech? I'd like to say this phrase in Polish.' That usually meant trouble because he was a hawk, and tried to insert aggressive remarks."

Brzezinski's motives soon became clear. The reception was attended by foreign officials, including Anatoly Dobrynin, Soviet ambassador to the United States. Brzezinski wanted to tell the Soviets that both the pope and the United States wanted them out of Poland. "When Carter spoke to the Pope in Polish, Brzezinksi is smirking at Dobrynin because Polish resistance to Russia has just been revived," Stewart says. "Three Poles—Walesa, the pope, and Brzezsinski—

(continues)

(continued)

were going to stir up the Poles and defy [the Soviets] to shoot them. There are dimensions that make this unlike any other job. There are moments, like the pope's visit, where something historical moved forward."

Stewart's most famous speech marked the signing of the second Strategic Arms Limitation Treaty with the Soviet Union in 1979. The treaty never actually took effect, but reduced the threat of nuclear war. Carter, voicing Stewart's words, told the U.S. Congress: "The central truth of the nuclear age is that we and the Soviet Union will either live in peace, or we will not live at all."

Powerful words from the president can change the world. That's why many working for the president want to influence his speechwriter. Fortunately for Stewart, meddling was minimal under Carter. "There's an enormous amount of jockeying and struggling over presidential words because people want the president to say certain things and once he says them, he and we are stuck with them," Stewart says. "So you have to be careful about what's urged on you. Everybody wants control over speechwriting. The ones who really cared about what I did would go to great lengths to befriend, intimidate, co-opt, or get around me."

Stewart also wrote presidential toasts for state dinners. He often found inspiration in Lincoln, the greatest presidential speechwriter of them all. A portrait of Lincoln always hung over the fireplace just behind one of Carter's shoulders. "I was always looking up and seeing this sad, brooding, deeply compassionate gaze of Abraham Lincoln, and you know that whatever you have done is just a small attempt to be as good at that moment as he was at every moment," Stewart says. "You'll never succeed, but you keep trying to keep alive a function where Lincoln was excellent but that has been delegated to people like me. I'd look at the president with [British Prime Minister] Maggie Thatcher and [French President Valéry] Giscard d'Estaing and look up at this man and say: 'God, help me to do well.' "

Stewart joined the Carter delegation sent by Reagan to Germany after the 1981 inauguration to welcome home U.S. hostages who were held in Iran for more than a year. "They weren't as happy as we thought they should've been," Stewart recalls. "They didn't realize we'd been working our butts off for 444 days. They thought they'd been abandoned. They were kind of cranky. Then things got better. On the way back, I got a call telling me that [UN Secretary General] Kurt Waldheim was looking for a speechwriter. I said: 'I appreciate the referral, but I think I have written my last speech for another individual.' "

Currently, Stewart is secretary of the Judson Welliver Society of former presidential speechwriters. The society includes about 40 members and was founded by William Safire, a speechwriter for Richard Nixon. "We sit around and tell stories; who else would listen to us?" Stewart laughs. "We talk about how much better off the world would be if they'd done what we told them. Generally, it's a wonderful kind of camaraderie and one of the few times all that ideology gets checked at the door. It's an odd job filled by odd people who, in the right or wrong circumstances, can provide some really odd results."

who can deliver a great speech in front of a crowd.

Reagan used his acting experience and love of anecdotes to give popular speeches. He was known as the Great Communicator and pundits said he could read a phone book and make people cry. President Bill Clinton was an excellent speaker, although he drove his writers crazy by changing his speeches as he spoke. There's often been a religious tone to George W. Bush's speeches, which are written by Michael Gerson, an evangelical Christian.

Although speechwriters and advisers want everything in a presidential speech to be perfect, there can be comic moments. Clinton's press secretary, George Stephanopoulos, once put the wrong speech on the teleprompter for a nationally televised address. Clinton ad-libbed for 90 seconds before he was given the correct speech. Reagan once was speaking in the Rose Garden, outside the White House, without a teleprompter. His speech was written on file cards, but an aide dropped them and they were out of order when they were picked up. Reagan was such a gifted speaker that nobody seemed to notice that one point didn't logically follow another.

Pitfalls

Presidential speechwriters often face a lot of meddling. Other administration officials may try to bully you to change a speech to suit their own goals and ambitions.

Perks

This can be an amazing opportunity. You get to be part of history. You'll write speeches and experience events that can change the nation and the world. You'll develop a working relationship, and maybe even a personal friendship, with one of the most important leaders on the face of the earth.

Get a Jump on the Job

Develop a serious interest in political issues. Volunteer to work on a local, state, or federal election campaign. Take lots of speaking and writing courses in high school and college. Study the presidents and read some of their most famous speeches.

PROBATION OFFICER

OVERVIEW

Many first-time offenders and those who commit minor crimes are given probation instead of prison terms. Probation officers keep track of these individuals. During probation, offenders must stay out of trouble and meet with a probation officer, who supervises offenders—often in their homes and on the job. Some offenders must wear an electronic device so that the probation officer can monitor the person's location and movements. As a probation officer, you might arrange for offenders to get substance abuse rehabilitation or job training.

Probation officers also spend much of their time working for the courts, investigating the background of offenders brought before the court, writing presentence reports, and making sentencing recommendations for each offender. Officers review sentencing recommendations with offenders and their families before submitting them to the court, and may be required to testify in court about their recommendations. Probation officers also attend court hearings to update the court on the offender's compliance with the terms of the sentence and on rehabilitation efforts.

The number of cases a probation officer handles at one time depends on the needs of offenders and the risks they pose. Higher-risk offenders and those who need more counseling usually take up more of an officer's time. Caseload size can also vary from as few as 20 to more than 100 active cases at a time.

AT A GLANCE

Salary Range
Salaries range from less than $25,810 to more than $62,520, with an average for employees in local government of $39,450. Higher wages tend to be found in urban areas.

Education/Experience
Background qualifications for probation officers vary by state, but a bachelor's degree in social work, criminal justice, or a related field from a four-year college or university is usually required. Some employers require previous experience or a master's degree in criminal justice, social work, psychology, or a related field. A graduate degree, such as a master's degree in criminal justice, social work, or psychology, may be helpful for advancement.

Personal Attributes
Prospective probation officers should be in good physical and emotional condition and have strong writing skills due to the large numbers of reports they are required to prepare.

Requirements
Applicants usually are administered written, oral, psychological, and physical examinations, and most are required to complete a training program sponsored by their state government or the federal government, after which a certification test may be required. Most agencies require applicants to be at least 21 years old; for federal employment, applicants may not be older than 37. Those convicted of felonies may not be eligible for employment. Computer skills are required, as is an understanding of relevant laws and regulations.

Outlook
Employment growth, which is projected to be about as fast as average through 2012, depends on government funding. In addition to openings due to growth, many jobs will be created when others leave or retire. Prison overcrowding has increased

---

AT A GLANCE

the probation population, as judges and prosecutors search for alternate forms of punishment, such as electronic monitoring and day reporting centers. The number of offenders released on parole also is expected to increase to create room in prison for other offenders. The increasing prison, parole, and probation populations should spur demand for probation and parole officers. However, the job outlook depends primarily on the amount of government funding given to probation systems. Although community supervision is far less expensive than keeping offenders in prison, a change in political trends toward more imprisonment and away from community supervision could result in fewer employment opportunities.

Probation officers may telecommute from their own homes; other technological advancements (such as electronic monitoring devices and drug screening) have helped probation officers supervise and counsel offenders.

Most probation officers work for state or local governments; those who work for the federal government are employed by the U.S. courts and the Federal Bureau of Prisons.

Pitfalls

Relatively low salary, heavy workload, and high stress combine to make this a tough job. Probation officers work with criminal offenders, some of whom may be dangerous, and officers typically interact with family members and friends of their clients who may be angry, upset, or difficult to work with. Moreover, you may be assigned to work in high-crime areas or in institutions where there is a risk of violence or communicable disease. The stress can be severe, since you're required to meet many deadlines, most of which are imposed by courts.

In addition, extensive travel and fieldwork may be required to meet with offenders who are on probation or parole. You may need to carry a weapon for protection, and you may be on call 24 hours a day to supervise and help offenders. You also may be required to collect and transport urine samples of offenders for drug testing.

Perks

Although the high stress levels can make these jobs very difficult at times, the work can also be very rewarding. Many workers obtain personal satisfaction from counseling members of their community and helping them become productive citizens.

Get a Jump on the Job

The best way to get an idea of what it takes to do this job is to read widely in the field, and then major in criminal justice or law enforcement and corrections in college.

Wanda Miller, former probation officer

As a probation and parole officer for the Impaired Driver Program in Lancaster County, Pennsylvania, Wanda Miller came to the job via a circuitous route—with a degree in English and an interest in mental health. She and the other probation officers in her department supervised people who had been arrested for drinking while under the influence—a motor vehicle offense.

Most of her clients were on "accelerated rehabilitative disposition," which meant that if they completed specific requirements, the district attorney would not prosecute the case and the person's arrest record would be erased. The requirements typically included a six-month loss of license, payment of fines and other costs, impaired driver classes, drug and alcohol treatment, and two years' probation. However, the driving record with the state would not be erased, so that any subsequent driving under the influence (DUI) charge would be handled as a second offense—with more severe consequences.

"Others clients were repeat offenders," she explains, "and many were also on supervision with [county] adult probation or state parole for criminal offenses ranging from shoplifting to murder. My caseload included a lot of sex offenders."

Miller says she was lucky enough to work for a department that encouraged probation officers' participation in mental health education workshops, seminars, and clinics, as well as criminal justice–related educational activities, including self defense. "What I found most rewarding was the opportunity to help people recognize and address areas in their lives that were causing them difficulty," she explains. "The most frustrating aspect was being not just a witness but a party to the injustices that people experience based on demographics. 'Underprivileged' almost always meant 'underserved' with regard to access to quality legal services or mental health care." She also notes the frustration involved in dealing within an entrenched bureaucracy and all that it typically entails.

For anyone interested in the probation field, Miller recommends a criminal justice major in college to get your foot in the door, with a strong minor or even a double major in social work. "You might also consider internships or summer jobs working with disenfranchised populations, such as mental health/mental retardation group homes or Habitat For Humanity to increase sensitivity to issues specific to folks not prepared to negotiate the system."

STAFF ASSISTANT TO THE FIRST LADY

OVERVIEW

Working with the first lady, meeting the president, and attending state functions with international leaders. For young staff assistants to the first lady, this job carries a heady sense of incredible opportunity. Staff assistants in the inner offices of the White House carry out a range of duties, but often center on arranging events and handling the voluminous correspondence sent to the first lady.

There's no way that the wife of the president of the United States could sit down and answer several hundred letters a week, some praising, some criticizing, some asking for advice or assistance or political intervention. Instead, she relies on her staff assistants to help sift through the correspondence, providing her with a summary of what the letters are saying with perhaps a handful of carefully chosen excerpts to read herself.

With a good sense of what the first lady would want to say, the staff assistant writes a reply in her name, always showing every letter to another pair of eyes before it's sent out on White House stationery. A mistake in a letter, even a typo, would not reflect well on either the White House or the first lady, and since most of these letters are treasured by their recipients, the smallest mistake would be noticed.

As a staff assistant, you'd also be responsible for helping to plan and carry out the many functions and events for which

she is responsible. Every detail, from the placement of the table decorations to the management of the guest list, could be your responsibility. And it would be up to you to make sure everything goes off without a hitch, functioning smoothly and flawlessly.

Pitfalls

By its very nature, working at the White House is a very public job where every potential mistake is magnified. Working in this kind of environment can be extremely stressful and involve very long hours.

Perks

What could be more exciting than working in the White House, face to face with the first lady, attending state functions and getting to meet political leaders and international heads of state? This job is a

---

AT A GLANCE

Salary Range
$30,000 to $50,000.

Education/Experience
A degree in communications, writing, or political science is helpful. Washington, D.C., office experience is also helpful.

Personal Attributes
Discretion, loyalty, excellent oral and written communication skills, and attention to detail.

Requirements
A bachelor's degree is required, as are political connections and the ability to communicate effectively.

Outlook
Fair. Competition for these jobs is tight.

Sheryl Eberly, former staff assistant to First Lady Nancy Reagan

As staff assistant and deputy director of projects for Nancy Reagan, Sheryl Eberly had a front-row seat at the making of history from 1980 to 1984. It was heady stuff for a young woman in her mid-20s, going to work every day in the White House.

Her degree was in communications with an emphasis on writing. After having some articles published in magazines, she landed a job with a Republican congressman, responsible for helping to draft responses to letters. Before long, she was promoted to administrative assistant, the top position involved in running a Congressional office.

Eberly heard that Mrs. Reagan was hiring staff assistants for the White House, and she was hoping for a crack at the job, but she knew she needed a reference from someone in the Republican campaign. Fortunately, her boss had served as the Republican campaign chair in Oklahoma during Ronald Reagan's successful election campaign.

"I asked him would he be willing to recommend me to the person doing the interviewing for Mrs. Reagan," Eberly says, "and he did." But her success was more than being in the right place at the right time or just knowing the right people. "I needed both my background in writing, professional experience, and a political sponsor," she explained. "You don't just apply at the White House and walk in. As a political appointee, you need someone to help you."

In her new job, Eberly was responsible for planning and handling events, planning the schedule of the first lady, and helping with the first lady's considerable correspondence, answering letters from fans and critics alike. "Mrs. Reagan would see many of the letters herself and she would write responses to them," Eberly explains. "Many others, I would answer." Keeping up with the constant flood of hundreds of notes a week kept a number of assistants busy. "We had a person who would read them, and that was another aspect of my job. She would often get letters saying: 'When you see the president tonight, would you get him to . . . .'"

"She really paid a lot of attention to her correspondence," Eberly says. "I gave her weekly reports: 'You had 50 letters from people saying thank you for promoting the foster grandparent program.'" But Mrs. Reagan also wanted to hear the criticism. "She wanted to know what all the letters were saying, she wanted to know everything," Eberly notes.

As staff assistant, Eberly and her office also handled scheduling. "She got a lot of requests to speak at various organizations, many more than she could attend," Eberly explains. "I would prepare a letter with her greetings that could be read by someone who was part of the sponsoring organization. The notes would say something like: 'I'm sorry I could not be there, I commend you for your event.'"

Eberly also was responsible for planning events within the White House related to the first lady's projects, such as the foster grandparents program linking the elderly to children with disabilities, or the anti-drug Just Say No campaign. She also was expected to host visitors to the White House at Christmas, putting them at ease as they toured rooms decorated for the holidays. "Mrs. Reagan believed the White House was the people's house, and belonged to everyone," she explained. Sometimes that meant helping ordinary citizens, and sometimes she was called on to assist celebrities. "I helped [NBC *Today Show* former weatherman] Willard Scott get into his Santa costume one year," she recalls, "as he helped welcome the press corps on a tour of the White House at Christmas."

But working at the White House is more than getting to participate in holiday celebrations. The primary requirement of a staff assistant in the White House is to be able to handle any eventuality, calmly and effectively. Eberly remembered one event honoring state Teachers of the Year, held in the first lady's rose garden on the east side of the White House. The tables were beautifully decorated with black velvet cloths to best showcase the Steuben crystal birds decorating each table, which were to be given to the guests. It was a glorious summer day, Eberly recalls, with the sun blazing down and no threat of rain to mar the event.

And then—"I noticed smoke coming from some of the tablecloths," she says. "The tablecloths were starting to burn!" It turned out that the brilliant sun, beaming through the crystal birds, was focused to laser-like intensity by the crystal, igniting the black velvet cloths. "Needless to say, the birds went back into their boxes!" she laughed. "As staff assistants, we had to take care of all the details—no matter what they were!"

As exciting as the job could be, it was also a daily challenge, given the public nature of the job. "It was kind of like being in a fish bowl," she explains. "I was writing letters on White House stationery. When people get a letter like that from the White House, they frame it, it gets published in their local newspaper. So I had to be very careful about what I said, and to make sure everything was correct."

Still, there was an occasional hiccup. "The first lady had a few favorite recipes, and we had the head calligrapher create recipe cards to mail out with some of the recipes. There was one for pull-apart bread. I was only in my mid-20s and I didn't have much cooking experience, so I didn't notice that I had put '1 tablespoon of salt' instead of '1 teaspoon' in the recipes that got mailed out."

As a political appointee, Eberly worked very hard, but to her the heroes in the White House are the civil servants. "I gained an amazing appreciation for the people who run the White House," she says. "I was a political appointee; you're appointed because of your political affiliation. But the White House is run by amazingly gifted civil servants who made our lives a lot easier. The chef, the calligrapher, the photographers, the curator, all kinds of people who understand the workings of this historic building, and what it takes to maintain it."

Today, Eberly works as a leadership consultant for North & Schanz Consulting Group in Lancaster, Pennsylvania, but she recalls her time spent in Washington with special fondness. "I loved working at the White House," she says simply. "We worked long, hard hours. Mrs. Reagan had an idea of what she wanted. She paid attention to details, so as her staff members, we did as well. It was an amazing experience to be on her staff, to be able to attend state events, see leaders from foreign governments."

once-in-a-lifetime opportunity to have an insider's view into the everyday functioning of the nation's leaders.

Get a Jump on the Job

If you're interested in working someday as a staff assistant at the White House, you can start by landing a college internship in Washington and making political contacts. You'll also need to get a solid education in communications, writing, or public affairs.

STATE EDUCATION COMMISSIONER

OVERVIEW

If you work in public education, you'll need to be prepared to stand in the eye of a storm. Few other areas in government generate as much emotion and controversy. Because most Americans have attended public schools, they consider themselves experts on education, and most have their own ideas about how their children should be educated.

Any one of these people can get their opinions heard because public education is among our nation's most democratic institutions. Local school board members and many state board members owe their jobs to voters, and must be responsive to them. School board meetings are open to the public and often include highly opinionated statements from students, parents, and anybody else who wishes to speak out on public education.

Most major issues in education cause controversy. School funding is always a hot topic as politicians often debate whether to raise taxes or cut money for schools. There's also plenty of debate over school curriculum, discipline, standardized testing, and the performance of teachers, principals, superintendents, board members, and other administrators. Public education became an even hotter topic in 2002, with the signing of the No Child Left Behind Act, an unprecedented federal involvement with education. The law, passed by Congress, set standards for

AT A GLANCE

Salary Range
$130,000 to $250,000.

Education/Experience
A doctorate in education is required. Teaching experience is also required, as is prior experience as an administrator at the local, state, or federal level.

Personal Attributes
You should have a genuine interest in seeing children perform well in school. You'll need political savvy, because you'll need help from elected officials to get things done. A thick skin also helps, because you'll probably face the criticism and controversy that comes with almost any job in public education.

Requirements
Depending upon what state you live in, you'll need the approval of the governor, state board of education, or the voters before you can get hired. This means you'll have to convince key people that you're the right person to improve the education of children in your state.

Outlook
Administrative jobs in education should remain plentiful as federal, state, and local officials continue to emphasize the need to improve schools. However, states may cut funding for education to balance their budgets, and this will mean fewer jobs and lower salaries.

achievement and established penalties for schools found to be deficient. Similar laws had already been passed by several states. Because states govern their public schools, a state education commissioner has an enormous responsibility and faces intense pressure and criticism.

So how does a state education commissioner meet such challenging goals? He or she must be an expert in education

Dr. Robert Bartman, state education commissioner

Robert Bartman became Missouri's top education official just when the job was becoming really, really interesting: It was 1987, about the time that his state and the rest of the country woke up to the fact that many of the nation's schoolchildren were not receiving a high-quality education. "There was a 'We're doing O.K.,' feeling," Bartman recalls. "That meant the top 10 to 15 percent of students were doing well, and maybe you had a good football team. It was kind of a calm time in the country and people enjoyed that, except you didn't have a high performance level for our kids."

Bartman's eyes also were opened when his children, who attended school in the state capital of Jefferson City, visited a rural school. "They told me the kids at this school did not have to work very hard," he recalls. "They had to finish after-school activities at a certain time because they had little bus service. If most of those kids were going to grow up in that district, they'd be fine. But not if they were to go somewhere else and compete at the best schools in the state and nation."

When Bartman became commissioner, the Missouri legislature already had passed a bill to raise standards in education. But it became clear to Bartman that much more needed to be done. A study showed that during the 1980s, school funding had doubled in Missouri but high school seniors hadn't improved their scores on the ACT, a standardized college admissions exam. "I wanted to create some urgency that we had to get better," Bartman says. In late 1992, he organized a conference of state political leaders to discuss how to improve education. This conference led to the state legislature passing the Outstanding Schools Act in 1993. This was a wide-ranging law that increased school funding, set standards for academic performance and established a system for reporting and auditing student achievement.

and have the political savvy to bring people together, including parents, teachers, students, administrators, elected officials, and community leaders. A state education commissioner can't get much done without the support of the governor and state legislature.

You can't run a school system without adequate resources, so an education commissioner will spend time trying to convince legislators and the public that public schools need more money. He or she has a better chance to raise that money if there's a solid plan in place. A commissioner may have to come up with a master plan that

establishes the curriculum for all public school districts.

The commissioner may call in officials from local districts and use encouragement or pressure to get them to improve student achievement. The commissioner may revoke accreditation of a deficient district or reinstate accreditation of an improving district. The commissioner conducts public hearings in which education issues are addressed and parents, teachers, administrators, and students are among those likely to speak. Because each state is required by federal law to give standardized tests, the commissioner may help

Now Bartman's plans had momentum. He created the Missouri School Improvement Plan, which included a difficult standardized test and set 11 criteria that school districts had to meet to be accredited. This didn't make Bartman very popular in districts found to be deficient. Of the state's more than 500 districts, 19 failed to meet standards for accreditation. Bartman sent letters to superintendents of those districts advising them of their problems and invited them to meet with him to discuss plans for improvement.

"This was the notion of shaming people into getting better," Bartman says. "Some superintendents could hardly believe I had the audacity to invite them to Jefferson City, and they didn't know how serious to take us. We gave them a method to focus more on performance and got the list (of unaccredited districts) down to five or six. I got hate mail from some teachers—the audacity of me to say they were not doing a good job. There was nobody from the outside hammering them to get better. Once they got over being mad, they got together and said: 'This is what we have to do.' They refocused on student performance and it went up."

Bartman went to work on the other side of the fence in 2004 when he became superintendent of the Center School District in Kansas City. He found himself required to meet the same performance standards that he'd established. "You could say the worm's turned," he joked. Bartman received a doctorate in secondary school administration at the University of Missouri and taught high school English for two years. In 1973, he became an intern in the Missouri Department of Elementary and Secondary Education and remained there until he retired as the commissioner in 2000. "It was a wonderful job and a great experience, in spite of all the challenges," he says. "And the challenges also made it a great job. I never went to work wondering about what I was going to do that day. Every day was different. It's been an interesting journey."

determine the kind of test that is challenging, yet fair for students.

Pitfalls

You'll seldom find everybody agreeing on anything you do. You'll often face angry and emotional critics, especially during public meetings. In addition, trying to achieve progress that requires the passage of state legislation can be slow and frustrating.

Perks

You'll feel tremendous satisfaction knowing that you've made a positive difference in a child's education. The variety of challenges is stimulating, and the pay is good.

Get a Jump on the Job

If you're in school, you're already getting a jump on the job. Take a serious look at what you're being taught, how it's being taught, and if these methods work. Read newspapers and magazines and visit Web sites to understand the important issues that face public education.

TEST PILOT

OVERVIEW

If you love flying and become very good at it, then test pilot might be the career for you. You'll enjoy the fun, challenge, and satisfaction of helping to develop new designs and systems for planes.

Test pilots fly new and modified planes and test them to make sure they can safely achieve what they were designed to do before other pilots and passengers travel in them. Being an exceptional military or civilian pilot doesn't automatically qualify you to become a test pilot, however. A U.S. military pilot who shows an aptitude for test piloting will be sent to a training center, such as the U.S. Naval Test Pilot School.

Candidates receive specialized training on a wide variety of planes so that they'll be prepared to test virtually any aircraft.

Most test pilots have at least one engineering degree because they're expected to understand planes well enough to evaluate designs and performance and suggest improvements. Once they graduate, test pilots work at flight centers operated by the military, the National Aeronautics and Space Administration (NASA), or private aerospace firms. Civilian test pilots may enter this field by working for an aircraft company. They usually make 20 to 40 flights during a research project and must start their homework long before the first flight.

If you've made it this far, you'll meet with the project engineers six months before testing, and visit the factory where the new plane or equipment is being built.

There you'll operate a flight simulator to get a feel for how to operate the research plane. The plane won't be ready for testing until the hardware, software, and data collection are all ready to go. A week before the first flight, you'll practice again on a simulator to make sure there have been no changes in the plane since your earlier practices. You'll go through a two-hour briefing before the first flight.

On the first day of testing, you may need to make three or four flights, each 30 to 45 minutes long. Each research project

Dick Ewers, test pilot

Dick Ewers was getting close to 59 years old and 10,000 hours of flight experience at the time of this interview. He'd been flying for more than 36 years and been a NASA test pilot at Dryden Flight Research Center since 1998. For someone who loves flying as much as Ewers, test pilot is the dream job. "Absolutely, it's like the icing on the cake," he says. "I did not come into flying ever thinking I'd graduate to this level. It was too much fun to quit and the best way to keep going is to become the resident expert."

Ewers loves being a test pilot so much that he's passed up better-paying flying opportunities. A commercial airline pilot, for instance, might earn twice as much as a government test pilot. Ewers, though, will even test planes when he's supposed to have the day off. "I would pay them to fly some of these things around here," he says one morning at Dryden after strong winds had forced cancellation of his test flight. "As you get older, you're usually looking for less work and more pay. But I was willing to sacrifice that for something I like so much. It's not a job. It's an experience and fun. You stand around the scheduling board in the office trying to weasel your way on a flight. [You say,] 'Vacation next week? No, no, I'll come off vacation to fly that.' "

Ewers came to NASA after eight and a half years as an engineering test pilot with Northrop Grumman's Sensors and Systems Division, formerly the Westinghouse Electronic Systems Group. His jobs included testing new radar systems for military and civilian use. Before joining Westinghouse, Ewers served more than 21 years as a U.S. Marine Corps fighter and test pilot before he retired in 1989 as a lieutenant colonel. His military flying included combat service in Vietnam. He and other Marine Corps pilots also joined U.S. Navy and U.S. Air Force squadrons flying F-4s around the world. They sometimes used aircraft carriers, which are very tricky for takeoffs and landings.

Ewers graduated from the U.S. Naval Test Pilot School in 1981 and served two tours as a test pilot at the Naval Air Test Center in Patuxent River, Maryland. Even for an experienced fighter pilot, test pilot school was an eye opener for Ewers. He wasn't accustomed to flying so many different planes. "You come in with a narrow focus," he recalled. "In the test pilot arena, you get exposed to any number of different airplanes and you're a better pilot for it. I can bring to the table exposure in everything from blimps to B-52s, more than just a single airplane. Today the guys aren't getting exposed to as much. Pilots before me flew a lot more than I did and the ones trained after me fly a lot less."

Ewers earned an undergraduate degree in engineering mechanics from the U.S. Air Force Academy in 1968 and a graduate degree in aeronautical systems from the University of West Florida in 1970. He underwent flight training at the Naval Air Station in Pensacola, Florida, in 1969–70 and was assigned to fighter and reconnaissance squadrons. Then he commanded a fighter squadron for two years.

When Ewers trained to become a test pilot, he found his engineering background was almost a must. Engineers are always asking pilots for highly technical opinions about the performance of the planes and systems being tested. "We have very, very few liberal arts majors," Ewers says. "Typically, by the time you get here, you're engrossed in a lot of engineering studies so you can intelligently talk to the engineers. If you can't converse on a

(continues)

uses a team of pilots to help test planes. Besides the pilot flying the research plane, there may be another following in a "chase plane" and still another on the ground in the control room to monitor data on the research plane's performance. The chase pilot is a lookout for the pilot in the research plane. He looks out for damage, smoke, or other aircraft that may be flying too close.

If you're very experienced, you might get to work on a project like the Autonomous Formation Flight Project, which aims to improve fuel mileage by copying the aerodynamics of birds flying in formation. NASA worked with scientists at UCLA and the Boeing Company to develop a system that would allow planes to fly in V-formation over long distances, yet not require the pilot to handle the stick. The V-

(continued)

mechanical, aeronautical, or engineering level, you get lost real quick. Test pilot school is literally a graduate level school in aeronautical engineering."

Ewers figured he'd be more comfortable remaining a test pilot than trying another job in flying, like becoming an airline pilot. Fighter pilots tend to be fiercely independent and Ewers is no exception. "You're typically a one-man show and you're opinionated," he says. "Most guys who get hired in the airline world conform to a quiet, mild-mannered style. You don't want a cowboy who's used to doing belly rolls and acrobatic maneuvers all his life. Airline flying is a different world, a bus driving, administrative world where you're trying to be absolutely as smooth and benign as possible so the people in the back don't even know they're flying."

Not that Ewers is reckless, mind you. He's always mindful of the danger involved in being a test pilot. "Absolutely," he says. "You never can explore the boundaries without recognizing you could stub your toe and trip. We don't step out in large leaps. We try it in simulation and we ease our way in. I always have the ability to say, 'It doesn't feel right, let's stop and regroup and take a look at it.' In today's world, we don't have the luxury of losing our asset. Each one of these [test planes] is one of a kind. The last plane we actually lost was about 15 years ago."

It's ironic that after all his years as a combat and test pilot, Ewers's only crash involved routine training on a twin-engine Lear Jet flying from Dryden. He was giving a new pilot a few practice flights and on landing, the plane veered out of control and its nose struck the tarmac. The impact caused the right side landing gear to collapse and the wing slammed into the ground. The fuel tank exploded and the plane left a trail of flame and smoke before it came to rest about 600 feet from the runway. Both pilots and a passenger walked away unharmed.

"That was probably the stupidest point in my career," Ewers recalls. "It happened in the blink of an eye and I still don't know what he did. It acted like it hit a little wind turbulence just before it reached the runway. That's the problem you get flying with two pilots. You think it's a walk in the park. I was daydreaming and gawking. It's still embarrassing and I had to change my resume from 'accident-free,' to 'only crashed once.' It's still embarrassing and I clench my teeth every time I remember it. But I'm too old to worry about my resume now."

formation, flown by many species of birds, helps each of the trailing birds to fly in the draft of the bird just ahead. Each trailing bird enjoys a decrease in drag and uses less energy to keep flying at a given speed. This allows migratory birds in formation to cover longer distances than birds flying solo. The Autonomous Formation Flight Project tested whether a trailing plane also could save fuel by flying in formation. The project tried to develop an automatic pilot system because it's exhausting for a pilot to hold the exact position needed to save fuel over long distances. When a plane gets into the right position, it's almost like riding a wave.

During one test with the F/A-18 fighter planes at NASA's Dryden Flight Research Center at Edwards, California, the pilot controlled the trailing plane and kept the left wing only 15 yards from the lead plane's right wing. The planes had computer systems to coordinate their positions. During a 96-minute flight to Nevada and back, the plane burned 600 fewer pounds of fuel than a third jet flying outside the formation. A later test showed a 14 percent fuel savings before the project ended in late 2001.

These days, test pilots now spend a lot of time testing systems for unmanned airplanes. They're taking planes such as old F/A-18s and putting in the latest computers, global positioning systems, or tracking devices, trying to find the solutions for tomorrow's problems. They're putting computers into unmanned airplanes, chasing them, and watching them work.

It's the wave of the future. If government agencies want do use high-altitude drones (unmanned planes) for weather or forest fire surveillance, how do those drones fly without crashing or hitting other airplanes? Test pilots are working on the projects that will make sure that doesn't happen. Maybe someday, you will too.

Pitfalls

No matter how much experience a test pilot may have, the job is always dangerous. Test pilots can't ever get careless or take their skills for granted. It can be tense and stressful work.

Perks

Test pilots get to fly on the cutting edge of new technology, and many move into highly paid jobs as commercial airline pilots. Because experience is so valuable for test pilots, they're allowed to work long past normal retirement age.

Get a Jump on the Job

If you think one day you might like to be a test pilot, you can start now by reading up on the subject. Check out books on airplanes and pilots, and take as many science classes as you can (especially physics). You might consider taking flying lessons, too, to see if you really do enjoy being behind the controls of a plane.

TRIAL CONSULTANT

OVERVIEW

When a lawyer is trying a case with billions of dollars at stake or an important criminal case, he or she is looking for all the help he can get. The lawyer may understand the law inside and out, but probably doesn't understand people as well as the experts who've spent years studying human behavior.

That's why trial consultants often have advanced degrees in psychology, sociology or psychiatry, and have worked in those fields. They have learned not only to understand how people behave, but how to use research methods that reveal a person's opinions and characteristics. One of a trial consultant's biggest jobs is advising a lawyer about which individuals, if selected for a jury, could help or hurt the case. They also advise lawyers on how to present a case that will make the best impression on judges and juries.

Trial consultants size up jurors the way most of us size up people, except that they're better trained. We can tell a lot about people by their age, race, religion, job, and whether they're married or have children. If you rely too much on one trait, you may be stereotyping somebody and get the wrong impression. But when a trial consultant considers a range of traits and listens to the lawyer ask potential jurors how they feel about certain issues, their answers and backgrounds can give the consultant a good idea of how they'd feel about a case.

If you're a lawyer, you don't want a juror who has a lot in common with the other side. For example, if your client is suing a hardware store for an injury suffered while shopping, you probably won't want a small business owner on the jury. A lot of potential jurors are perfectly willing to admit to a lawyer how they'd probably feel about a case. But not everybody is quite so forthcoming, however, and that's where a trial consultant's skills are important. In a civil case where a plaintiff is suing for damages, it may be enough for an attorney to know what potential jurors do for a living, how much they earn, and if they've ever been sued.

A trial consultant faces different challenges in a criminal case. Whether working for the prosecution or defense, consultants need to examine a person's religious and moral beliefs, plus the person's attitude toward the justice system and the police. Many potential jurors believe a person wouldn't have been arrested if not guilty of a crime. Many individuals also think they should always believe the testimony

of a police officer and not the defendant. A prosecutor wants those kinds of people on the jury—the defense lawyer does not.

Trial consultants say that what they really do is deselect jurors. That's because lawyers don't get to pick jurors, they can only reject the potential jurors likely to hurt them. Both sides get a number of challenges (called dismissals), and when they've used them up the people who are left get on the jury. Consultants may sit with lawyers in the courtroom and help them decide which jurors they don't want. They may prepare written and oral questions for lawyers to ask. They may help lawyers understand

George Kich, trial consultant

George Kich has consulted on cases that have made big headlines and won big verdicts. In his biggest cases, he's worked for lawyers who sued major tobacco companies because clients became seriously ill after smoking for many years. One verdict originally was for $28 billion and another for $3 billion.

"I enjoy the work," Kich says. "[I enjoy] developing themes and results at a quick pace, the learning and processing of massive amounts of information, and the support that attorneys and clients feel from my work. I really enjoy the sense of victory on the faces of attorneys' clients, and I feel personal satisfaction in using my skills for good causes."

Kich, like most top trial consultants, is a licensed psychologist, not a lawyer. He has bachelor's degrees in both English and education from DePaul University, and a doctorate in social-clinical psychology from the Wright Institute in Berkeley, California. "My history includes many years of [administering] psychotherapy in private practice, where I mostly saw individual adults and couples," he says. "My role was to help them understand their own personal dynamics, competencies, and wishes, and help them achieve the goals they want in their lives. I also taught graduate psychology students and did consultations and supervisions of other therapists in training, as well as wrote articles. I was involved in executive coaching and later did some diversity training for corporations to help them with racial and gender issues that often could lead to productivity problems, or worse." In 1998, he joined the consulting firm National Jury Project in Oakland, California, and he's been a trial consultant ever since.

Any case is only as strong as a lawyer's ability to connect with the jury. Kich uses his vast background in human behavior to help a lawyer make that connection. "This work is active and involves rapid learning of many different types of case facts and is a way to use my

(continues)

the attitudes of people in the place where the trial is held (known as the venue). Consultants may already have worked on similar cases in that area, or they may conduct phone surveys in the area to get an idea of what kinds of people are likely to appear in the jury pool.

Trial consultants also try to help a lawyer understand how jurors will respond to legal arguments. A lawyer may think he or she has an open-and-shut case, based on laws that he or she thoroughly understands. Consultants can help her realize that jurors may see the case differently because they aren't experienced in the law, and need to have the issues simplified.

Consultants often put together a focus group, in which people similar in makeup to the jurors hear a lawyer practice the case. The group's reaction will help the lawyer fine-tune the arguments. Trial consultants also help witnesses and even experts to be more effective when they testify.

After the trial, consultants may get the court's approval to interview jurors and find out why the case was won or lost. This helps the consultants and their lawyers do a better job next time.

Pitfalls

The hours and travel are grueling, and there's a lot of pressure to win a case.

(continued)

psychological, people, and analytical skills and experiences," he says. "There is a lot about the law—about the court systems, about judges and their various protocols, about the different types of claims and lawsuits. This is an ongoing learning experience. What is important is that I know many basics about all this. However, my role is to assist and help the attorneys, who are the ones who really know the law."

It's easier for a lawyer to see a case as another lawyer would than to see it as a juror might. Kich is there to remind a lawyer of that. "We often say that we are the eyes and ears of the jurors," he says. "Often, attorneys have been steeped in the case facts, the details of the events and the evidence that must be organized and presented at trial. We can help by allowing them to take a step back, and get the perspective of the juror who is entirely new to the case, and to help the lawyer to teach the case to the jurors." For some attorneys, the case seems simple since they know the complexities of the laws and legal positions that are being argued, Kich explains. But the jurors don't.

"All of us tend to have relatively simplistic and pragmatic rules about what is right and wrong and how people should resolve problems," Kich says. "And we use our personal experiences to make future decisions." At a trial, however, jurors need to be able to understand and follow the law as it is, or as the judge gives it to them. They can only use the evidence as it is presented. "They cannot search the news or the Internet," Kich explains. "They can't ask Aunt Martha or Father Murphy to give them guidance. In fact, they can't talk about the case to anyone, until the judge tells them to go to the jury room and deliberate. All of these factors are part of what we, as trial consultants, keep in mind and use as ways to assess the attorneys' presentations."

Lawyers pay a lot for trial consulting and expect to get their money's worth.

Perks

Trial consultants have the satisfaction of being an important part of the legal system. You'll feel good about helping a cause or a person you believe in. Everybody likes to share in the thrill of victory, and the pay can be terrific. Consultants, like lawyers, are paid by the hour.

Get a Jump on the Job

Between Court TV and all the legal dramas on TV, you can get a fairly good idea of how trials work. You can also read about important trials in newspapers, magazines, or online, or you can visit a courtroom and watch a civil or criminal trial in person.

VICTIM ADVOCATE

OVERVIEW

No so very long ago, the victim of a crime faced a rocky road to justice in this country's judicial system, and was often victimized twice: once during the crime, and a second time during trial. But with new victims' rights laws, plus the recognition that victims have as many rights as the criminals who have harmed them, things began to change. Local towns and villages, recognizing the special situation of the victim, began hiring specialists to work with victims to help them navigate the legal system. Eventually, a few states—notably Alaska and Connecticut—also began making striking changes in the field of victim rights.

Part legal expert and part counselor, the victim advocate does just what the title implies: advocates for and supports the victim. This might include accompanying a victim to the hospital, doctor's office, police department, judicial proceedings, or counselor. Victim advocates on a college campus might also contact the victim's instructors, explaining that the student has experienced a crisis and asking instructors to help accommodate the student by allowing late assignments, overlooking missed classes and scheduling makeup exams. State victim rights advocates take on a larger role, also working with state legislatures to write legislation reinforcing victims' rights.

Many victim advocates have a background in psychology, social work, or counseling, because their job requires them

to be empathetic and supportive to clients who may sometimes be defiant, angry, or difficult. But many advocates also have a background in criminal justice so as to be able to better negotiate the often-complex judicial system. As part of their job, advocates can provide appropriate referrals to individual counseling services and support groups, and for medical services for evidence collection and follow-up, STD testing, pregnancy exams, or physical injuries exams. The advocate might offer helpful reading material that may aid the victim's recovery. A victim advocate might arrange for temporary housing if the victim is living in an unsafe condition. At the same time, the advocate will probably maintain contact with the police department and state attorney's office regarding the student's case, and can be present to offer support at any legal interview with the victim, and at any legal proceeding related to the crime.

The advocate makes sure the victim knows when a trial is coming up, explains information about victim compensation, and tries to help solve the case. The victim advocate also provides support as the prosecuting attorney develops the case, trying to convince reluctant victims to testify and supporting victims who do testify during their ordeal. They also offer information to the public with questions about legal issues related to ongoing cases.

But the job doesn't stop once the criminal is convicted and shipped off to jail. Every inmate (except those serving a life sentence or on death row) eventually will get out of prison. Victim advocates help the victim prepare for the inmate's release, which in some cases can trigger a severe crisis reaction in the victim. Victim advocates can help during this time.

Pitfalls

It can be emotionally difficult to deal with victims all day, every day, and to provide support for people in very trying circumstances. The workload can be rough and the problems insurmountable.

Perks

If you're attracted to a job as victim advocate you're probably a sensitive, warm and caring person, and few jobs can provide such a feeling of accomplishment. Supporting individuals who have been

---

James Papillo, J.D., Ph.D., Connecticut state victim advocate

Jim Papillo started out in the direction of psychology, obtaining a Ph.D. from the State University of New York at Stony Brook, where he specialized in behavioral medicine and health psychology. A postdoctoral fellow at Columbia University and at the University of California at Los Angeles, he also published numerous scientific articles and book chapters in the field of psychology—before going back to school for his law degree (with honors) from the University of Connecticut Law School in 1991.

Eight years later, he was appointed by Governor John G. Rowland as Connecticut's first victim advocate—and it's a job he's dedicated himself to ever since. "There's a tremendous amount of rewards that comes from helping people who are in distress interact with the criminal justice system," he says, "which can sometimes be [a] very sterile, cold, confusing entity. The justice system hasn't always been truly friendly to victims' concerns. Defendants have many rights, but the idea of victims' rights is new."

Papillo explains that Connecticut was the first state in the country to establish an independent state agency dedicated to the idea of furthering victims' rights. As the state's victim advocate, Papillo evaluates the services to victims by state agencies, and handles their complaints. He works with other agencies concerned with the constitutional rights of victims, and can file a limited special appearance in any court proceeding to help advocate for any right guaranteed to a crime victim by the state constitution. At the same time, he's got legislative duties, responsible for recommending changes in state policies concerning victims and working with the public to help them understand the concept that a victim does have rights.

(continues)

(continued)

"The reward definitely comes from helping victims assert their rights, achieve closure, and see that justice is done," he says. His background in psychology is invaluable in helping them from an emotional point of view move forward as they take part in the criminal justice system. That doesn't mean that his job is all thank-yous and roses. "There's a reason why this agency was created," he explains. "Things weren't working for victims. It can be somewhat frustrating to deal with the criminal justice system that sometimes resists the idea of victims' rights. So the rewards are working with the victims, but on the other side—well, it involves butting heads with criminal justice professionals to make sure those rights are asserted."

Because the idea of victim rights is new, Papillo figures it will take time to make a lot of headway. "It's my job to serve as a catalyst to get the victims' rights honored and respected," he says. "It's my job to serve as a watchdog, and in that sense, Connecticut is in the forefront of victims' rights."

If the idea of working to help victims of crimes is appealing, it's a good idea to get some experience in the helping professions, Papillo believes—sociology, psychology, and so on. "You have to have compassion for people," he says, "as well as a strong understanding of the criminal justice system. You have to be able to work with people who don't understand the system, and help walk the victim through it. You'll need a great deal of compassion and people skills. It can be a demanding job, but it's also tremendously rewarding."

victims to violent crimes can be an enormously satisfying way to feel that you're making a difference.

Get a Jump on the Job

As soon as you're old enough, try volunteering for a crisis hot line, woman's shelter, or intervention center. Take every course you can in the field of criminal justice and psychology or counseling, women's issues, or law.

VOICE OF AMERICA BROADCASTER

OVERVIEW

Wouldn't it be weird to become a celebrity almost everywhere in the world except your own country?

That could be your situation if you become one of the Voice of America (VOA) broadcasters who regularly broadcast to 94 million people around the world in 53 different languages. Yet despite its huge audience, VOA is not allowed to broadcast directly to American citizens. That's because independent networks always have dominated U.S. broadcasting, and the idea of a state-run TV or radio network has never been popular here. So some of the most famous American broadcasters in history have been strangers at home.

Willis Conover, a VOA disc jockey who played jazz two hours a night for listeners in Communist Europe, was known as the most famous American most Americans never knew. When he died from lung cancer in May 1996, his obituary in the *New York Times* read: "In the long struggle between the forces of Communism and democracy, Conover, who went on the air in 1955 and who continued broadcasting until a few months ago, proved more effective than a fleet of B-29s."

Until World War II, the United States was the only world power without a government-sponsored international radio network. During World War II, the Voice of America was organized under the Office

AT A GLANCE

Salary Range

$40,000 to $115,000.

Education/Experience

You'll need a background in the history, customs, economy, and outlook of your viewers or listeners. That usually means you're a native of their country or have spent several years there. You'll need professional broadcasting skills, as well as a college degree.

Personal Attributes

You must be likeable and believable, with an international outlook. You should be able to understand cultures much different than your own.

Requirements

You must speak the language of your viewers and listeners, being familiar with their figures of speech and current slang. You must be able to write and speak English for your research and scriptwriting, and you'll need a college degree.

Outlook

Opportunities should keep expanding because Voice of America audiences should get bigger as more and more people overseas get satellite TV dishes and Internet access.

of Wartime Information. Broadcasting became a powerful wartime weapon and the VOA tried to undermine German support by broadcasting to occupied areas of Europe and North Africa. VOA began broadcasts to the Soviet Union in 1947 and during the Cold War delivered propaganda to Communist countries. Since the Cold War, however, VOA has evolved into a respected news organization. That means broadcasters will need experience or a degree in print or broadcast journalism. Or you might want to study foreign languages, history, political science, or economics.

VOA today is one of the most popular international networks. People who live in countries where governments control the news are hungry for outside viewpoints, especially from the United States. Even those who may oppose U.S. policies are interested in American fashions, music, and lifestyle, all presented on VOA programs.

The VOA charter requires that broadcasts be accurate and objective, represent many parts of American society, and present the official policies of the United States. These are difficult goals to reach because it's hard to agree on what is "accurate" and "objective." In this

Setareh Sieg, nightly news anchor

The best compliment that Setareh Sieg ever received for *News and Views*, her daily VOA TV show beamed to Iran, came from an Iranian guest. He compared her show to *The Fugitive*, a popular 1960s TV show in which the star was wrongfully convicted of his wife's murder and kept searching for a one-armed man he believed to be the killer. So what's the connection between a 40-year-old TV thriller and *News and Views*, a show featuring reporting from inside Iran, world news roundups, and news analysis?

Sieg's guest mentioned that in the 1960s, when *The Fugitive* was on TV, "the streets in Iran emptied out because everyone was watching the show," says Sieg, who works in Washington, D.C. "He says that's what's happening now whenever our show comes on. The streets are empty."

Sieg gets many e-mails from fans, so she knows how popular her show is becoming. "The [Iranian] media is government controlled, so there is a hunger for accurate news," she explained. "This is a fantastic opportunity for us to tell Iranians what's happening in the world and how the world sees them."

Since the overthrow of the Shah in 1979, Iran has been ruled by religious leaders who restrict the press and consider the United States an enemy. Sieg tells Iranians about nations that recently have had their first democratic elections. On May 3, 2005, the anniversary of World Press Freedom Day, she interviewed an activist whose husband had spent more than 5,000 days in Iran's prisons since 1981. He kept writing newspaper articles the government did not like.

"Our mission at VOA is, we have to give our audience an opportunity to receive information that's relevant to them," Sieg says. "That's why we talk to people in similar cultural situations. Since [Iranians] feel the regime is quite intrusive, we've covered the elections in Iraq, Afghanistan, and Ukraine. We cover segments of Iranian life—women in society, business, and various other things. We tell people about the U.S. as a society, a culture, and a democracy." Iranians are also interested in cinema, music, space research, and everything that happens in the United States, she noted. "Satellite dishes are illegal in Iran, but everybody watches the show," she says. "It comes on the Internet, too. You cannot control the flow of information at this point."

Today, in addition to her broadcasting, she teaches a course in culture and politics of 20th-century France at Georgetown University. On her show, she often conducts phone interviews with Iranians who criticize their government. While those interviews may get them in some trouble, Sieg says, it's harder for the government to punish them once they've gotten worldwide country, where Americans pride themselves on fair and honest reporting, major news networks often are accused of slanting the news and other programs to favor one political viewpoint.

VOA has several sister radio and TV networks, which all are operated by the Broadcasting Board of Governors. Radio Sawa is an around-the-clock, Arabic-language service aimed at listeners under 30. Alhurra, which means "the free one," is an Arabic-language TV service that broadcasts news, talk shows, documentaries, and entertainment to the Middle East. Radio Farda, which means "Radio Tomorrow" in Persian, combines news with popular Iranian and Western music. Radio and TV Marti broadcasts Spanish-language news

exposure. "Once their voice is out there, there's not much the government can do about them," she explained. "I've had many interviews with political prisoners when they're out on furlough. Under law, they have to send them home for two days. When they're out, they talk. They are given a hard time but at the same time, it's protection for them."

Sieg has special sympathy for political prisoners because her father, Mohamad Derakhshesh, was jailed under both the Shah and Ayatollah Khomeini, who deposed the Shah. Her father served in parliament during the 1950s and served in the Shah's cabinet during the 1960s. "Under the Shah, he was jailed several times," Sieg says. "He was trying to help create a more civil and democratic society. He was asked to cooperate with the regime, which he didn't. He didn't cooperate with the Khomeini regime, either, and was put in jail."

Sieg was born in Tehran, Iran, and left for Paris when she was 15 years old. After graduating from high school in Paris, she earned a law degree from the University of Paris and a doctorate from the Sorbonne. During graduate school, she came to the United States on vacation and was joined by her father, who had recently gotten out of prison. "They gave him political asylum, then he had a heart attack and had to stay," Sieg says. She knew someone at VOA who suggested that she apply for part-time work. "They told me to come in and they didn't let me go," she says, laughing. "And I got hooked because I was always interested in what they were doing. When my father was jailed under Khomeini, I first heard about it on VOA. I started in radio and I moved to television in 1993."

Besides reading the news and conducting interviews, Sieg has been helping to produce *News and Views* since it started in 2003. The show was so popular that it was soon expanded from 30 minutes to an hour. "They gave us 10 days and told us to put together a TV show," she says. "They brought in consultants to help us and they were fabulous. We worked 30 days nonstop; the show's been fun ever since."

Sieg broadcasts at noon in Washington, which is 8:30 p.m. in Iran. At the end of one show, she almost immediately starts preparing for the next show. "It took a lot of time to put together the half-hour show, and it takes twice as long now," she says. Sieg also has other VOA duties. For the first 2004 presidential debate between President George W. Bush and challenger John Kerry, she served as a studio analyst, discussing what the debate meant for the rest of the world. "I never thought I'd wind up so far from Iran," she says.

and entertainment to Cuba. Radio Free Europe/Radio Liberty broadcasts to the former Soviet bloc and Afghanistan. Radio Free Asia broadcasts in 10 languages to China, Tibet, Burma, Vietnam, Laos, Cambodia, and North Korea.

VOA is even getting a U.S. audience now because its programs can be picked up on shortwave radios and over the Internet. So who knows? By the time you become a successful VOA broadcaster, you may be just as famous at home as abroad.

Pitfalls

Because VOA has a 24-hour, seven-days-a-week schedule, your workload may be heavy. You may work odd hours because of worldwide time zones. When it's listening time for your audience, it might be the middle of the night for you.

Perks

As a VOA broadcaster, you'll be an important voice in some of the world's hot spots.

You may become a celebrity to your listeners. The job's very satisfying for those broadcasting back to their native countries, especially if those countries have government-controlled news.

Get a Jump on the Job

Broadcasting experience is helpful. If your school has a radio station, try for a production or broadcast position. For instance, you might try out as a disc jockey. Or you might seek an internship or summer job with a local TV or radio station. If you were born overseas and want to broadcast back to your native land, learn to speak and write English as a native, and learn all you can about world affairs.

APPENDIX A: ASSOCIATIONS, ORGANIZATIONS, AND WEB SITES

GENERAL

U.S. Merit Systems Protection Board
1615 M Street, NW
Washington, DC 20419
(800) 209-8960
http://www.mspb.gov

For current research on employment practices in the federal government, see the reports and newsletters of the U.S. Merit Systems Protection Board.

AEROSPACE ENGINEER

American Institute of Aeronautics and Astronautics
1801 Alexander Bell Drive
Suite 500
Reston, VA 20191-4344
(800) 639-AIAA
custserv@aiaa.org
http://www.aiaa.org

The AIAA is a professional society of approximately 31,000 members, making it the largest group of aerospace engineers and scientists in the world. The AIAA's technical interests cover 66 specialties, ranging from aerodynamic deceleration to underwater propulsion. The AIAA provides technical communication to all members of the aerospace community and hopes to stimulate the personal development of individual engineers and scientists. The AIAA holds a full schedule of national and local meetings each year. The AIAA publishes a monthly magazine,

Aerospace America, as well as technical journals and the AIAA Student Journal. The institute recognizes outstanding professional achievements through its program of honors and awards.

AIR TRAFFIC CONTROLLER

Airline Dispatchers Federation
700 13th Street, Suite 950
Washington, DC 20005
(800) OPN-CNTL
http://www.dispatcher.org

The only national organization representing the professional interests of the dispatch profession, working for licensed aircraft dispatchers and operational control professionals from 103 aerospace companies including every major U.S. airline. It has been estimated that about 92 percent of airline passengers traveling each day in the United States do so under the eye of ADF members.

AviationNow: Careers
http://www.aviationnow.com/content/careercenter/global/car2001f.htm

A Web site with a selection of the latest news and analysis from the industry's leading publications, as well as complementary content created by AviationNow.com's team of editors. The careers section includes information about jobs, news on upcoming conferences and workshops, with job listings and bulletin boards.

FAA Air Traffic Control Division
http://www.ama500.jccbi.gov

A Web site discussing "how to become an air traffic controller."

Federal Aviation Administration
800 Independence Avenue, SW
Washington, DC 20591
http://www.faa.gov

This primary Web site of the FAA, the governmental agency with the responsibility for providing a safe, secure, and efficient global aerospace system that contributes to national security and the promotion of US aerospace safety. The FAA is the leading authority in the international aerospace community.

National Air Traffic Controllers Association
1325 Massachusetts Avenue, NW
Washington, DC 20005
(202) 223-2900
http://www.natca.org/about/career.msp

This Web page discusses: "So you want to be an air traffic controller?"

National Association of Air Traffic Specialists
11303 Amherst Avenue, Suite 4
Wheaton, MD 20902
(301) 933-6228
http://www.naats.org

This Web site offers lots of information for air traffic controllers.

ATF SPECIAL AGENT

Federal Law Enforcement Officers Association
PO Box 326
Lewisberry, PA 17339

(717) 938-2300
services@fleoa.org
http://www.fleoa.org

FLEOA is the largest nonpartisan professional organization representing only federal law enforcement officers. It represents more than 20,000 federal agents from more than 50 different agencies. The association was founded in 1977 mainly to provide legal help to federal officers. FLEOA also tries to encourage legislation that benefits federal agents. The association has helped to increase death benefits, provide scholarships for children of officers killed in the line of duty, helped raise pay scales and encouraged passage of a bill that makes federal officers eligible for a Congressional Medal of Honor. The association's officers are active duty federal agents who are required to conduct association business while they are off duty or on leave.

BANK EXAMINER

Association of Certified Fraud Examiners
716 West Avenue
Austin, TX 78701
(800) 245-3321
info@acfe.com
http://www.acfe.com

The ACFE is the world's biggest provider of antifraud training and education. It has about 33,000 members in 25 countries, sponsors more than 100 chapters and provides antifraud educational materials to more than 100 universities. Certified fraud examiners on six continents have investigated more than a million suspected cases of civil and criminal fraud. A certified fraud examiner is a specialist in the prevention and detection of fraud. The association gives a CFE exam, which is self-administered and online. It covers fraudulent financial transactions, the legal elements of fraud, fraud investigation, and criminology and ethics. The ACFE puts antifraud professionals in touch with each other through seminars, conferences, online forums, chapter events, and e-newsletters.

BORDER PATROL SEARCH AND RESCUE AGENT

National Association of Emergency Medical Technicians
PO Box 1400
Clinton, MS 39060-1400
(800) 34-NAEMT
info@naemt.org
http://naemt.org

NAEMT's mission is to represent and serve emergency medical services personnel through advocacy, educational programs, and research. NAEMT annually gives research grants worth as much as $1,500 each. The association has a code of ethics, which says, in part, that the EMT's responsibility is "to conserve life, to alleviate suffering, to promote health, to do no harm, and to encourage the quality and equal availability of emergency medical care." NAEMT also offers educational programs in advanced life support, pre-hospital trauma life support, and pre-hospital pediatric care. More than 30,000 people around the world participate annually in these programs. The association holds an awards banquet each year to recognize excellence in various areas of emergency medical services.

CENSUS BUREAU STATISTICIAN

American Statistical Association
1429 Duke Street
Alexandria, VA 22314
http://www.amstat.org

A nonprofit organization that provides information about careers in statistics.

American Mathematical Society
201 Charles Street
Providence, RI 02940
http://www.ams.org

A nonprofit organization that provides information on doctoral-level careers and training in mathematics, a field closely related to statistics.

CITY PLANNER

American Planning Association
122 South Michigan Avenue, Suite 1600
Chicago, IL 60603
(312) 431-9100
customerservice@planning.org
http://www.planning.org

The APA includes 30,000 practicing planners, citizens, and elected officials interested in community planning. APA is a nonprofit public interest and research organization committed to urban, suburban, regional, and rural planning. APA also has a professional institute, the American Institute of Certified Planners. This institute promotes innovations in planning and oversees certification of professional planners. AICP also deals with ethics, professional development, and education. About 2,700 APA members are students who receive reduced membership rates. Students are active in local APA chapters, participate in APA governance through the Student Representatives Council, and meet and exchange ideas on campus through planning student organizations.

CONGRESSIONAL PRESS SECRETARY

National Association of Government Communicators
10366 Democracy Lane, Suite B
Fairfax, VA 22030
(703) 691-0377
info@nagc.com
http://www.nagc.com

The National Association of Government Communicators (NAGC) is a national nonprofit professional network of federal, state, and local government employees who disseminate information within and outside government. Its members are editors, writers, graphic artists, video professionals, broadcasters, photographers, information specialists, and agency spokespersons. The NAGC is the only organization for, by, and about government communicators and communications. Its members are guided by a professional code of ethics that demands complete and timely communication between government and the people it serves.

National Press Club
529 14th Street, NW, 13th Floor
Washington, DC 20045
(202) 662-7500
http://www.press.org

The National Press Club has been a part of Washington life for more than 90 years. Its members have included 17 consecutive presidents of the United States, from Theodore Roosevelt to Bill Clinton. To many of the men and women who belong to the National Press Club today, it is primarily one of the world's foremost news forums, the sanctum sanctorum of American journalists.

Society of Professional Journalists
Eugene S. Pulliam
National Journalism Center
3909 North Meridian Street
Indianapolis, IN 46208
(317) 927-8000
http://www.spj.org/students.asp

The Society of Professional Journalists works to improve and protect journalism. The organization is the nation's most broad-based journalism organization, dedicated to encouraging the free practice of journalism and stimulating high standards of ethical behavior. Founded in 1909 as Sigma Delta Chi, the SPJ promotes the free flow of information vital to a well-informed citizenry; works to inspire and educate the next generation of journalists; and protects First Amendment guarantees of freedom of speech and press.

CORONER

The International Association of Coroners and Medical Examiners (IACME)
PO Box 44834
Columbus, OH 43204-0834
(614) 276-8384

This organization of elected lay and physician coroners also includes a small number of physician medical examiners.

The International Homicide
Investigators Association (IHIA)
http://www.ihia.org/

This organization is the largest and fastest growing organization of homicide and death investigation professionals in the world and has representation from the United States and 16 other nations.

The National Association
of Medical Examiners (NAME)
430 Pryor Street SW
Atlanta, GA 30312
(404) 730-4781
http://www.thename.org/

This organization includes mainly physician medical examiners and other members of their death investigation teams. Physician pathologists and some physician coroners are also members. The NAME Web site below includes a page, "So You Want To Be A Medical Detective?" that explains the differences between a coroner and a medical examiner and other experts who work on a death investigation: http://www. thename.org/medical_detective.htm

COURT INTERPRETER

National Association of Judiciary
Interpreters and Translators
603 Stewart Street, Suite 610
Seattle, WA 98101
(206) 267-2300
headquarters@nagit.org
http://www.najit.org

Ever since NAJIT was formed in 1978, it has aimed to promote high-quality interpreting and translating in the judiciary system for those who aren't fluent in the language of the court.

Members are bound by a code of ethics and professional responsibilities. NAJIT has more than 900 members, mostly from the United States but also from Latin America, Europe, Asia, and Australia. Members include interpreters, translators, educators, researchers, students, and administrators. NAJIT holds periodic meetings and publishes a quarterly newsletter and other publications. The association also offers workshops and seminars, and sends representatives to university programs and institutes for court interpreters to learn new skills and share experiences.

COURT REPORTER

National Court Reporters Association
8224 Old Courthouse Road
Vienna, VA 22182
(800) 272-6272
msic@ncrahg.org
http://www.ncraonline.org

The NCRA is committed to advancing the profession of court reporting through ethical standards, testing and certification, educational programs, contacts with lawmakers, research, and analysis. NCRA members are offered certification exams in May and November. The association promotes a code of professional ethics. The NCRA also offers information about online training for court reporters. It has a Virtual Mentors program that allows high school or college students to get in touch with court reporters. Through the National Court Reporters Foundation, the NCRA uses charitable support to promote research, technology, and education in court reporting. The NCRA works on behalf of an international membership to influence legislation that will affect court reporters.

DISASTER ASSISTANCE EMPLOYEE

International Association of Emergency Managers
201 Park Washington Court
Falls Court, VA 22046-4527
(703) 538-1795
info@iaem.com
http://www.iaem.com

IAEM membership is for professionals in the field of emergency management. It provides members with up-to-date information to help them fulfill their roles. The IAEM is aimed at emergency managers interested in protecting lives and property, concerned with national security, and having an emergency management or civil defense job in the government, military, private industry, or a volunteer organization. The association has created a certified emergency manager program to raise and maintain professional standards. The IAEM has a scholarship program for college students studying emergency management. It also holds an annual conference.

GSA ASSOCIATE

National Contract Management Association
8260 Greensboro Drive, Suite 200
McLean, VA 22102
(800) 344-8096
http://www.ncmahq.org

The NCMA was formed in 1959 to promote the growth and educational advancement of its members. The association aims to lead and represent the contract management profession. It believes that businesses will grow through improved buyer and seller relationships based on common values, practices, and professional standards. The NCMA offers a code of ethics and an accredited certification program. Through its international chapters, publications, programs, and activities, it provides the tools and resources to help members grow in their jobs. The NCMA holds an annual conference that features an educational program on federal, state, and local management and procurement. Speakers include top government officials and executives from private industry.

INTERNATIONAL ELECTION OBSERVER

Association of Election Officials in Bosnia-Herzegovina
Terezija 16
71000 Sarajevo
Bosnia and Herzogovina
(033) 250-810
IrenaH@aeobih.com.ba
http://www.aeobih.com.ba

This association was formed to develop a democratic process in Bosnia-Herzegovina, which was formerly part of Yugoslavia. Association members work with the Organization for Security and Cooperation in Europe to conduct free elections, which were first held in Bosnia-Herzegovina in 2000. The association has more than 750 regular and associate members who live in this area, as well as election officials from around the world. Most members hold law degrees and attend courses and seminars to study Western standards for elections. The

association helps train officials to serve on municipal election commissions and work at polling stations. It also holds voter education meetings and initially registered more than 10,000 voters.

IRS AGENT

**American Institute of
Certified Public Accountants**
1211 Avenue of Americas
New York, NY 10036-8775
(888) 777-7077
http://www.aicpa.org

The AICPA is the national professional organization for all certified public accountants. Its mission is to provide members with the resources, information, and leadership that enables them to give valuable services to the public, employers, and clients. It serves as the national representative of CPAs before governments, regulatory bodies, or other organizations in protecting and promoting members' interests. It seeks the highest possible level of uniform certification and licensing standards. It promotes public awareness of the professionalism of CPAs. It establishes and enforces professional standards. It encourages people to become CPAs and provides information to students about career paths, hiring trends, and internship opportunities.

LOBBYIST

Association of Junior Lobbyists
1130 Connecticut Avenue, Suite 650
Washington, DC 20036
(202) 822-3815
info@juniorlobbyists.com
http://www.juniorlobbyists.com

The AJL is dedicated to the advancement of those who are new to lobbying. The association promotes the idea that effective government depends on a high level of participation by professional lobbyists. The AJL provides educational and employment opportunities, sponsors programs and seminars on public policy issues, encourages advancement of ethical lobbying practices, distributes information on hot topics, represents the interest of lobbying professionals, and provides speakers to explain and discuss the lobbying process. Other benefits include a monthly newsletter, a monthly congressional calendar, and such resources as periodicals, links to useful Web sites, and lobbying registration information. The AJL also holds a yearly meeting that features a well-known guest speaker.

MAYOR

U.S. Conference of Mayors
1620 Eye Street, NW
Washington, DC 20006
(202) 293-7330
info@usmayors.org
http://www.usmayors.org

A national nonprofit association for mayors in cities and towns throughout the United States.

MILITARY DENTIST

American Dental Association
211 East Chicago Avenue
Chicago, IL 60611-2678
(312) 440-2500
http://www.ada.org

The ADA is the professional association of dentists and is committed to the public's oral health and the ethics, science, and professional advancement of dentistry. It began in 1859 when 26 dentists met in Niagara Falls, New York, to form a professional society. ADA leads initiatives in advocacy, education, research, and the development of professional standards. The association works for effective legislative and regulatory advocacy on behalf of the public and profession to facilitate access to care, encourage interstate mobility for qualified dentists and dental hygienists and preserve the integrity of the doctor-patient relationship. ADA also tries to ensure that decision makers who affect the practice of dentistry are required to base their decisions on credible scientific data.

MILITARY LAWYER

American Bar Association
740 15th Street, NW
Washington, DC 20005-1019
(202) 662-1000
askaba@abanet.org
http://abanet.org

The ABA is the largest voluntary professional association in the world. With more than 400,000 members, the ABA provides law school accreditation, continuing legal education, information about the law, programs to assist lawyers and judges in their work, and initiatives to improve the legal system for the public. The ABA's mission is to be the national representative of the legal profession, serving the public and the profession by promoting justice, professional excellence and respect for the law. It publishes the ABA Journal, a news and business magazine about the law and its practice, as well as Your

Law, a newsletter for clients. The ABA also sponsors awards and contests that recognize outstanding efforts to foster public understanding of the law by individuals and institutions in education, law, media, and the arts.

PARKS DIRECTOR

National Recreation and Parks Association
22377 Belmont Ridge Road
Ashburn, VA 20148
(703) 858-0784
info@nrpa.org
http://www.nrpa.org

For more than 100 years, NRPA has advocated making parks, open space, and recreational opportunities available to all Americans. The association encourages the use of millions of acres of open space for hiking and biking trails, community parks, and local recreation centers. NRPA's mission is, "to advance parks, recreation and environmental conservation efforts that enhance the quality of life for all people." NRPA has a 70-member board of trustees made up of citizens and professionals who represent diverse areas within the parks and recreation industry. NRPA's annual awards recognize outstanding programs and people whose work in parks and recreation helps to improve Americans' quality of life. The awards are presented at the NRPA's annual congress and exposition.

POLITICAL CONSULTANT

American Association of Political Consultants
600 Pennsylvania Avenue, SE, Suite 330
Washington, DC 20003

(202) 544-9815
info@theaapc.org
http://www.theaapc.org

The AAPC, founded in 1969, is a bipartisan organization of political professionals. It has more than 1,100 members. They include political consultants, media consultants, pollsters, campaign managers, corporate public affairs officers, professors, fund-raisers, lobbyists, congressional staffers, and vendors. The AAPC was formed partly to highlight and promote political consulting as a career. The AAPC is open to everyone associated with politics from the local level to the White House. The organization maintains a code of professional ethics for members. Those who apply for membership are required to sign the code and live up to its standards. The AAPC also gives out annual Pollie Awards, which recognize those who've distinguished themselves during recent campaigns.

POLYGRAPH EXAMINER

American Polygraph Association
PO Box 8037
Chattanooga, TN 37414-0037
(800) APA-8037
president@polygraph.org
http://www.polygraph.org

Established in 1966, the APA has more than 2,500 members. The APA says it is dedicated to providing a valid and reliable means to verify the truth and establish standards of moral, ethical, and professional conduct in the polygraph field. The APA lists these goals: serving the cause of truth with integrity, objectivity, and fairness to all; encouraging and supporting research, training, and education to benefit members; establishing and enforcing standards for admission and continued membership to the APA; and governing the conduct of members by requiring they obey a code of ethics and a set of standards and principles of practice. The APA gives annual awards for service to members, advancement of APA ideas and goals, and for research, teaching, and writing.

PRESIDENTIAL SPEECHWRITER

Judson Welliver Society
Insurance Information Institute
110 William Street
New York, NY 10038
(212) 346-5500
http://iiidev.iii.org

The Judson Welliver Society includes about 40 former presidential speechwriters, going back half a century. The society was formed by William Safire, a former speechwriter for Richard Nixon and a long-time political journalist. The secretary, Gordon Stewart, wrote speeches for Jimmy Carter. Society members meet periodically and swap stories about speeches they wrote and the presidents and characters in the administrations they served. Party loyalties usually are checked at the door, though they sometimes flare up. The society has heard notable speakers, including Michael Gerson, chief speechwriter for President George W. Bush. The society is named for the man believed to be the first full-time presidential speechwriter. Welliver worked for Warren Harding in the 1920s.

PROBATION OFFICER

**American Probation
and Parole Association**
PO Box 11910
Lexington, KY 40578
http://www.appa-net.org

*The American Probation and Parole
Association is an international
association composed of individuals from
the United States and Canada actively
involved with probation, parole, and
community-based corrections, in both
adult and juvenile sectors. All levels
of government including local, state/
provincial, legislative, executive, judicial,
and federal agencies are counted among
its constituents. By taking the initiative,
the APPA has grown to become the
voice for thousands of probation and
parole practitioners including line
staff, supervisors, and administrators.
Educators, volunteers, and concerned
citizens with an interest in criminal
and juvenile justice are also among
the APPA's members. The APPA will
continue to effectively provide services
to its constituents. The association
represents a strong, unified voice for the
field of community corrections.*

American Correctional Association
4380 Forbes Boulevard
Lanham, MD 20706
http://www.aca.org

*The oldest and largest international
correctional association in the world.
ACA serves all disciplines within the
corrections profession and is dedicated
to excellence in every aspect of the
field, from professional development
and certification to standards and
accreditation, from networking and
consulting to research and publications,
and from conferences and exhibits to
technology and testing*

STAFF ASSISTANT TO THE FIRST LADY

**International Association
of Protocol Consultants**
Post Office Box 6150
McLean, VA 22106
(703) 759-4272
http://www.iapcmembers.org/

*The International Association of
Protocol Consultants is an executive
education and certification nonprofit
membership organization that is
committed to increasing higher learning
opportunities for everyone interested
in corporate/international protocol,
diplomatic/government protocol, business
etiquette, and civility. Members include
experienced producers and directors of
events involving world leaders, heads of
state, foreign dignitaries, and corporate
executives. Some have worked directly
with U.S. presidents, White House
officials, and State Department officials.*

**National Active and Retired
Federal Employees Association**
606 North Washington Street
Alexandria, VA 22314
(703) 838-7760
http://www.narfe.org/

*NARFE's mission is to protect and
improve the retirement benefits of federal
retirees, employees, and their families.*

STATE EDUCATION COMMISSIONER

**National Association of
State Boards of Education**
277 South Washington Street
Suite 100
Alexandria, VA 22314
(703) 684-4000

boards@nasbe.org

http://www.nasbe.org

The NASBE is a national organization that speaks for the nation's State Boards of Education. A nonprofit organization founded in 1958, the association works to strengthen state leadership in educational policy making, promote excellence in the education of all students, advocate equality of access to educational opportunity, and assure continued citizen support for public education. NASBE's membership is kept abreast of the latest developments in public policy through a weekly federal update, monthly legislative and legal briefs, and monthly policy updates. NASBE also sponsors study groups that bring together education experts, state education policy makers, and national education officials to produce in-depth reports on timely education topics.

TEST PILOT

Society of Experimental Test Pilots
PO Box 986
Lancaster, CA 93584-0986
setpe@setp.org
http://setp.org

The SETP seeks to be the recognized world leader in promoting safety, communication, and education in the design and flight test of aerospace vehicles and their related systems. The society also seeks to maintain a professional international society for all test pilots and aerospace corporations. It strives to strengthen professional relationships through the sharing of ideas and experiences. It also strives to prevent accidents and deaths by improving safety. SETP also aims to provide a forum within the aerospace

industry to emphasize test pilots' integrity, ethical behavior, professional reputation, experience, expertise, and the need for fair dealing between pilots and employers. SETP holds an annual symposium in which members may present papers about important issues.

TRIAL CONSULTANT

American Society of Trial Consultants
1941 Greenspring Drive
Timonium, MD 21093
(410) 560-7949
ASTCOffice@aol.com
http://www.astcweb.org

ASTC members come from the fields of communication, psychology, sociology, linguistics, political science, and law. As trial consultants working with attorneys, and as researchers and educators in academic settings, ASTC members share an interest in understanding the workings of the trial process, the decision making of juries and judges, and all methods of dispute resolution. The ASTC's national membership includes long-established firms, pioneers in trial consulting and research since the 1970s, and people who've recently come into the field. Membership includes access to a library of trial consulting work, a subscription to a quarterly online newsletter, and an invitation to the national annual conference.

VICTIM ADVOCATE

The National Organization for Victim Assistance
510 King Street, Suite 424
Alexandria, VA 22314
(703) 535-NOVA
http://www.trynova.org

The National Organization for Victim Assistance (NOVA) is a private nonprofit organization of victim and witness assistance programs and practitioners, criminal justice agencies and professionals, mental health professionals, researchers, former victims and survivors, and others committed to the recognition and implementation of victim rights and services.

National Center for Victims of Crime
2000 M Street NW, Suite 480
Washington, DC 20036
(202) 467-8700
http://www.ncvc.org/ncvc/Main.aspx

The nation's leading resource and advocacy organization for crime victims that since 1985 has worked with more than 10,000 grassroots organizations and criminal justice agencies serving millions of crime victims.

VOICE OF AMERICA BROADCASTER

White House Correspondents Association
1920 N Street, NW, Suite 300
Washington, DC 20036
(202) 452-20036
http://www.whca.net

The WHCA, founded in 1914, represents the White House press corps in dealing with the administration on coverage-related issues. A nine-member board of directors, elected by correspondents, addresses access to the president, costs for press travel when accompanying the president, and arrangements for coverage opportunities and work space. The WHCA offers a four-year scholarship, worth $6,000 a year, to recognize the achievement and potential of a high school senior. The award is presented at the annual WHCA dinner, along with three major journalism awards that include cash prizes. The dinner is usually attended by the president and vice president. In 1924, Calvin Coolidge became the first president to attend and George W. Bush became the 13th.

APPENDIX B:
ONLINE CAREER RESOURCES

This volume offers a look inside a wide-range of unusual and unique careers that might appeal to someone interested in working in government. Although this book highlights general information about each job, it can really only give you a glimpse into these careers. These entries are intended to whet your appetite and provide you with some career options you maybe never knew existed.

Before jumping into any career, you'll want to do more research to make sure that it's really something you want to pursue for the rest of your life. You'll want to learn as much as you can about the careers in which you're interested; that way, as you continue to do research and talk to people in those particular fields, you can ask informed and intelligent questions that will help you make your decisions. You might want to research the education options for learning the skills you'll need to be successful, along with scholarships, work-study programs, and other opportunities to help you finance that education. If you search long enough, you can find just about anything using the Internet, including additional information about the jobs featured in this book.

✳ **A word about Internet safety:** The Internet is also a wonderful resource for networking. Many job and career sites have forums where students can interact with other people interested in and working in that field. Some sites even offer online chats where people can communicate with each other in real time. They provide students and jobseekers opportunities to make connections and maybe even begin to lay the groundwork for future employment.

But as you use these forums and chats, remember that anyone could be on the other side of that computer screen, telling you exactly what you want to hear. It's easy to get wrapped up in the excitement of the moment when you're on a forum or in a chat, interacting with people who share your career interests and aspirations. Be cautious about what kind of personal information you make available on the forums and in the chats; never give out your full name, address, or phone number. And above all, never agree to meet with someone you've met online.

SEARCH ENGINES

There are many different search engines that will help you to find out more about these jobs. While you probably already have a favorite search engine, you might want to take some time to check out some of the others we'll show you here. Some have features that might help you find information not located with the others. Several engines will offer suggestions for ways to narrow your results, or related phrases you might want to search along with your search results. This is handy if you're having trouble locating exactly what you want.

Another good thing to do is to learn how to use the advanced search features of your favorite search engines. Knowing that might help you to zero in on exactly the information for which you are searching without wasting time looking through pages of irrelevant hits.

As you use the Internet to search information on the perfect career, keep in mind that like anything you find on the Internet, you need to consider the source from which the information comes.

Some of the most popular Internet search engines are:

AllSearchEngines.com
http://www.allsearchengines.com

This search engine index has links to the major search engines along with search engines grouped by topic. The site includes a page with more than 75 career and job search engines at http://www. allsearchengines.com/careerjobs.html.

AlltheWeb
http://www.alltheweb.com

AltaVista
http://www.altavista.com

Ask.com
http://www.ask.com

Dogpile
http://www.dogpile.com

Excite
http://www.excite.com

Google
http://www.google.com

HotBot
http://www.hotbot.com

LookSmart
http://www.looksmart.com

Lycos
http://www.lycos.com

Mamma.com
http://www.mamma.com

MSN Network
http://www.msn.com

My Way
http://www.goto.com

Teoma
http://www.directhit.com

Vivisimo
http://www.vivisimo.com

Yahoo!
http://www.yahoo.com

HELPFUL WEB SITES

The Internet has a wealth of information on careers—everything from the mundane to the outrageous. There are thousands of sites devoted to helping you find the perfect job for you and your interests, skills, and talents. The sites listed here are some of the most helpful ones that the authors discovered while researching the jobs in this volume. The sites are listed in alphabetical order, and are offered for your information. Their inclusion does not imply endorsement by the authors.

All Experts
http://www.allexperts.com

"The oldest and largest free Q&A service on the Internet," AllExperts.com has thousands of volunteer experts to answer your questions. You can also read replies to questions asked by other people. Each expert has an online profile to help you

pick someone who might be best suited to answer your question. Very easy to use, it's a great resource for finding experts who can help to answer your questions.

America's Career InfoNet
http://www.acinet.org

A wealth of information! You can get a feel for the general job market; check out wages and trends in a particular state for different jobs; learn more about the knowledge, skills, abilities, and tasks for specific careers; and learn about required certifications and how to get them. You can search over 5,000 scholarship and other financial opportunities to help you further your education. A huge career resources library has links to nearly 6,500 online resources. And for fun, you can take a break and watch one of nearly 450 videos featuring real people at work.

Backdoor Jobs: Short-Term Job Adventures, Summer Jobs, Volunteer Vacations, Work Abroad, and More
http://www.backdoorjobs.com

This is the Web site of the popular book by the same name, now in its third edition. While not as extensive as the book, the site still offers a wealth of information for people looking for short-term opportunities: internships, seasonal jobs, volunteer vacations, and work abroad situations. Job opportunities are classified into several categories: Adventure Jobs; Camps, Ranches & Resort Jobs; Ski Resort Jobs; Jobs in the Great Outdoors; Nature Lover Jobs; Sustainable Living and Farming Work; Artistic & Learning Adventures; Heart Work; and Opportunities Abroad.

Boston Works—Job Explainer
http://bostonworks.boston.com/globe/job_explainer/archive.html

For nearly 18 months, the Boston Globe ran a weekly series profiling a wide range of careers. Some of the jobs were more traditional, but with a twist, like the veterinarian who makes house calls. Others were very unique and unusual, like the profile of a superior of a society of monks. The profiles discuss an "average" day, challenges of the job, required training, salary, and more. Each profile gives an up-close, personal look at that particular career. In addition, the Boston Works Web site (http://bostonworks.boston.com/) has a lot of good, general employment-related information.

Career Planning at About.com
http://careerplanning.about.com

Like most of the other About.com topics, the career planning area offers a wealth of information and links to other information on the Web. Among the excellent essentials are career planning A to Z, a career planning glossary, information on career choices, and a free career planning class. There are many great articles and other excellent resources.

Career Voyages
http://www.careervoyages.gov

"The ultimate road trip to career success," sponsored by the U.S. Department of Labor and the U.S. Department of Education. This site features sections for students, parents, career changers, and career advisors with information and resources aimed to that

specific group. The FAQ offers great information about getting started, the high-growth industries, how to find your perfect job, how to make sure you're qualified for the job you want, tips for paying for the training and education you need, and more. Also interesting are the Hot Careers and the Emerging Fields sections.

Dream Jobs
http://www.salary.com/careers/ layouthtmls/crel_display_Cat10.html

The staff at Salary.com takes a look at some wild, wacky, outrageous, and totally cool ways to earn a living. The jobs they highlight include pro skateboarder, computer game guru, nose, diplomat, and much more. The profiles don't offer links or resources for more information, but they are informative and fun to read.

Find It! in DOL
http://www.dol.gov/dol/findit.htm

A handy source for finding information at the extensive U.S. Department of Labor Web site. You can search by broad topic category, or by audience, which includes a section for students.

Fine Living: *Radical Sabbatical*
http://www.fineliving.com/fine/episode_ archive/0,1663,FINE_1413_14,00. html#Series873

The show Radical Sabbatical *on the Fine Living network looks at people willing to take a chance and follow their dreams and passions. The show focuses on individuals between the ages of 20 and 65 who have made the decision to leave successful, lucrative careers to start over, usually in an unconventional career.*

Free Salary Survey Reports and Cost of Living Reports
http://www.salaryexpert.com

Based on information from a number of sources, Salary Expert will tell you what kind of salary you can expect to make for a certain job in a certain geographic location. Salary Expert has information on hundreds of jobs; everything from the more traditional white- and blue-collar jobs, to some unique and out-of-the-ordinary professions. With sections covering schools, crime, community comparison, community explorer, and more, the Moving Center is a useful area for people who need to relocate for training or employment.

Fun Jobs
http://www.funjobs.com

Fun Jobs has job listings for adventure, outdoor, and fun jobs at ranches, camps, ski resorts, and more. The job postings have a lot of information about the position, requirements, benefits, and responsibilities so that you know what you are getting into ahead of time. And, you can apply online for most of the positions. The Fun Companies link will let you look up companies in an A-to-Z listing, or you can search for companies in a specific area or by keyword. The company listings offer you more detailed information about the location, types of jobs available, employment qualifications, and more.

Girls Can Do
http://www.girlscando.com

"Helping girls discover their life's passions," Girls Can Do has opportunities, resources, and a lot of other cool stuff for girls ages 8 to 18.

Girls can explore sections on Outdoor Adventure, Sports, My Body, The Arts, Sci-Tech, Change the World, and Learn, Earn, and Intern. In addition to reading about women in all sorts of careers, girls can explore a wide range of opportunities and information that will help them grow into strong, intelligent, capable women.

Great Web Sites for Kids

http://www.ala.org/gwstemplate.cfm?section=greatwebsites&template=/cfapps/gws/default.cfm

Great Web Sites for Kids is a collection of more than 700 sites organized into a variety of categories, including animals, sciences, the arts, reference, social sciences, and more. All of the sites included here have been approved by a committee made up of professional librarians and educators. You can even submit your favorite great site for possible inclusion.

Hot Jobs: Career Tools Home

http://www.hotjobs.com/htdocs/tools/index-us.html

While the jobs listed at Hot Jobs are more on the traditional side, the Career Tools area has a lot of great resources for anyone looking for a job. You'll find information about how to write a resume and a cover letter, how to put together a career portfolio, interviewing tips, links to career assessments, and much more.

Job Descriptions and Job Details

http://www.job-descriptions.org

Search for descriptions and details for more than 13,000 jobs at this site. You can search for jobs by category or by industry. You'd probably be hard pressed to find a job that isn't listed here, and you'll probably find lots of jobs you never imagined existed. The descriptions and details are short, but it's interesting and fun, and might lead you to the career of your dreams.

Job Hunter's Bible

http://www.jobhuntersbible.com

This site is the official online supplement to the book What Color Is Your Parachute? A Practical Manual for Job-Hunters and Career-Changers, *and is a great source of information with lots of informative, helpful articles and links to many more resources.*

Job Profiles

http://www.jobprofiles.org

A collection of profiles, where experienced workers share about rewards of their job; stressful parts of the job; basic skills the job demands; challenges of the future; and advice on entering the field. The careers include everything from baseball ticket manager to pastry chef and much, much more. The hundreds of profiles are arranged by broad category. While most of the profiles are easy to read, you can check out "How to browse JobProfiles.org" (http://www.jobprofiles.org/jphowto.htm) if you have any problems.

Major Job Web Sites at Careers.org

http://www.careers.org/topic/01_jobs_10.html

This page at the Careers.org Web site has links for more than 40 of the Web's major job-related Web sites. While you're there, check out the numerous links to additional information.

Monster Jobs
http://www.monster.com

Monster.com is one of the largest, and probably best known, job-resource sites on the Web. It's really one-stop shopping for almost anything job-related that you can imagine. You can find a new job, network, update your resume, improve your skills, plan a job change or relocation, and so much more. Of special interest are the Monster: Cool Careers (http://change.monster.com/archives/coolcareers/) and Monster: Job Profiles (http://jobprofiles.monster.com/) sections where you can read about some really neat careers. The short profiles also include links to additional information. The Monster: Career Advice section (http://content.monster.com/) has resume and interviewing advice, message boards where you can network, relocation tools and advice, and more.

Occupational Outlook Handbook
http://www.bls.gov/oco

Published by the U.S. Department of Labor's Bureau of Labor Statistics, the Occupational Outlook Handbook *(sometimes referred to as the OOH) is the premiere source of career information. The book is updated every two years, so you can be assured that the information you are using to help make your decisions is current. The online version is very easy to use; you can search for a specific occupation, browse through a group of related occupations, or look through an alphabetical listing of all the jobs included in the volume. Each of the entries highlights the general nature of the job, working conditions, training and other qualifications, job outlook, average earning, related occupations, and sources of additional information. Each entry covers several pages and is a terrific source to get some great information about a huge variety of jobs.*

The Riley Guide: Employment Opportunities and Job Resources on the Internet
http://www.rileyguide.com

The Riley Guide is an amazing collection of job and career resources. Unless you are looking for something specific, one of the best ways to maneuver around the site is with the A-to-Z Index. You can find everything from links to careers in enology to information about researching companies and employers. The Riley Guide is a great place to find just about anything you might be looking for, and probably lots of things you aren't looking for. But be forewarned—it's easy to get lost in the A-to-Z Index, reading about all sorts of interesting things.

USA TODAY Career Focus
http://www.usatoday.com/careers/dream/dreamarc.htm

Several years ago, USA TODAY ran a series featuring people working in their dream jobs. In the profiles, people discuss how they got their dream job, what they enjoy the most about it, they talk about an average day, their education backgrounds, sacrifices they had to make for their jobs, and more. They also share words of advice for anyone hoping to follow in their footsteps. Most of the articles also feature links where you can find more information. The USATODAY .com Job Center (http://www.usatoday .com/money/jobcenter/front.htm) also has links to lots of resources and additional information.

CAREER TESTS AND INVENTORIES

If you have no idea what career is right for you, there are many resources available online that will help assess your interests and maybe steer you in the right direction. While some of the assessments charge a fee, there are many out there that are free. You can locate more tests and inventories by searching for the keywords *career tests*, *career inventories*, or *personality inventories*. Some of the most popular assessments available online are:

Campbell Interest and Skill Survey (CISS)
http://www.usnews.com/usnews/edu/careers/ccciss.htm

Career Explorer
http://careerexplorer.net/aptitude.asp

Career Focus 2000 Interest Inventory
http://www.iccweb.com/careerfocus

The Career Interests Game
http://career.missouri.edu/students/explore/thecareerinterestsgame.php

The Career Key
http://www.careerkey.org

Career Maze
http://www.careermaze.com/home.asp?licensee=CareerMaze

Career Tests at CareerPlanner.com
http://www.careerplanner.com

CAREERLINK Inventory
http://www.mpc.edu/cl/cl.htm

FOCUS
http://www.focuscareer.com

Keirsey Temperament Test
http://www.keirsey.com

Motivational Appraisal of Personal Potential (MAPP)
http://www.assessment.com

Myers-Briggs Personality Type
http://www.personalitypathways.com/type_inventory.html

Princeton Review Career Quiz
http://www.princetonreview.com/cte/quiz/default.asp

Skills Profiler
http://www.acinet.org/acinet/skills_home.asp

GOVERNMENT JOBS

Career Guide to Industries: Government
http://stats.bls.gov/oco/cg/cg10010.htm
Publication from the U.S. Bureau of Labor Statistics including information about employment in the federal, state, and local government, describing federal agencies and the industry's occupations, earnings, and employment prospects.

Federal Employment of People with Disabilities
http://www.opm.gov/disability
Provides information tailored to job applicants with disabilities.

Occupational Outlook Handbook
http://www.bls.gov/oco
Publication from the government describing the job duties, earnings, employment prospects, and training requirements for hundreds of occupations, including many in government.

Partnership for Public Service
1725 Eye Street, NW, Suite 900
Washington, DC 20006
(202) 775-9111

http://www.ourpublicservice.org

The Partnership for Public Service is a good source of information that encourages college graduates to work for the federal government. It publishes advice for students on how to get internships and permanent jobs. Many of its resources are customized for people with specific majors. The Partnership also conducts research on federal employment and helps career counselors and federal recruiters.

Studentjobs.gov
http://www.studentjobs.gov

Provides information about jobs for students.

USAJOBS
http://www.usajobs.opm.gov

The official job site of the U.S.Federal Government.

Veterans Employment Information
http://www.opm.gov/veterans

Provides information about how military skills relate to civilian jobs in the Federal Government and about applying for hiring preferences.

APPENDIX C: GETTING A JOB IN THE FEDERAL GOVERNMENT

There's no magic formula for getting a job in the federal government—you need to find a vacancy and submit a resume or application, as with any other job. But at the same time, landing a position with Uncle Sam can be more a lot more complicated. Applying for a civil service job can feel as if you're endlessly jumping through hoops and choking on red tape. Lots of these regulations were designed to make the federal job search more fair, but knowing that doesn't make the application process any easier.

It's important to understand the federal government's rules, because if you follow them, you'll have a much better chance of getting the job you want, no matter how unusual. And there should be something that strikes a chord with you, since there are more than 1.7 million jobs and 400 occupational specialties—and that's not even counting postal service and military workers. In fact, the federal government offers more job choices than any other single employer in the United States. Whether you're interested in buying and selling, writing reports, or taking care of sick animals, you can probably find a government career to match.

Of course, all those choices can make actually *finding* the job of your dreams a challenge, since these jobs are located in more than 100 agencies and bureaus, each with its own responsibilities and each with its own way of going about getting new employees. And the government, with its old-fashioned job titles, doesn't make it any easier. When looking for a job in the vast federal government job pool, the broader your search, the better. Don't get hung up on one job title, only looking under "writer" and ignoring "PR specialist" or "communications expert." You might want to check out the Bureau of Labor Statistics (http://www.bls.gov/oco) for an in-depth discussion of a wide range of jobs in the federal government.

QUALIFICATIONS

If there's one thing you can count on, it's that the federal government is going to require that you be a U.S. citizen before they hire you. Other than that, qualifications vary with the job, ranging from high school students with no experience to Ph.Ds with established careers. Obviously, for some professional jobs (such as lawyer), you'll need a graduate degree; other jobs require a bachelor's or master's degree and credit for specific college classes. Some jobs, such as entry-level clerks, assistants, or secretaries, don't list any education or experience requirements at all.

The "vacancy announcements" that advertise job openings will give you all the details you need about the specific qualifications for each job. And of course, it wouldn't be the government without codes—each job will list a code that corresponds to its minimum requirements. Most agencies use the common General Schedule (GS) designation from 1 to 15, which corresponds to the minimum level of education and experience you'll need to do the job. Jobs on the bottom rung of the employee ladder requiring no experience or education are graded a GS-1. Jobs for which you need a bachelor's degree but no experience would be about a GS-5 or GS-7. For occupations requiring general college-level skills, you'll qualify with a bachelor's degree in any subject, but other jobs require a specific major. For example, if you have a master's degree in English, that doesn't mean you'll qualify for that grade level in the fish and game department requiring a degree in wildlife management.

If you've gotten some work experience under your belt, you'll probably qualify for higher GS levels. In general, most clerical and technician employees can figure that one year of job-related experience might boost their GS level by one grade. Administrative, professional, and scientific positions rise in increments of two GS levels until GS-12; after that, GS level increases one level at a time. Your GS level could continue to increase with each additional year of experience at a higher level of responsibility, until you reach the maximum for your occupation.

HOP ON THE INFORMATION HIGHWAY

If you've got a computer, applying for a federal job is going to be a lot easier, letting you search, download, and even submit your application electronically. For one-stop shopping, visit USAJOBS (http://www.usajobs.opm.gov), the official job site for all federal government jobs. Here you can explore the more than 19,000 job openings, as well as create and store your resume.

In most cases, agencies are required to advertise job openings on the USAJOBS system. The USAJOBS Web site lets you sort ads by occupation, location, occupational group, keyword, grade level, salary, and agency. The site may highlight a particular job, and will box a "jobs in demand" section for areas that are really hot right now. The site also typically will highlight one department or agency to provide more in-depth information.

And because the federal government loves forms, you'll find them all here—standard forms, SF15 forms (for veterans), OPM forms, optional forms, qualifications and availability forms—and even brochures to help you fill out their forms. Much of this information is also available in Spanish. The site also offers a helpful (and extensive) FAQ, answering all sorts of questions, from "where do I take a civil service exam" to "can I get a job if I have a jail record."

If you've got a specific job in mind, you can look for it by occupational series, but if you're mystified by the federal job title logic, you can always search for jobs using a keyword, which checks each vacancy announcement for the words you ask it to look for. You can also use this keyword function to identify jobs that require a certain level of education or experience, or you can specify a particular GS level.

Don't limit yourself to just one agency; engineers may work for the Army Corps of Engineers but they'll also be hired by the U.S. Navy; the Environmental Protection Agency; the Air Force; the Army Test and Evaluation Command; the Indian Health Service; the Army Research, Development & Engineering Command; and many other agencies. You can even direct the USAJOBS site to repeat your search automatically and e-mail you the results on a daily or weekly basis.

USAJOBS also offers an automated phone research system at (703) 724-1850. It lists the same openings 24 hours a day; customer service representatives are available weekdays from 8 a.m. to 8 p.m. EST. It will help if you know the occupational titles and series codes for jobs you're interested in, since you can start a job search by punching in the code on the phone keypad. You also search by occupation type, length of job, or hiring agency, location, or pay range. The telephone system gives a few details about each job opening.

The U.S. Department of Labor also offers a toll-free career information line: (877) USA-JOBS (872-5627).

If you wish, you can simply contact any federal agency directly and avoid the Web site entirely, which is a good idea for jobs that may not be required to be posted on USAJOBS. However, you might still want to check out USAJOBS, which often has more up-to-the-minute information than either the agency Web sites or the agency's own human resources specialists. It's a good idea to combine both strategies, since human resources specialists might be able to direct you to some job openings right away and may be better at helping you match your skills with job openings. (Sometimes it's just nice to be able to talk to a real human, and get his or her advice.) Human resources specialists might be able to give you more information about programs you've not even thought about, such as the Outstanding Scholar Program for people who graduated with academic honors or with grade point averages of at least 3.45. Other programs give priority to people applying to certain jobs, people who speak Spanish or have important cultural knowledge; or to jobs with a shortage of qualified workers. Some human resource specialists in most agencies also focus on helping certain individuals, such as minority groups and people with disabilities.

But the federal government Web site or individual agencies aren't the only place you can search for federal jobs. Federal employers often advertise for jobs in newspapers and journals, at job fairs, and on private job boards. Many government agencies also provide school career centers with information about jobs and special programs for students and recent graduates.

A few agencies and occupations don't have to list their openings on USAJOBS, including the U.S. Postal Service, the Federal Bureau of Investigation, and the intelligence services. A few occupations, such as attorneys and Foreign Service workers, are also exempt from some of the procedures described here, and so are temporary positions that won't last more than 180 days. Nevertheless, even when they don't have to, many of these agencies still follow the standard procedures and go ahead and list openings on USAJOBS.

And of course, a few positions in the federal government are set aside for political appointees. You get one of these jobs by being appointed by an elected official. For these assignments, it pays to know someone.

APPLYING FOR THE JOB

Once you've located a few jobs in which you're interested, you need to apply for the job. To do this, you need to follow the government's requirements, and submit your information exactly the way the vacancy announcement has stipulated you should. Many federal agencies have developed their own online application forms that they insist you use, but a few are more lenient, and will accept any sort of resume as long as you list the information they want. If you are applying to one of these more flexible agencies, you can submit a paper resume or you can use one of the official forms that the government provides.

USAJOBS Resume Builder

You may find it easiest to simply use the online resume builder on the USAJOBS Web site, which allows you to submit or update your application quickly and painlessly. (Visit the resume builder at: https://my.usajobs.opm.gov/new.asp?ID=e nableRedirect&redirect=%2Findex%2Ea sp.) By logging on and becoming a member (it's free), you can post your resume online and wait for employers to contact you, apply for jobs using this form, and receive automated job alerts. You can either fill out the form online, or cut and paste the details from your own electronic resume in a word processed document.

Agency-Specific Resume Builders

Some agencies have their own resume builders. Because many of these use automated systems to check resumes, you can boost the likelihood of being considered if you use as many keywords from the job ad as you can. That's because the more keywords from the ad that the computer finds in your resume, the higher

your resume will score. You'll rise to the head of the pack. Of course, that isn't a license to lie. Don't go crazy and stick in all kinds of keywords that don't fit your skills, because eventually your application will be read by a real, live person.

Once you've completed the resume builder for a specific agency, you can submit a resume for every job in which you're interested in that agency. You'll have to submit a new resume for each new job at the agency.

Paper Resumes

If an agency doesn't have its own form, or if it does have a form but you prefer paper, you can submit your own resume in hard copy—making sure to follow the government's requirements. Always remember to include the job announcement number and your name and Social Security number on every page of the resume.

If you're creating your own paper resume for a federal job, you'll want to include all of the information you'd normally add in a standard resume—with some extra details. Don't worry if your resume is longer than the one- to two page resumes typical in the private sector. A four-page federal government resume is about normal, because federal agencies want more information than do most other employers.

Contact Information

In addition to your full name, address, and telephone number, you'll also need to provide your Social Security number and citizenship, and indicate your willingness to relocate (if you are).

Job Details

Make sure to include the job's announcement number, position title, and the lowest grade level you would accept. For example, if the announcement describes the job as "GS-8/10," you'll need to decide whether you could live with a GS-8, or whether you would only settle for GS-10—assuming, of course, that you actually qualify for GS-10. If you aim too high and hope that no one will notice, you won't make it past the first hurdle. However, if you aim too low, it's likely that the agency will automatically upgrade you.

Experience

In addition to the standard information about past jobs you've had, you also need to add whether it was full time, what your salary was, and contact details for your supervisor. Any past government jobs should list the occupational series numbers and the starting and ending grades. Relevant volunteer experience counts here, so describe your job title and what you did. Describe how your past job experience matches the requirements for this federal government job, using words from the job vacancy ad.

The nice thing about a paper resume is that you can tailor it to emphasize your strengths and disguise your weaknesses. If you're a recent graduate, for example, you can emphasize your education over your work experience, which is probably limited. However, the federal government does insist that you list information in reverse chronological order, starting with your most recent job or educational experience.

So if you've not had much on-the-job experience, use your most impressive educational accomplishments first. You could indicate that you earned a 4.0 average in all of your major courses in environmental science, which would appeal to the human resources people reading your resume at the Environmental Protection Agency. Talk about school awards, or how—as an intern—you saved your company money by coming up with a better way to handle invoices. Try to be as specific as possible. If you interned at an art museum and you organized a successful fund-raiser, tell the government exactly how much money you brought in. If you were in charge of the membership drive for your local nonprofit, indicate how many new members you were able to wrangle.

Education and Training

Although many companies in the private sector don't care much about what you did in high school, the federal government does. Nearly all agencies want details about where you went to high school (including address), along with the typical details of degrees, year they were conferred, and your major areas of study. Details are desirable; include the number of credits you've earned in any subjects that are at all related to the job you're aiming for. The federal government considers 24 credits in one subject to be equivalent to a major. Also be sure to list specific courses you've taken that relate to the job.

If you're not required to list your grade point average, it's a good idea to include it if you think that it will help. If you've attained at least a 2.5 or 3.0, you may qualify for higher starting pay; you may also qualify for some programs based on class rank, honor society membership, or grade point average. If your average is below 2.5 and you can avoid it, it's best just not to mention it at all.

Other Qualifications

If you've got any special skills, such as fluency in another language or unusual computer skills, it's a good idea to include it. You never know what might spark the interest of the human resources person reading your resume, and anything that helps you stand out from the crowd (in a good way) is desirable.

Qualification Summary

It's a good idea to summarize your qualifications in a separate section of your resume, especially if you have a long, complex, or varied work history. Try to tailor this section to focus on the desired qualifications in the vacancy announcement.

OF-612 Form

Many government jobs give you the option of filling out the government's optional application form: the OF-612. Using this paper form means you don't have to create a resume from scratch. You can download a form at the USAJOBS Web site or get a hard copy by visiting a U.S. government personnel office.

Knowledge, Skills, and Abilities Statement (KSA)

In addition to a resume, the job might require a "knowledge, skills, and abili-ties statement" (a KSA) that allows you to show how your qualifications match the job requirements. For example, an announcement for a PR specialist might ask you to describe your oral and written communication skills. An announcement for an engineer might ask about math-ematics ability or knowledge of engineer-ing. Writing a KSA lets you show that you have all the qualifications the government is looking for. A KSA is usually about a half to a page long, single-spaced, written in paragraph form.

THE WAITING GAME

This being the government, you should expect to wait quite a while after submitting an application before you hear anything. In fact, it could take months, partly because of the federal job search process required by law. Agencies have managed to cut the waiting time down to a few weeks.

In the meantime, if your agency uses an automated hiring system, you can check the status of your application by logging on to its employment Web site, or you could call the contact person in human resources. This is important because sometimes jobs are cancelled and then re-listed later. It's probably a good idea, however, to wait at least three weeks after the closing date to give the agency time to wade through all the applications.

HANDLING THE INTERVIEW

If you make the first cut and you're called in for an interview, you'll want to learn as much as you can about the job and the agency before you get there. The age of the Internet has made this much easier; you can skim the "about us" section of the agency

Web site, reading over its publications and checking out the organizational chart. Read any news releases it has posted, and review the job announcement.

You'll want to bring photo identification as well as any materials that the hiring manager requests, and give yourself plenty of time on the day of the interview to find your way in the building and make it through the security procedures.

NEGOTIATING SALARY

Congratulations! You've got the job. At this point, a human resources specialist will telephone you with an offer. Keep in mind that salary negotiations aren't quite the same as if you were getting a nongovernmental job, since pay ranges are set by law. However, agencies do have some flexibility—if you have experience, they can start you at the higher end of the pay range, and some can provide signing bonuses, offer to pay your student loans, or give you some relocation funds.

Once the money details are out of the way, the human resources specialist will explain the process of getting any necessary security clearances or other background check. Ask for time to decide whether to accept the job if you wish, but if you want the job, you'll be told when to start.

And enjoy your new career with the federal government!

APPENDIX D: GRADUATE SCHOOL PROGRAMS

ALABAMA

Auburn University
MPA program
8030 Haley Center
Auburn, AL 36849-5208
(334) 844-5371
hartzmm@auburn.edu
http://www.auburn.edu/academic/liberal_
arts/poli_sci/mpa/

Auburn University at Montgomery
Master of Public Administration
Dept of Political Science and Public
Administration
PO Box 244023
Montgomery, AL 36124-4023
(334) 244-3698
vocino@strudel.aum.edu

University of Alabama at Birmingham
Department of Government
238 Ullman Building
1212 University Boulevard
Birmingham, AL 35294
(205) 934-9680
mpa@uab.edu
http://main.uab.edu/show.asp?durki=
26532

University of Alabama
MPA Program
Department of Political Science
Box 870213
Ten Hoor Hall
Tuscaloosa, AL 35487-0213
(205) 348-5980
http://www.as.ua.edu

ALASKA

University of Alaska–Anchorage
3211 Providence Drive
Anchorage, AK 99508
(907) 786-1786
afgjp@uaa.alaska.edu
http://www.scob.alaska.edu/dept/
mpadept.asp?page=public

University of Alaska SE
11120 Glacier Highway
Juneau, AK 99801
(907) 465-6356
jonathan.Anderson@uas.alaska.edu
http://www.uas.alaska.edu/mpa

ARKANSAS

Arkansas State University
Department of Political Science
State University, AR 72467-1750
(870) 972-3048
pstewart@astate.edu
http://polsci.astate.edu/
degree%20Information/mpapage.htm

University of Arkansas
Clinton School of Public Service
1200 President Clinton Avenue
Little Rock, AR 72201
(501) 683-5228
mmhawkins@clintonschool.uasys.edu
http://www.clintonschool.uasys.edu

University of Arkansas at Little Rock
Institute of Government

2801 South University
Little Rock, AR 72207
(501) 569-3037
mxwinn@ualr,edu
http://www.ualr.edu/~iog/

University of Arkansas–Fayetteville
MPA Program
Department of Political Science
428 Old Main
Fayetteville AR 72701
(479) 575-3356
mreid@uark.edu
http://plsc.uark.edu/grad

ARIZONA

Arizona State University
School of Public Affairs
PO Box 870603
Tempe, AZ 85287-0603
(480) 965-3926
spa@asu.edu
http://spa.ahsu.edu

The University of Arizona
School of Public Administration and
Policy
Eller College of Business and Public
Administration
McClelland Hall, 405
PO Box 210108
Tucson, AZ 85721-0108
(520) 621-7965
padams@eller.arizona.edu
http://publicadmin.eller.arizona.edu

CALIFORNIA

**California State Polytechnic University–
Pomona**
Department of Political Science

CSU Pomona
3801 West Temple Avenue
Pomona, CA 91768
(909) 869-4739
smemerson@csupomona.edu
http://www.csupomona.edu/~lnelson/
mpaprogram

California State University–Bakersfield
Department of Public Policy and
Administration
9001 Stockdale Highway
Bakersfield CA 93311-1099
(661) 664-2181
rdaniels@csub.edu
http://www.csub.edu/bpa

California State University–Chico
Department of Political Science
Chico, CA 95929
(530) 898-5734
dkemp@csuchico.edu
http://www.csuchico.edu/catalog/
programs/pols/mpa_puba.html

**California State University–Dominguez
Hills**
Department of Public Administration
and Public Policy
1000 East Victoria Street
Carson, CA 90747
(310) 243-3444
jwaters@csudh.edu
http://som.csudh.edu/depts/public/info

California State University–East Bay
Department of Public Affairs and
Administration
Hayward, CA 94542
(510) 885-3282
http://www.csuhayward.edu

California State University–Fullerton
Department of Political Science
PO Box 6848

Fullerton, CA 92886-6848
(714) 278-3521
yting@fullerton.edu
http://hss.fullerton.edu/polisci/programs/
Mpa/pa-index.htm

California State University–Long Beach
Graduate Center for Public Policy and
Administration
1250 Bellflower Boulevard
Long Beach, CA 90840
(562) 985-4178
sbauer@csulb.edu or quirk@csulb.edu
http://www.csulb.edu/~beachmpa

California State University–Los Angeles
Department of Political Science
5151 State University Drive
Los Angeles, CA 90032-8226
(323) 343-2230
gandran@calstatela.edu
http://www.calstatela.edu/dept/pol_sci/
MSPA1.html

California State University–Northridge
Master of Public Administration
Northridge, CA 91330-8362
(818) 677-5635
veena.bassi@csun.edu
http://www.csun.edu/~urb49619

**California State University–San
Bernardino**
Department of Public Administration
5500 University Parkway
San Bernardino, CA 92407
(909) 880-5758
dbellis@csusb.edu
http://www.cbpa.csusb.edu

California State University–Stanislaus
Department of Politics and Public
Administration
Turlock, CA 95382
(209) 667-3388

ahejka-ekins@csustan.edu
http://www.csustan.edu/ppa/index.html

Golden Gate University
Executive Master of Public
Administration (EMPA) Program
Edward S. Ageno School of Business
536 Mission Street
San Francisco, CA 94105-2968
(415) 442-6576
jgonzalez@ggu.edu
http://www.ggu.edu

**Monterey Institute of
International Studies**
460 Pierce Street
Monterey, CA 93940
(831) 647-4123
admit@miis.edu
http://www.miis.edu

Naval Postgraduate School
Graduate School of Business & Public
Policy
CDR Roger D. Lord, Program Officer
555 Dyer Road
Monterey, CA 93943
(831) 656-3953
rdlord@nps.edu
http://www.nps.navy.mil/gsbpp

San Diego State University
School of Public Administration and
Urban Studies
5500 Campanile Drive
San Diego, CA 92182-4505
(619) 594-4546
lrea@mail.sdsu.edu
http://psfa.sdsu.edu/spaus

San Francisco State University
Master of Public Administration
1600 Holloway Avenue
San Francisco, CA 94132
(415) 338-2985

mpa@sfsu.edu
http://bss.sfsu.edu/~mpa

University of California—Los Angeles
Department of Policy Studies
UCLA School of Public Affairs
3250 Public Policy Building
Box 951656
Los Angeles, CA 90095-1656
(310) 825-0448
mppinfo@sppsr.ucla.edu
http://www.spa.ucla.edu

University of La Verne
Department of Public Administration
2220 Third Street
La Verne, CA 91750
(909) 593-3511 x4942
schildtk@ulv.edu
http://www.ulv.edu/padm

University of San Francisco
Office of Graduate and Adult Admission
2130 Fulton Street
San Francisco, CA 94117-1047
(415) 422-6000
workingadults@usfca.edu
http://www.cps.usfca.edu

University of Southern California
School of Policy, Planning, and
Development
Los Angeles, CA 90089-0626
(213) 740-6842
sppd@usc.edu
http://www.usc.edu/sppd

COLORADO

University of Colorado
Graduate School of Public Affairs
1380 Lawrence Street, Suite 500
Denver, CO 80204-2054
(303) 556-5970

pete.wolfe@cudenver.edu
http://www.cudenver.edu/gspa

CONNECTICUT

University of Connecticut
MPA Program
Department of Public Policy
1800 Asylum Avenue
West Hartford, CT 06117
(860) 570-9343
MPA@UConn.edu
http://www.mpa.uconn.edu/uconn/mpa/
mpa.nsf/indexstart?openform

University of New Haven
300 Post Road
West Haven, CT 06518
(203) 932-7133
egormley@newhaven.edu
http://admissions.newhaven.edu/grad/

DISTRICT OF COLUMBIA

American University
School of Public Affairs
Washington, DC 20016
(202) 885-6230
spagrad@american.edu
http://spa.american.edu

Georgetown University
Georgetown Public Policy Institute
3600 N Street, NW, Suite #200
Washington, DC 20007
(202) 687-9186
gppiadmissions@georgetown.edu
http://gppi.georgetown.edu

The George Washington University
School of Public Policy and Public
Administration

Media Public Affairs Building
805 21st Street, NW, Suite 601
Washington, DC 20052
(202) 994-6295
spppa@gwu.edu
http://www.gwu.edu/~spppa

Howard University
Department of Political Science
2441 6th Street NW
Frederick Douglass Hall, Room 144
Washington, DC 20059
(202) 806-6720

Southeastern University
Department of Public Administration
501 I Street, SW
Washington, DC 20024
(202) 488-8162 x188
apharr@admin.seu.edu
http://www.seu.edu/gen/Academic/pub/
Admin/pubAdmin/default.htm

DELAWARE

University of Delaware
School of Urban Affairs & Public Policy
Admissions Office
182 Graham Hall
Newark, DE 19716
(302) 831-1687
suapp@udel.edu
http://www.udel.edu/suapp

FLORIDA

Florida Atlantic University
Public Administration
111 East Las Olas Boulevard
Fort Lauderdale, FL 33301
(954) 762-5667
lleip@aol.com
http://www.fau.edu/spa

Florida Gulf Coast University
College of Professional Studies
Division of Public Affairs
10501 FGCU Boulevard South
Ft. Myers, FL 33965-6565
(239) 590-7841
rwalsh@fgcu.edu
http://www.fgcu.edu

Florida International University
School of Policy and Management
AC 1-267
North Miami, FL 33181
(305) 919-5890
howardf@fiu.edu
http://www.fiu.edu

Florida State University
Askew School of Public Administration
and Policy
Tallahassee, FL 32306-2032
(904) 644-3525
http://askew.fsu.edu

Nova Southeastern University
H. Wayne Huizenga School of Business
and Entrepreneurship
Carl DeSantis Building
3301 College Avenue
Ft. Lauderdale, FL 33314-7796
(954) 262-5100
prestonj@huizenga.nova.edu
http://www.huizenga.nova.edu

University of Central Florida
Department of Public Administration
238 Health & Public Affairs Building II
Orlando, FL 32816
(407) 823-2604
http://www.cohpa.ucf.edu/pubadm

University of Miami
Department of Political Science
PO Box 248047
Coral Gables, FL 33134
(305) 284-2401

jwest@miami.edu
http://www.miami.edu

University of North Florida
Dept. of Political Science and Public
Admin.
4567 St. Johns Bluff Road South
Jacksonville, FL 32224-2645
(904) 620-1928
pplumlee@unf.edu
http://www.unf.edu/coas/polsci-
pubadmin

University of South Florida
Department of Government and
International Affairs
Public Administration Program
4202 East Fowler Avenue, SOC 107
Tampa, FL 33620-8100
(813) 974-2510
http://www.cas.usf.edu/pad/index.html

University of West Florida
11000 University Parkway
Pensacola, FL 32514
(850) 474-2184
adminstudies@uwf.edu
http://www.uwf.edu

GEORGIA

Albany State University
Department of History, Political Science
and Public Administration
Albany State University
504 College Drive
Albany, GA 31705
(229) 430-4873
http://www.asurams.edu

Augusta State University
Department of Political Science
2500 Walton Way
Augusta, GA 30904
(706) 737-1710

sreinke@aug.edu
http://www.aug.edu/mpa

Clark Atlanta University
Department of Public Administration
223 James P. Brawley Drive
Atlanta, GA 30314
(404) 880-6650
http://www.cau.edu

Columbus State University
4225 University Avenue
Columbus, GA 31907-5645
(706) 568-2055
chappell_bill@colstate.edu
http://www.colstate.edu

Georgia College & State University
MPA Program
Department of Government
Milledgeville, GA 31061
(478) 445-4562
chris.grant@gcsu.edu
http://www.gcsu.edu

Georgia Institute of Technology
School of Public Policy
685 Cherry Street
Atlanta, GA 30332-0345
(404) 894-0417
grad@pubpolicy.gatech.edu
http://www.spp.gatech.edu

Georgia Southern University
Statesboro, GA 30460-8101
(912) 871-1400
mpa@gasou.edu
http://www.georgiasouthern.edu

Georgia State University
Department of Public Administration &
Urban Studies
Andrew Young School of Policy Studies
PO Box 3992
Atlanta, GA 30303-3992
(404) 651-3662

ayspsacademicassist@gsu.edu
http://www.gsu.edu/~wwwpau

Kennesaw State University
Department of Political Science &
International Affairs
Box 2302
1000 Chastain Road
Kennesaw, GA 30144
(770) 423-6631
mgriffit@kennesaw.edu
http://www.kennesaw.edu/pols

Savannah State University
The MPA Program at SSU
PO Box 20385
Savannah, GA 31404
(912) 351-6787
wilsonz@savstate.edu
http://www.savstate.edu/class/mpa/

University of Georgia
Department of Public Administration
and Policy
School of Public and International
Affairs
Athens, GA 30602
(706) 542-2057
jlegge@uga.edu
http://www.uga.edu/pol-sci/

University of West Georgia
Department of Political Science and
Planning
Carrollton, GA 30118-2100
(770) 836-6504
mhirling@westga.edu
http://www.westga.edu/~polisci/mpa

Valdosta State University
1500 N. Patterson Street—WH 101
Valdosta, GA 31698-0058
(229) 293-6058
nargyle@valdosta.edu
http://www.valdosta.edu/mpa

HAWAII

University of Hawaii
Public Administration Program
2424 Maile Way
Saunders Hall 631
Honolulu, HI 96822
(808) 956-8260
http://www2.soc.hawaii.edu/puba

IDAHO

University of Idaho
Department of Political Science
Moscow, ID 83844-3164
(208) 885-6563
fheffron@uidaho.edu
http://www.uidaho.edu

ILLINOIS

Governors State University
College of Business and Public
Administration
University Park, IL 60466
(708) 534-4391
BPA-INFO@govst.edu
http://www.govst.edu/users/gcbpa/
degreeprog/mpa.htm

Northern Illinois University
Division of Public Administration
DeKalb, IL 60115-2854
(815) 753-6149
vclarke@niu.edu
http://www.niu.edu/pub_ad/paweb.html

Southern Illinois University–Carbondale
Department of Political Science
SIUC MC 4501
Carbondale, IL 62901-4501
(618) 453-3177

mpaprog@siu.edu
http://www.siu.edu/departments/cola/
polysci

Southern Illinois University–Edwardsville
Department of Public Administration
and Policy Analysis
Campus Box 1457
Edwardsville, IL 62026-1457
(618) 650-3762
http://www.siue.edu/PAPA

The University of Chicago
The Irving B. Harris Graduate School of
Public Policy Studies
1155 East 60th Street
Chicago, IL 60637
(773) 702-8400
harrisschool@uchicago.edu
http://www.harrisschool.uchicago.edu

University of Illinois–Chicago
College of Urban Planning and Public
Affairs
UIC Graduate Program in Public
Administration
412 South Peoria Street,
130 CUPPA Hall (mc 278)
Chicago, IL 60607
(312) 996-3109
eali@uic.edu
http://www.uic.edu/cuppa/pa

University of Illinois at Springfield
Department of Public Administration
One University Plaza, MS PAC 418
Springfield, IL 62703
(217) 206-6310
mpa@uis.edu
http://www.uis.edu/publicadministration

INDIANA

Indiana State University
Department of Political Science
Holmstedt Hall, Room 306

Terre Haute, IN 47809
(812) 237-2430
http://www.indstate.edu/polisci/

Indiana University–Bloomington
School of Public and Environmental
Affairs
Graduate Programs
SPEA 260
Bloomington, IN 47405-2100
(800) 765-7755
speainfo@indiana.edu
http://www.spea.indiana.edu

Indiana University Northwest
Division of Public & Environmental
Affairs
School of Public Environmental Affairs
400 Broadway
Gary, IN 46408
(219) 980-6695
jpelli@iun.edu
http://www.iun.edu/~speanw

Indiana University South Bend
School of Public and Environmental
Affairs
1700 Mishawaka Ave. PO Box 7111
South Bend, IN 46634
(574) 520-4131 jherr@iusb.edu
http://www.iusb.edu/~sbspea/

**Indiana University–Purdue University,
Fort Wayne**
School of Public Environmental Affairs
801 West Michigan Street BS/SPEA 3027
Indianapolis, IN 46202
(877) 292-9321
infospea@iupui.edu
http://www.spea.iupui.edu

IOWA

Drake University
College of Business and Public
Administration

Aliber Hall
2507 University Avenue
Des Moines, IA 50311-4505
(515) 271-2188
cpba.gradprograms@drake.edu
http://www.cbpa.drake.edu

Iowa State University
Public Policy and Administration
Program
Department of Political Science
529 Ross Hall
Ames, IA 50011-1204
(515) 294-7256
http://www.iastate.edu

KANSAS

Kansas State University
Department of Political Science
226 Waters Hall
Manhattan, KS 66506-4030
(913) 532-6842
polsci@ksu.edu
http://www.ksu.edu/polsci

University of Kansas
Department of Public Administration
1541 Lilac Lane, #318
Lawrence, KS 66045-3177
(785) 864-3527
padept@ku.edu
http://www.ku.edu/~kupa/

Wichita State University
Hugo Wall School of Urban and Public
Affairs
Wichita, KS 67260-0155
(316) 978-7240
http://hws.wichita.edu/

KENTUCKY

Eastern Kentucky University
Department of Government

McCreary 113
Richmond, KY 40474
(859) 622-5931
Terry.Busson@eku.edu
http://www.eku.edu

Kentucky State University
334 Academic Services Building
Frankfort, KY 40601
(502) 597-6117
glake@gwmail.kysu.edu
http://www.kysu.edu

Northern Kentucky University
Department of Political Science
Nunn Drive
Highland Heights, KY 41099
(859) 572-5326
mpa@nku.edu
http://www.nku.edu/~psc/

University of Kentucky
Martin School of Public Policy and
Administration
413 Patterson Office Tower
Lexington, KY 40506-0027
(859) 257-5594
pub718@pop.uky.edu
http://www-martin.uky.edu

University of Louisville
School of Urban and Public Affairs
426 West Bloom Street
Louisville, KY 40208
(502) 852-7906
upa@louisville.edu
http://supa.louisville.edu

LOUISIANA

Grambling State University
Department of Political Science
Grambling, LA 71245
(318) 274-2310 x2714
sim4@ALPHAD.Gram.edu
http://www.gram.edu

Louisiana State University
Public Administration Institute
E.J. Ourso College of Business
Administration
3200 CEBA Building
Louisiana State University
Baton Rouge, LA 70803
(225) 578-6743
parich@lsu.edu
http://www.bus.lsu.edu/pai

Southern University
The School of Public Policy and Urban
Affairs
PO Box 9656
Baton Rouge LA 70813
(504) 771-3092
http://www.subr.edu/aboutsubr.html

University of New Orleans
College of Urban and Public Affairs
New Orleans, LA 70148-2910
(504) 280-6277
dstrong@uno.edu
http://www.uno.edu

MAINE

University of Maine
5754 North Stevens Hall
Orono, ME 04469-5754
(207) 581-1872
umpubadm@umit.maine.edu
http://www.umaine.edu/pubadmin

MARYLAND

Johns Hopkins University
Institute for Policy Studies, Wyman
Building
3400 North Charles Street
Baltimore, MD 21218-2696
(410) 516-4167

maps@jhu.edu
http://www.jhu.edu/~ips/

University of Baltimore
School of Public Affairs
1304 St. Paul Street
Baltimore, MD 21201
(410) 837-6094
http://www.ubalt.edu/cla_spa

University of Maryland College Park
School of Public Policy
2101 Van Munching Hall
College Park, MD 20742
(301) 405-6330
ze2@umail.umd.edu
http://www.puaf.umd.edu

MASSACHUSETTS

Clark University
950 Main Street
Worcester, MA 01610
(508) 793-7212
http://copace.clarku.edu

Harvard University
John F. Kennedy School of Government
79 John F. Kennedy Street
Cambridge, MA 02138
(617) 495-1155
ksg_admissions@harvard.edu
http://www.ksg.harvard.edu/apply

Northeastern University
Department of Political Science
303 Meserve Hall
Boston, MA 02115
(617) 373-4404
wkay@neu.edu
http://www.polisci.neu.edu/

Suffolk University
Department of Public Management
8 Ashburton Place

Boston, MA 02108
(617) 573-8330
mmatava@suffolkpad.org
http://www.suffolkpad.org

University of Massachusetts–Amherst
Center for Public Policy and
Administration
Thompson Hall
Amherst, MA 01003 USA
(413) 545-3940
info@pubpol.umass.edu
http://www.masspolicy.org

MICHIGAN

Eastern Michigan University
MPA Program
Department of Political Science
Ypsilanti, MI 48197
(734) 487-2522
Joseph.Ohren@emich.edu
http://www.emich.edu/public/polisci/
pubad/about.htm

Northern Michigan University
1401 Presque Isle Avenue
Marquette, MI 49855
(906) 227-1815
bcherry@nmu.edu
http://www.nmu.edu/mpa

University of Michigan
Gerald R. Ford School of Public Policy
440 Lorch Hall
611 Tappan Street
Ann Arbor, Michigan 48109-1220
(734) 764-0453
fsppadmit@umich.edu
http://www.fordschool.umich.edu

Wayne State University
Department of Political Science
2049 FAB
Detroit, MI 48202

(313) 577-2668
ad5179@wayne.edu
http://www.cla.wayne.edu/polisci

MISSISSIPPI

Mississippi State University
Department of Political Science and
Public Administration—Box PC
Mississippi State, MS 39762
(601) 325-7852
ejc1@ps.msstate.edu
http://www.msstate.edu/dept/
politicalscience/programs

MISSOURI

Saint Louis University
McGannon Hall
3750 Lindell Boulevard
St. Louis, MO 63108
(314) 977-3934
domahimr@slu.edu
http://www.slu.edu/colleges/cops/pps

University of Missouri–St. Louis
406 Tower
One University Boulevard
St. Louis, MO 63121-4400
(314) 516-5145
glassberg@umsl.edu
http://www.umsl.edu/divisions/graduate/
mppa

MONTANA

Montana State University
Department of Political Science
Room 2-143 Wilson Hall
MSU-Bozeman
Bozeman, MT 59717

(406) 994-5167
aponp@montana.edu
http://www.montana.edu/wwwpo/
mpaprogram

NEVADA

University of Nevada, Las Vegas
Department of Public Administration
CDC Building 7
Las Vegas, NV 89154-6026
(702) 895-4828
lee.bernick@ccmail.nevada.edu
http://www.unlv.edu/Colleges/Urban/
pubadmin

NEW JERSEY

Fairleigh Dickinson University
The Public Administration Institute
Teaneck-Hackensack Campus
Teaneck, NJ 07666
(201) 692-7177
http://fduinfo.com/gradbull/ncpa-mpa-
pubadmin.php

Rutgers University
PA Department
701 Hill Hall
360 M.L. King Jr. Boulevard
Newark, NJ 07102
(973) 353-5093 x11
pubadmin@andromeda.rutgers.edu
http://pubadmin.newark.rutgers.edu/

NEW MEXICO

The University of New Mexico
The School of Public Administration
1924 Las Lomas NE
Albuquerque, NM 87131-1221
(505) 277-3312

spagrad@unm.edu
http://www.unm.edu/~spagrad/

NEW YORK

Binghamton University
Master of Public Administration
PO Box 6000
Binghamton, NY 13902
(607) 777-2719
smarrow@binghamton.edu
http://mpa.binghamton.edu

Columbia University
408 International Affairs Building
MC 3325
420 West 118th Street
New York, NY 10027
(212) 854-6216
sipa_admission@columbia.edu
http://www.sipa.columbia.edu

Cornell University
Institute for Public Affairs
472 Hollister Hall
Ithaca, New York 14853
(607) 255-8018
cipa@cornell.edu
http://www.cipa.cornell.edu

New School University
Milano Graduate School
Urban Policy Analysis and Management
Program
72 Fifth Avenue
New York, NY 10011
(212) 229-5311
ednsu@newschool.edu
http://www.newschool.edu/milano

New York University
Robert F. Wagner Graduate School of
Public Service
295 Lafayette Street, 2nd floor
New York, NY 10012-9604

(212) 998-7414
wagner.admissions@nyu.edu
http://wagner.nyu.edu

Syracuse University
Department of Public Administration
Maxwell School of Citizenship and
Public Affairs
215 Eggers Hall
Syracuse, NY 13244
(315) 443-4000
comolino@maxwell.syr.edu
http://www.maxwell.syr.edu/pa

NORTH CAROLINA

Duke University
Terry Sanford Institute of Public Policy
Box 90243
Durham, NC 27708-0243
(919) 613-7325
DukeMPP@duke.edu
http://www.pubpol.duke.edu/graduate/
mpp

North Carolina State University
Raleigh, NC 27695-8102
(919) 515-5159
http://www.chass.ncsu.edu/pa/MPA.htm

**University of North Carolina–Chapel
Hill**
Institute of Government
CB# 3330, Knapp Building
Chapel Hill, NC 27599-3330
(919) 962-0426
mpastaff@iogmail.iog.unc.edu
http://www.mpa.unc.edu

OHIO

Kent State University
Department of Political Science
Kent, OH 44242

(330) 672-2060
jdrew@kent.edu
http://www.kent.edu/mpa

Ohio State University
School of Public Policy and Management
110 Page Hall
1810 College Road
Columbus, OH 43210-1336
(614) 292-8696
admitppm@osu.edu
http://www.ppm.ohio-state.edu

PENNSYLVANIA

Carnegie Mellon University
H. John Heinz III School of Public Policy
and Management
5000 Forbes Avenue
Pittsburgh, PA 15213
(412) 268-2164
Heinz-admissions@andrew.cmu.edu
http://www.heinz.cmu.edu

University of Pennsylvania
The Fels Center of Government
3814 Walnut Street
Philadelphia, PA 19104
(215) 898-8216
http://www.fels.upenn.edu

University of Pittsburgh
Graduate School of Public and
International Affairs
Pittsburgh, PA 15260
(412) 648-7640
gspia@pitt.edu
http://www.gspia.pitt.edu

Widener University
Master of Public Administration
Program
One University Place
Chester, PA 19013
(610) 499-1120

james.e.vike@widener.edu
http://www.science.widener.edu/grad/
mpamain.html

RHODE ISLAND

Brown University
Taubman Center for Public Policy
67 George Street
Providence, RI 02912-1977
(401) 863-2201
Melissa_Nicholaus@brown.edu
http://www.brown.edu/Departments/
Taubman_Center

SOUTH CAROLINA

Clemson University
PO Box 5616
Greenville, SC 29606
(864) 656-3233
rws@clemson.edu
http://business.clemson.edu/mpa

TENNESSEE

University of Tennessee–Knoxville
UT Department of Political Science
1001 McClung Tower
Knoxville, TN 37996-0410
(865) 974-0802
dfolz@utk.edu
http://web.utk.edu/~polisci/

TEXAS

Texas Tech University
Program for Master of Public
Administration
Center for Public Service
Box 41015 T

Lubbock, TX 79409
(806) 742-3125
ldicke@ttacs.ttu.edu
http://www.ttu.edu

The University of Texas at Austin
Graduate and International Admissions
Center
PO Box 7608
Austin, TX 78813-7608
(512) 475-7390
http://www.utexas.edu/lbj

UTAH

Brigham Young University
George W. Romney Institute of Public
Management
760 Tanner Building
Provo, UT 84602
(801) 422-4516
mpa@byu.edu or empa@byu.edu
http://marriottschool.byu.edu/mpa

VIRGINIA

The College of William and Mary
Thomas Jefferson Program in Public
Policy
Jamestown Road, Morton Hall,
Room 140
Williamsburg, VA 23185
(757) 221-2368
tjppp@wm.edu
http://www.wm.edu/tjppp

George Mason University
Department of Public and
International Affairs
Fairfax, VA 22030-4444
(703) 993-1411
mpa@gmu.edu
http://mpa.gmu.edu

George Mason University
School of Public Policy
3401 North Fairfax Drive, MS 3B1
Arlington, VA 22201
(703) 993-8099
spp@gmu.edu
http://policy.gmu.edu

WASHINGTON

University of Washington
Daniel J. Evans School of Public Affairs
Box 353055
Seattle, WA 98195-3055
(206) 543-4900
Evansuw@u.washington.edu
http://www.evansuw.org

WEST VIRGINIA

West Virginia University
Division of Public Administration
PO Box 6322
Morgantown, WV 26406-6322

(304) 293-2614
dwillia6@wvu.edu
http://www.as.wvu.edu/pubadm

WISCONSIN

University of Wisconsin–Madison
Robert M. La Follette School of Public
Affairs
1225 Observatory Drive
Madison, WI 53706
(608) 262-3582
chapin@lafollette.wisc.edu
http://www.lafollette.wisc.edu

WYOMING

University of Wyoming
Department of Political Science
Laramie, WY 82071
(307) 766-6484
mpa.info@uwyo.edu
http://uwadmnweb.uwyo.edu/Pols/

READ MORE ABOUT IT

The following sources and books may help you learn more about government careers. Libraries and career centers also provide information on the federal government, including books about how to get government jobs. When choosing books, look for those with recent publication dates because employment regulations change from time to time.

GENERAL CAREERS

Axelrod-Contrada, Joan. *Career Opportunities in Politics, Government, and Activism*. New York: Ferguson, 2003.

Culbreath, Alice N., and Saundra K. Neal. *Testing the Waters: A Teen's Guide to Career Exploration*. New York: JRC Consulting, 1999.

DeGalan, Julie, and Stephen Lambert. *Great Jobs for Foreign Language Majors*. Lincolnwood, Ill.: VGM Career Books, 2001.

Endicott, William T. *An Insider's Guide to Political Jobs in Washington*. New York: Wiley, 2003.

Farr, Michael, LaVerne L. Ludden, and Laurence Shatkin, *200 Best Jobs for College Graduates*. Indianapolis, Ind.: Jist Publishing, 2003.

Fogg, Neeta Paul Harrington, Thomas Harrington. *College Majors Handbook with Real Career Paths and Payoffs: The Actual Jobs, Earnings, and Trends for Graduates of 60 College Majors*. Indianapolis, Ind.: Jist Publishing, 2004.

Goldberg, Jan. *Careers for Patriotic Types & Others Who Want to Serve Their Country*. Lincolnwood, Ill.: VGM Career Horizons, 2000.

Hiam, Alex, and Susan Angle. *Adventure Careers: Your Guide to Exciting Jobs, Uncommon Occupations and Extraordinary Experiences* (2nd ed.). Franklin Lakes N.J.: Career Press, 1995.

Krannich, Ronald L., and Caryl Rae Krannich. *The Best Jobs for the 1990s and into the 21st Century*. Manassas Park, Va.: Impact Publications, 1995.

JIST Works, Inc. *Guide to America's Federal Jobs*. Indianapolis, Ind.: JIST Works, 2001.

Mannion, James. *The Everything Alternative Careers Book: Leave the Office Behind and Embark on a New Adventure (Everything: School and Careers)*. Boston: Adams, 2004.

Mariani, Mack. *The Insider's Guide to Political Internships: What to Do Once You're in the Door*. Boulder, Colo.: Westview Press, 2002.

McCarthy, William. *Vault Guide to Capitol Hill Careers: An Inside Look Inside the Beltway*. New York: Vault, 2003.

Porter, Christopher. *How to Get a Job in Congress without Winning an Election*. Arlington, Va.: Blutarsky Media, 2000.

Rowh, Mark. *Great Jobs for Political Science Majors*. New York: McGraw-Hill, 2003.

U.S. Bureau of Labor Statistics. *Occupational Outlook Handbook, 2006–07 Edition*. Available online at http://stats.bls.gov/search/ooh.asp?ct=OOH.

AEROSPACE ENGINEER

American Institute of Aeronautics and Astronautics. *Aerospace Design Engineers Guide*. Reston, Va.: AIAA, 2003.

Smith, David Albert. *NASA and the Aerospace Industry: A Study of Federal Influences on Industrial Location*. Pittsburgh: University of Pittsburgh, 1972.

AIR TRAFFIC CONTROLLER

Maples, Wallace. *Adventures in Aerospace Careers*. New York: McGraw-Hill, 2002.

ATF SPECIAL AGENT

Moore, Jim. *Very Special Agents: The Inside Story of America's Most Controversial Law Enforcement Agency–The Bureau of Alcohol, Tobacco and Firearms*. Champaign, Ill.: University of Illinois Press, 2001.

U.S. Department of Treasury. *ATF Investigation of Vernon Wayne Howell, Also Known as David Koresh*. Washington, D.C.: Department of Treasury, 1993.

BANK EXAMINER

Myers, Forest E. *Basics for Bank Directors*. Kansas City, Mo.: Division of Supervision and Risk Management, Federal Reserve Bank of Kansas City, 2001. Also available online at http://www.kc.frb.org/BS&S/publicat/PDF/dirbasics.pdf.

Spong, Kenneth. *Bank Regulation: Its Purposes, Implementation and Effects*. Kansas City, Mo.: Division of Supervision and Risk Management, Federal Reserve Bank of Kansas City, 2000.

Also available online at http://www.kc.frb.org/BS&S/publicat/PDF/Regs-Book2000.pdf.

BORDER PATROL SEARCH AND RESCUE AGENT

Krauss, Erich. *Inside the U.S. Border Patrol*. New York: Citadel Books, 2004.

Maril, Robert Lee. *Patrolling Chaos: The U.S. Border Patrol in Deep South Texas*. Lubbock, Tex.: Texas Tech University Press, 2004.

CENSUS BUREAU STATISTICIAN

Rowland, Donald T. *Demographic Methods and Concepts*. London: Oxford University Press, 2003.

Preston, Samuel H., Patrick Heuveline, and Michel Guillot. *Demography: Measuring and Modeling Population Processes*. Oxford, U.K.: Blackwell Publishers, 2000.

CITY PLANNER

Levy, John M. *Contemporary Urban Planning*. New York: Prentice Hall, 2002.

Perlman, Dan L., and Jeffrey Milder. *Practical Ecology for Planners, Developers and Citizens*. Washington, D.C.: Island Press, 2004.

CONGRESSIONAL PRESS SECRETARY

Nelson, Dale. *Who Speaks for the President: The White House Press Secretary from Cleveland to Clinton*. Syracuse, N.Y.: Syracuse University Press, 2000.

Jamieson, K., and P. Waldman. *The Press Effect: Politicians, Journalists, and the Stories That Shape the Political World*. New York: Oxford University Press, 2002.

CORONER

Cohen, Paul, and Shari Cohen. *Careers in Law Enforcement and Security*. New York: The Rosen Publishing Group, Inc., 1995.

Echaore-McDavid, Susan. *Career Opportunities in Law Enforcement, Security, and Protective Services*. New York: Checkmark Books, 2000.

Lee, Mary Price, Richard S. Lee, and Carol Beam. *100 Best Careers in Crime Fighting*. New York: Macmillan, 1998.

Stinchcomb, James. *Opportunities in Law Enforcement and Criminal Justice*. Lincolnwoood, Ill.: NTC./VGM, 1996.

COURT INTERPRETER

Berk-Seligson, Susan. *The Bilingual Courtroom: Court Interpreters in the Judicial Process*. Chicago: University of Chicago Press, 2002.

Carr, Silvana, editor. *The Critical Link: Interpreter in the Community*. Philadelphia: John Benjamins Publishing Co., 1997.

COURT REPORTER

Chipkin, Wendy Mapstone. *Successful Freelance Court Reporting*. Albany, N.Y.: Thomson Delmar Learning, 2000.

Knapp, Mary H. *The Complete Court Reporter's Handbook*. New York: Prentice Hall, 1998.

DISASTER ASSISTANCE EMPLOYEE

Barnes, Jay. *Florida's Hurricane History*. Chapel Hill, N.C.: University of North Carolina Press, 1998.

Williams, Jack. *Hurricane Watch: Forecasting the Deadliest Storms on Earth*. New York: Vintage, 2001.

GSA ASSOCIATE

Keyes, W. Noel. *Government Contracts In A Nutshell*. St. Paul, Minn.: West Group, 2004.

Stanberry, Scott. *Federal Contracting Made Easy, Second Edition*. Vienna, Va.: Management Concepts, 2004.

INTERNATIONAL ELECTION OBSERVER

Diamond, Larry, ed. *Consolidating the Third Wave Democracies*. Baltimore: Johns Hopkins University Press, 1997.

Stojanovic, Svetozar. *Serbia: The Democratic Revolution*. Amherst, N.Y.: Prometheus Books, 2003.

IRS AGENT

Tyson, Eric, et al. *Taxes for Dummies 2005*. Hoboken, N.J.: Wiley, 2004.

Yancey, Richard. *Confessions of a Tax Collector: One Man's Tour of Duty Inside the IRS*. New York: Harper Collins, 2004.

LOBBYIST

Goldstein, Kenneth M. *Interest Groups, Lobbying and Participation in America.* Cambridge, U.K.: Cambridge University Press, 1999.

McKean, David. *Peddling Influence: Thomas 'Tommy the Cork' Corcoran and the Birth of Modern Lobbying.* Hanover, N.H.: Steerforth, 2005.

MAYOR

Axelrod-Contrada, Joan. *Career Opportunities in Politics, Government, and Activism.* New York: Facts On File, 2003.

Bennis, Warren. *On Becoming A Leader: The Leadership Classic.* New York: Perseus Publishing, 2003.

MILITARY DENTIST

Kenny, David J., and Michael J. Casas. *Wet Fingered Dentistry: Practical Advice from Experienced Dentists.* Chicago: Quintessence Publishing, 2002.

Rules, James T., and Muriel J. Bebeau. *Dentists Who Care: Inspiring Stories of Professional Commitment.* Chicago: Quintessence Publishing, 2005.

MILITARY LAWYER

Davidson, Michael J. *A Guide to Military Criminal Law.* Annapolis, Md.: Naval Institute Press, 1999.

Shanor, Charles A. *National Security and Military Law in a Nutshell.* Eagan, Minn.: West Group, 2003.

PARKS DIRECTOR

Dahl, Bernard, and Donald J. Molnar. *Anatomy of a Park: Essentials of Recreation Area Planning and Design.* Long Grove, Ill.: Waveland Press, Inc., 2003.

Harnik, Peter. *Inside City Parks.* Washington, D.C.: Urban Land Institute, 2000.

POLITICAL CONSULTANT

Cannon, Carl, et al. *Boy Genius: Karl Rove, the Architect of George W. Bush's Remarkable Political Triumphs.* New York: Public Affairs, 2005.

Carville, James, and Paul Begala. *Buck Up, Suck Up...and Come Back When You Foul Up: 12 Winning Secrets from the War Room.* New York: Simon & Schuster, 2003.

POLYGRAPH EXAMINER

Kleiner, Murray, ed. *Handbook of Polygraph Testing.* San Diego: Academic Press, 2001.

Lieberman, David J. *Never Be Lied To Again: How to Get the Truth in 5 Minutes or Less in Any Conversation or Situation.* New York: St. Martin's Griffin, 1999.

PRESIDENTIAL SPEECHWRITER

Noonan, Peggy. *What I Saw at the Revolution: A Political Life in the Reagan Era.* New York: Random House Trade Paperbacks, 2003.

Safire, William, ed. *Lend Me Your Ears: Great Speeches in History.* New York: W.W. Norton & Company, 2004.

PROBATION OFFICER

Cree, Vivienne E. *Sociology for Social Workers and Probation Officers.* New York: Routledge, 2000.

Rush, Jeffrey P. *Arco Probation Officer/ Parole Officer Exam (Arco Civil Service Test Tutor)*. New York: ARCO, 2001.

STAFF ASSISTANT TO THE FIRST LADY

Burke, Michelle. *The Valuable Office Professional: For Administrative Assistants, Office Managers, Secretaries, and Other Support Staff*. New York: American Management Association, 1996.

Faber, Doris. *Smithsonian Book of the First Ladies: Their Lives, Times, and Issues*. New York: Henry Holt & Company, 1996.

STATE EDUCATION COMMISSIONER

Dewey, John. *Experience and Education*. New York: Free Press, 1997.

Mendler, Allen N. *Motivating Students Who Don't Care: Successful Techniques for Educations*. Leicestershire, U.K.: NES, 2001.

TEST PILOT

Cook, LeRoy. *101 Things To Do After You Get Your Private Pilot's License*. New York: McGraw-Hill Professional, 2003.

Schiff, Barry. *Test Pilot: 1,001 Things You Thought You Knew About Flying*. Newcastle, Wash.: Aviation Supplies and Academics, 2001.

TRIAL CONSULTANT

Ball, David. *Theater Tips and Strategy for Jury Trials*. South Bend, Ind.: National Institute for Trial Advocacy, 2003.

Varinsky, Howard. *Jury Persuasion: How to Package and Sell Your Case to a Jury*. Oakland, Calif.: Continuing Education of the Bar, 1998.

VICTIM ADVOCATE

Lew, Mike. *Victims No Longer: The Classic Guide for Men Recovering from Sexual Child Abuse*. New York: Harper, 2004.

Zimberoff, Diane. *Breaking Free from the Victim Trap: Reclaiming Your Personal Power*. Chicago: Wellness Press, 1989.

VOICE OF AMERICA BROADCASTER

Heil, Alan. *Voice of America*. New York: Columbia University Press, 2003.

Horton, Gerd. *Radio Goes to War: The Cultural Politics of Propaganda during World War II*. Berkeley: University of California Press, 2002.

INDEX

Page numbers in **bold** indicate main entries.